More Praise fo

The Siege is a Freudian descent into the moral ambiguity inherent in modern institutions. When it comes, as it must, the violence is as tangible and absurd as certain scenes in Cormac McCarthy's *Blood Meridian*. An excellent debut from a writer on the rise.

John M. Gist, Founding Editor, *Red Savina Review*

The Siege takes you on a thrilling journey into the world of a prison, exploring both the relationship between inmate and captor, as well as the politics and the players who pull the strings behind the scenes. It is terrifying in a way, because you know that this fiction can't be far from the reality of our prison system today."

E. Branden Hart, Executive Editor, *Empty Sink*

The Siege is gripping. It's obviously written by somebody with years of experience in the criminal justice system, so it rings with authenticity. It's like this is a debriefing of somebody who actually went through this experience. The wonder of it all is that the main character has preserved his humanity in an obviously anti-human environment.

James Rowland, San Francisco District Attorney, retired

A great read! Jim Hanna's writing is authentic and compelling. An extraordinary novel, *The Siege* conveys the tensions of the prison system as only an insider could. Painful emotions, thoughts and experiences of both the prisoners and their keepers come alive in the author's searing prose.

Judge Harold Kahn, Superior Court 16

THE SIEGE

James Hanna

THE SIEGE

James Hanna

Copyright © 2014 by James Hanna
Published by Sand Hill Review Press
www.sandhillreviewpress.com
P.O. Box 1275, San Mateo, CA 94401 (415) 297-3571

Library of Congress Control Number: 2012947803
Library of Congress Cataloging-in-Publication Data
Hanna, James The Siege / James Hanna
ISBN: 978-1-937818005

The Siege is a work of fiction. Its characters, scenes and locales are a
product of the author's imagination or are used fictitiously. Any similarity
to people alive or dead is purely cooincitental.

SHRP
Sand Hill Review Press

ERIC,

THANS SO MUCH FOR ALL
YOUR SUPPORT.

To Catherine, Mary, and Mickey

CONTENTS

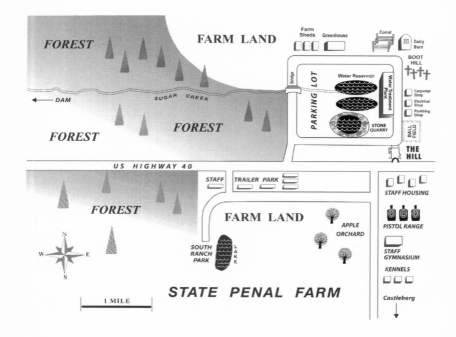

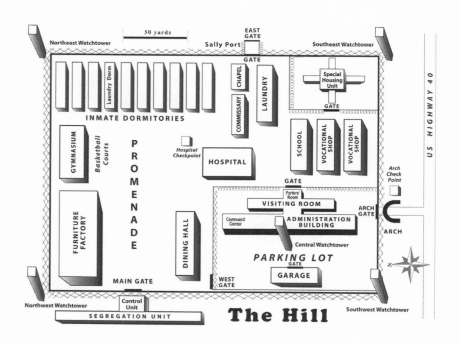

I

SMOKE

Turning and turning in the widening gyre,
The falcon cannot hear the falconer.
—William Butler Yeats

The Indiana Penal Farm, an 86-year-old penitentiary in the heart of the Hoosier state, is an icon to moderation. It houses medium security prisoners, produces furniture and brooms for state-use only, and rewards its staff with adequate benefits. Its dormitories, one-story red-brick buildings, resemble the fraternity houses on many college campuses, while its ball field and basketball courts offer modest variety since the inmates play the same teams day-after-day. Insulated by 20,000 acres of farmland and sycamore forest, it sits stolidly on Highway 40—a towered estate too foreboding to blend into the scarred communities surrounding it. Detached from the heart of the heartland, it is barely accessible to even the most rural of seductions: dogma, religion, and guns. Escapes, though they happen at times, are relatively rare, while the staffers, the Farm's most durable incumbents, tend to stay on even after their home mortgages are paid off and their pensions can be bolstered by Medicare and Social Security.

Clans and gangs are a fixture at the Farm, but mostly they just quarrel among one another, and even the inmate insurrections tend to be rather limited in scope: riots designed not to break down the gates but to acquire an extra concession or two from the state. But a notorious inmate uprising—the takeover of a laundry dormitory on the evening of November 22, 2000—might be viewed as an aberration: an opportunity for mundane men to acquire the fame of champions. How else could Chester Mahoney, a portly child molester with the gift of gab, be regarded as the leader of an insurgent nation? How else could Henry Yoakum, a petty grafter employed as a prison guard, acquire a commando's prestige? And how else could Tom Hemmings, a self-effacing dorm counselor, be given the immunities of a diplomat?

3

Guards took back the dormitory on November 25, following a four-day siege. The battle made national headlines.

November 23, 2000
9:00 a.m.

Tom Hemmings did not feel alarmed when the riot finally began, not even after the laundry dorm—the dormitory he was assigned to—had been taken over by the inmates. He instead felt a sense of vindication, a sentiment reminiscent of the antiwar marches of the sixties, but he knew his nostalgia was presumptuous since it was difficult to determine the purpose of the uprising. The bodies in the compound, several swollen bundles, suggested that the matter was intramural rather than seditious: a bloodletting by rival gangs that had seized the opportunity to settle scores. The divisions among the inmates were further evident when an envoy party—a few skinheads displaying a bed sheet as a truce flag—was clapped in shackles and frog-marched to the segregation building behind the Control Unit.

"They wanted to wear Bermuda shorts in their own time," said Captain Hawkins, the squat excitable commander of the prison emergency squads. "The moment I heard that I ordered 'em locked up. They're not *speakin'* for the inmate body." The captain, with his Charlie Chaplain waddle, looked comical as he walked back to the Command Center.

Tom glanced at Bret Brewer once Hawkins was out of earshot. He coughed before speaking. "The skinheads *knew* Harold Hawkins would lock them up. They didn't want to be part of it anymore."

Although a counselor at the medium-security facility, Tom was temporarily assigned to the Third Emergency Squad, two-dozen darkly clad men wearing spit shields, helmets, and body armor. The gear was reassuring but unnecessary since the assault would be made by the emergency squads from the state prison and reformatory.

4

These logistics were a comfort: reprisals from the inmates would be minimal if the head-busting was done by officers they didn't know. Tom's baton, for that matter, seemed too brittle to wield and he held it as if it were a vase. As the smoke began to clear, he was struck not by the imminence of the battle so much as the ghostly familiarity of the compound, a view he had seen every day for the last twenty years.

Brewer grunted, unsnapping his spit shield from his helmet. The smoke from the compound had darkened the Plexiglas and he rubbed it meticulously with a handkerchief. The plastic looked fragile in his large hands.

"Who have the inmates got collared in that dorm?" Brewer, the farm foreman, sounded as if he were pricing livestock.

"A dozen third shift officers," Tom said. "Most of them old men. They've got Henry Yoakum too."

Brewer snorted. "They're wearin' the *wrong* colors." His contempt, under the circumstances, seemed unusual for even a union steward, but it was clear that the smoldering compound impressed Brewer less than his sudden responsibility for members of a rival union. He continued rubbing the shield. "We owe them, I guess," he muttered. "For as long as they're hostages anyhow. 'Cept for that goddam Yoakum. He won't *live* long enough to get old."

"Give Yoakum a break. It's Thanksgiving day."

Brewer shook his head, squinting as he returned his gaze to the compound. A ground swell of heat was distorting their view, a blanket so heavy that the dead bodies appeared to be afloat.

"Then break bread with the *inmates*, Hemmings. Have yerself a powwow. You could probably spring *Yoakum* for a pack of cigarettes." Brewer spat on the face shield then continued polishing it. "A rogue officer ain't *worth* more 'an a *pack*."

"He is during a free-for-all."

"Then offer 'em a carton. Whatever it takes. But that's one fucker I *won't* risk my neck for."

5

The contempt in Brewer's voice was disturbing, perhaps because it undermined Tom's hope that staff rivalries would dissolve in the face of an inmate insurrection. That tensions between the unions seemed destined to endure could only suggest trouble. Tom wondered which clans were more united, the union cliques or the inmate gangs. The question made him tremble.

Tom looked toward the compound as it began to emerge through the smoke. It seemed like a facade—not a prison—a false front belonging to a movie set. The buildings, wavering in the heat, were almost like mirages about to float away. He felt further removed from the emergency squads, the K-9 Unit, and the sharpshooters perched like crows on the roof of the Administration Building.

Tom spoke hopefully. "I can't *give* them any bargains."

Brewer grunted. "Then why'd the brass let Chester out of the hole? The fucker's no good for anything *but* bargainin'."

"Maybe the brass wants his throat cut. Maybe he got the better of them once too often."

That it could come down to Chester Mahoney, a backwoods preacher with a flowery tongue, was a possibility Tom did not wish to consider. The release of his informant from the Special Housing Unit, where he had been locked up days ago for a rule infraction, seemed amateurish, a violation of the first principle of negotiating that had been drummed into him at the Correctional Academy several months ago. *Make 'em pay a price for everything*, the instructor had emphasized time and again. *You don't do that, they'll just accelerate their demands*. It therefore aggravated Tom that an unearned concession had already been given to the hostage takers. If called on to negotiate with the inmates, Tom would surely be facing a power-drunk lot with an inflated set of demands. He almost hoped that Brewer was right—that the facility had released Chester from the hole only so he would get his throat cut.

"You heard Captain Hawkins," Tom insisted. "He doesn't *want* the inmates bargaining. Least of all with *me*."

"And why *not* you?" Brewer said. "It's a shitkicker's job, ain't it?"

Tom squeezed his baton as though gripping a snake. "It isn't *my* job," he snapped.

Brewer chuckled tonelessly. "You told Hawkins you have a snitch, Hemmings. And you told him your snitch would speak for the inmates. Don't that *make* it your job?"

The observation was too obvious to be caustic, and Tom made no reply as he watched the compound. His career at the prison, a series of lateral transfers, could well be summed up as shitkicker duties. Even his status as a hostage negotiator, a position he had accepted at the urging of the Commissioner, seemed only a continuation of this norm. Negotiators were most effective if they were perceived as messengers rather than decision-makers.

"Company's comin'," Brewer remarked. His voice was once again neutral.

Tom returned his attention to the compound where some watery movement suggested a figure, perhaps two, staggering in their direction. "I hope they're not emissaries."

Brewer shrugged. "More Bermuda shorts if you ask me."

The men seemed adrift, as though caught in a current, and so it was several minutes before Tom was able to identify them as an officer and an inmate. But he could not be sure which of them was in charge or if they were even aware of one another. That the men looked nonthreatening was vaguely disturbing to him: an indictment of the complacency he had fallen into after twenty years at the penal facility. Had the clues been there all that time or was it only the events of the past few days that had given him any real premonitions of the riot?

"They're refugees," Brewer said. "But they're bringin' us a message." He tapped his baton on his palm as he spoke, a hollow emphasis since his observation was in no way supported by the random scene in front of them. The men approaching them were stumbling like drunkards and no longer seemed vested in the standoff.

Tom felt his scalp prickle "When did we start bargaining with vagrants?" he asked.

Brewer shrugged again. "It's one of them Muslims," he muttered. "He might just have something to *say* to you, Hemmings. And it looks like Cavanaugh's with him."

The comment was like a tune whistled in a graveyard. Although one of the men did resemble Cavanaugh, the heat-warped image bore little resemblance to the officer who had oriented Tom to the facility twenty years ago, chatting like a tour guide as he drove him past the cornfields, the dairy, and the water treatment plant. The person approaching them seemed superfluous, much like a chess piece that had been captured and discarded from the board. Tom was neither impressed by the second of the two men, an African-American clad in the dingy whites of a kitchen worker—probably one of the Muslims, although the man's slumped shoulders and pronounced limp suggested he was a castoff as well. Tom was tempted to remember the man's name, but there was little sense in calling out. The inmate was limping badly and needed to be in a hospital bed. Tom watched as the men drew closer, raising their hands above their heads when the Main Gate parted, then he saw them no more.

"The inmates want to meet with you," Brewer said.

"It's too late!" Tom muttered.

"Then why did they give us back a guard, Hemmings? And a lieutenant to boot."

"Maybe they got tired of him. Or maybe he just wandered away and they haven't figured it out yet." Tom made no attempt to disguise his irritability—not because of Brewer's smugness so much as Tom's personal belief that riots were bound by a natural order of events. The sequence was in fact Gospel to him: first came the outbreak, in this case the inmate seizure of the laundry dorm, then the massing of troops along the perimeter fence, and finally, once diplomacy had failed, the issuance of an ultimatum.

Since the ultimatum had already been issued and ignored—the inmates had been given one hour to surrender—it was time to launch the final phase: an attack upon the dormitory. This ultimate phase was in fact overdue; the dormitory had been seized twenty hours ago and no serious demands had been made by the inmates, nothing beyond the transparent request for Bermuda shorts and the rather patented insistence from the Devil's Disciples, the most radical of the black gangs, that its members be flown to "non-imperialistic countries." But men would soon die—that much was clear—and Tom wanted no part in the bloodshed.

It seemed like a death knell when the attack order—delivered by a bullhorn—echoed throughout the parking lot. The command struck Tom as a teasing of fate: a noise more likely to wake a slumbering beast than effectively rally the hunters to the kill. His apprehension grew when the Point Squad advanced noisily towards the Main Gate, its clomping half-step soliciting a crisp echo from the prison compound. As a novice member of the Third Emergency Squad, Tom had practiced the half-step only once, an experience that had caused him to approach Lieutenant Baldwin, his taciturn commander, with profound reservations. "Is *this* how we're taking back ground?" he had asked, grateful when Baldwin, shaking his head, had set his mind to rest.

"Not likely, Tom," Baldwin had wearily drawled. "Not unless ya wanna get hit with twice as many stones."

It was Baldwin who addressed them now, his voice unusually animated as he gave the secondary command. "Stand by, gentlemen. An' remember what we're fightin' for."

"Penal Health Services—what else?" Brewer grumbled. "An' that fuckin' Colonial Concession Company."

The complaint stirred Tom like a battle cry, giving him a vigor that Baldwin's sharp voice had been unable to inspire. This response was irrational since the two contractors, both models of inefficiency, had contributed to the discontent of the inmates. But Tom was grateful for the anger these contractors awoke in him—an emotion more welcome than ambivalence when it came to storming compounds. His anger was so reflexive, so utterly cleansing, that he felt only anticipation when he saw Captain Hawkins strutting back towards them.

"*Here's* your emissary," Brewer said, an observation that was surely another false alarm.

9

Tom felt heartened by the sour expression on Hawkins' face, an exasperation that suggested not diplomacy—not even tolerance—but a soldier's commitment to battle. He lifted his spit shield as Hawkins approached, the act of an observer rather than a participant, a fan to a blood sport that he would get to witness from the security of the bleachers. It was only when Hawkins spoke, uttering Tom's name as though it were that of a traitor, that his heart began to hammer.

"Hemmings!" barked Hawkins. His voice was like sandpaper.

Tom nodded slowly, determined to savor the last of his illusions—the notion that he could somehow sit this out.

"Yer goin' in, Hemmings," the captain muttered. "The inmates wanna talk."

Tom shook his head. "It's too *late*," he protested.

Hawkins spat on the ground. "That don't make no *difference*, Hemmings."

Tom felt his brow sweating. "Then get some one else."

Hawkins folded his arms. His face was now sulky—his eyes hard as ice. "The inmates are asking for *you*, Hemmings. *You* and *you* alone."

November 23, 2000
9:30 a.m.

Tom awaited his clearance to enter the compound, grateful for the sluggishness of the Command Center: an assurance that it would be at least an hour before the Main Gate rolled open for him. He suspected, as he waited, that the chaos was best defined by the incidents of the last few days: random events that were now so validated by hindsight that they could only have brought him to this particular crossroad. This was not to discount his two decades at the prison—nor to minimize his evolution from a Foreign Service brat to a dropout living abroad to a long-term prison employee—but because he had acquired, perhaps as a defense to his inconsistencies, the habit of living entirely in the present. It was therefore the blur of recent events—an inmate disciplinary hearing, a manhunt, his introduction to Chester Mahoney, #990624—that gave him some sense of the moment. The rest of his past, whatever its worth, now seemed a luxurious mist.

Tom was a finely boned man with a measured demeanor: a manner that suggested that he had squandered the best of himself long ago. But the sixties had been gentler to him, a paradox since his pursuits had been more radical at that time. His excesses had still protected him in those days: such poses as war resister, expatriate, aspiring hippie, had been too exhaustive to weigh upon him indefinitely. He was therefore poorly prepared for the role of centurion—a penal farm henchman and protector of what he considered to be the social comedy. That he had only risen to the level of a Dorm Counselor, a role attributable to a lingering idealism, did little to modify this status, at least not in the eyes of the inmates. "The Man," the Muslims called him, not always in jest, while the Aryan Brotherhood had dubbed him, "The Hog with the Big Balls." He suspected these factions liked him—he had always treated them with a callow consistency—but it still consoled him that Chester Mahoney was among the hundred or so inmates in his dorm. Chester was the most affable individual that Tom had ever met.

But Chester was only an inmate, after all. There were nobler castoffs around than Chester; there were his fellow employees: Jed Watkins, Omar Perkins, Chuck Baldwin, former GM workers whose factory foreclosures had driven them to take jobs as prison guards. And yet only Chester had captured Tom's affections. Not that this friendship was of consequence—friendship seemed ludicrous when extended to a felon involved with an antigovernment cult. The thought that the American Gospel Party was *led* by this pot-bellied man in his seventies, was not reassuring. It took only a glance at Chester to convince Tom that the devils he was guarding were only slightly less artful than the ones that had placed him in charge.

Still, Tom was grateful for the day the prison had interviewed him for a position—his job at the time, a

11

records inspector at Fort Ben Harrison, was boring him out of his skull. And so he had been eager to start when he had received a call twenty years ago from the facility's Personnel Director. The Interview Board, chaired by Harold Hawkins, had been so struck by his résumé that it practically hired him on the spot.

"You grew up abroad," Hawkins said when they met in the superintendent's office. "Your dad in the Military?"

"State Department," Tom replied.

"Then two years in the Army. Got yerself educated on the GI Bill. A *master's* degree in criminology. Impressive, sir."

"I'm interested in crime. Call it a nostalgia for foreign cultures." Tom let a smile touch the corners of his lips.

Harold smirked and shook his head. "So what did you do before the Army? Odd jobs?"

Tom nodded, relieved not to have to mention too much of his past: his suburban anomie, his anti-war activity, his leaving a mid-western college to roam Australia as a draft resister. Since he had spent a few weeks in federal custody before accepting a peacetime enlistment in the Army, he was not comfortable with intimate exchanges. The trauma of jail—its profound humiliation—had been much too hard to shake.

Hawkins studied him critically, as though sensing that something was out of whack. "Now how about *you*, Hemmings? You got any issues? I like a man to *know* what he's getting into before he joins our team."

Tom struggled to come up with a question. "How large *is* the place?" he finally blurted.

Hawkins chuckled sarcastically. "Over thirty square miles, sir. But the shops and factories are all on the Hill. That's so the watchtowers can keep an eye on the bojacks. 'Cept for the road gang and the farm workers, *no* one gets off the Hill."

Tom felt himself blush, stung by his own question. "Do they *need* that much watching?"

"Hell no, Hemmings. They need a whole lot *more*. We're gamblin' with a bad mix here. Killers and child rapers.

Robbers and pimps. And some of the best con men in the world."

Tom felt his blush deepen. "That *might* get dicey."

"There ain't no *might* about it, Hemmings. It *is* dicey. Most of the time the inmates will be watching *you*."

"How many of them are there?"

"Thirteen hundred and counting, sir. And most of 'em belong to gangs. We got three hundred staff members covering three shifts, but the unions won't let 'em do their jobs. We're *outnumbered* here, Hemmings, by agitators and cons. The only trump card we got is our guns."

Tom squirmed in his seat. "I'm glad might makes right." He was accustomed to making smart remarks, even at the risk of pissing others off. He could handle the anger his sharp tongue created, but too much candor chilled his soul. Why tell people that he had once been in custody himself?

Hawkins merely laughed. "The *inmates* have more rights than *you* do, Hemmings. But you don't have to tell 'em that. Here you *are* the law—judge, jury, and executioner all rolled into one. Keep that in mind and you just might last a month or two."

"What else keeps them busy—besides watching staff?"

"Not much. Kitchen work, furniture making, and gambling, mostly. Some of 'em are in a school dorm, but that's just makin' 'em smarter cons. The truth is, Hemmings, they got nothing but time on their hands. A lot more time than you."

"I can watch my own back," Tom said, shuffling once more in his chair.

"Do that, Hemmings. Don't count on the unions to do it for you. Too many ex-auto workers in our ranks—the only thing they can watch is a clock."

Tom smiled uneasily, unsure that he had passed the interview, but the final question thrown up by Hawkins convinced him that he would soon be getting a letter of employment.

"Can you say no to inmates, Hemmings? And to union agitators, too? You're gonna be meat here, you know?

Meat in a prison sandwich. The unions are on the top, the prisoners on the bottom, and you'll be right in the middle."

Tom answered uneasily—"I *can* say no"—and with that the interview ended.

Despite the challenge of his interview, the Hill itself, two dozen buildings surrounded by a single wire-mesh fence, seemed incidental at first impression, a stepping stone to greater ambitions rather than a destination in itself. The Hill, in fact, struck him as wholly pedestrian: a cracked promenade bordered by a row of inmate dormitories, a cafeteria-sized dining hall, a sagging gymnasium, a hospital, and a rickety factory for furniture and broom making. He was not impressed either by the deportment of the prison staff, a partisan demeanor that made his education seem a liability. It could only have been the fatigue of more careless adventuring, the seven taxing years he had spent roaming Australia, that delivered him so readily into the ranks of the state employee.

He was in fact embarrassed by the ease with which the Farm had claimed him, not merely by its climate of constraint but also by its vastness: twenty thousand acres of woodland and fields where a man could lose himself from time-to-time. Within this asylum, he traded greater ambitions for trail hiking, deer hunting, and fishing. He traded the prospects of promotion for stringers of largemouth bass, taken not only from the ponds and creeks but from a flooded limestone quarry, an epic excavation northwest of the Hill where prisoners had labored alongside mules before federal legislation had forbidden the facility to price building stone on the open market. The servility of this and other regulations did not seem uncomfortable enough, and so he found them convenient to ignore while moving through a series of lateral appointments: first a dorm counselor, later a parole board liaison, and until only recently the director of the facility's Work Release recruitment program. He had worked each of these jobs with a novice's zeal—a fresh but untested idealism.

And when the unions expanded, an inevitability given the frugal terms of state employment, its effect upon staffers less complacent than himself, he found himself embracing the causes, not because he himself was a sufferer of forced overtime or even the prepackaged suspension hearings, but because he still carried with him a mistrust of authority, a quality that had defined him so severely during the Vietnam Era that it refused, even now, to allow him a sense of irony. Still, there were times when Tom felt at least a tolerance towards the state, usually when walking alone across the basketball courts and noticing the emblems of smaller nations: the blood red handkerchiefs worn by the Devil's Disciples or the shaven heads and dark sunglasses that marked the members of the Aryan Brotherhood. These symbols, which seemed comical to him most of the time, would arouse him at such moments, perhaps because they smacked of a starker aggression, an assurance that their bearers, though the ultimate wards of the facility, were capable of striking with greater precision than the state. Walking alone, observing these tighter cliques, Tom would suppress a thrill of anticipation, quicken his step, and take comfort in the long shadows of the watchtowers.

Two decades would pass before he met Chester Mahoney, the man who would provide Tom with his consummate orientation to the Farm: a revelation he had once confused with his six weeks of training at the Correctional Academy, with the smooth accuracy of a Mini-14 at the qualification range, with the docility of the inmate work crews that departed the Hill in the morning, and with his first foray into an inmate dormitory, a military-style barracks where his every movement was noticed by a hundred pairs of eyes. His life, for all relevant purposes, had started just a week ago— the day that Chester, the first of several bleak heralds, had stood in front of him.

Having met the man only a week ago, Tom had viewed him at first as an oddity, not the nemesis that now awaited him in the compound—the man who had insisted that Tom negotiate the siege. When he had first met Chester, Tom had seen him as a candidate for charity, a commodity with which he was sadly overstocked. He could only be suspicious, after all, of an empathy that extended itself to a convicted child molester in search of a favor. Were his own misdeeds as epic, he could have made better sense of the matter, but Tom's sins were of the garden variety, sins too pedestrian to bind him to scoundrels.

Thankfully, his opportunities to grant favors had diminished dramatically over the past few months. The shrinkage had begun with a spousal killing by an inmate on a three-day pass—an embarrassment to Indiana's photogenic governor and a deathblow to the Work Release Program that had contented him for almost eight years. Things had further diminished with the surrender of the institution's commissary and medical services to private entrepreneurs. And so his job had shrunk from reviewing inmates for halfway house transfers to helping them acquire their commissary orders, a challenge no less formidable given the convoluted order forms of the Colonial Concession Company. But these smaller triumphs had begun to satisfy him as well, so much so that he had grown tolerant of the long line of inmates outside of his dorm office each commissary Thursday. It even amused him to see white and black gang members united in a common cause: an angry complaint about the irregularity with which their commissary orders arrived and, when they did acquire them, the predictable shoddiness of the goods for which they had paid market price. He had almost grown resigned to the daily mound of request slips in his dormitory mailbox, a pile that finally included a solitary gem of courtesy and composition. The note, distinguishable by its neat almost feminine handwriting, was a pleasure to read and he scanned it with gratitude as he sat in his office chair.

November 16, 2000
Mr. Thomas Hemmings:

> *It has come to my attention that you are among the few at this facility who will make an honest effort to assist a gentleman. I am*

16

*sure this is because you are first a Christian
and, only afterwards, a hireling of a pirated
state. I therefore feel comfortable in asking
you for a small piece of your time. If your
charity is available to even the minorities at
this facility, then how much greater might it
be if it extended to a member of your own race.
My request is a small one, Mr. Hemmings,
but sufficient, I daresay, to grant you another
brick in your heavenly mansion.*

> *Yours faithfully,*
> *C. H. Mahoney*
> *DOC-990624*

Since the facility was on lockdown, a constraint that allowed Tom to work uninterrupted at his desk, it was several days before he was able to meet the author of the note. The meeting would have been difficult to arrange in any case since Chester, a kitchen worker assigned to his dormitory, was exempt from the morning and noon dorm counts and would require an escort from an inmate porter to come to the office. Tom disliked using the porters, preferring instead to fetch an inmate from his bed pod after count, but on the third day of the lockdown he sighed, conceded to the additional paperwork, and filled out the pass and log entry necessary to bring Chester to the dorm.

It was an hour before the knock finally came, an interval during which he had discarded a memo, an assurance from the Governor that from here-on-out prison employees would be spot-tested for drug use, in favor of the Indianapolis Star. He did not read the sports page, his usual retreat, but an article depicting another shutdown, a General Motors subsidiary plant in the town of Anderson. Since downsizing had become a theme to him, the article seriously vexed him, and so it was several seconds before he grew aware of the startling presence in his office.

"*May* I interrupt you, sir?"

Tom looked up from the newspaper and noticed the little man standing in front of him. The resemblance to Colonel Sanders seemed laughable since his visitor, a church and cult leader from the village of Walnut Creek, was the antithesis of a corporate icon. The comparison was still irresistible: a snowy goat's beard dangled from his chin, as though it had been pasted there, and the white kitchen uniform was impeccably pressed, a clue that his visitor was paying off the laundry workers. His impression of the man, if speech and grooming were reliable indications, was that he was not a defector at all but a portly anachronism, possibly even a gentleman of the Old South.

Tom set the newspaper aside. "I could *use* an interruption. Shall we get acquainted?"

The man smiled seamlessly and coughed. "I *will* disregard your nickname, sir, although slander is bread to a Christian."

"The Hog," Tom replied. "I don't mind it all that much. In fact it's a bit of a compliment."

The little man nodded. "More so than Chester the Molester, I daresay. A fib, of course, but I *have* been promiscuous, sir. Had I not lusted for a bit of the pie, the mayorship of Parkersburg, the county prosecutor would have never conspired so effectively against me."

"Politics," Tom said, shaking his head. "A sorry business everywhere." He was familiar with his visitors' file, having retrieved it for their meeting, and had anticipated the rationalization. But he had not been prepared for the eloquence of the man—glibness more typical of an author than a dispossessed farmer and a small town evangelist. Chester Mahoney seemed to be a person of conspicuous accomplishment, a quality unaffected by even the triteness of his introspection. There could be no percentage, after all, in confessing to a tryst with a girl of fifteen.

"You talk like a thespian," Tom said.

The man bowed stiffly, apparently accustomed to the compliment. "I *have* no finer disguise, Mr. Hemmings. Blame it on the Good Book, sir, and the immortal Bard. Wonderful company for a widower of five years. Blame it also on South Bend Baptist College. Did you know I have a master's in divinity?"

Tom suppressed a smirk. "You're in the right place," he replied finally. "Think of the souls to be saved in a laundry dorm."

Chester bowed again. "That's not why I am here, gracious sir. I would *prefer* a reassignment." A cloud crept across his brow. "In fact, I believe I have earned one. I've been tutoring one of the little blacks, helping him with his math. I daresay he will soon have his General Education Certificate."

"Would Walnut Creek approve?"

The man fell silent; his cheeks were now flushed. Clearly, he was more embarrassed by his philanthropy than the dark allegation in his inmate file. "Probably not," he sighed. "But the conflict is between races, Mr. Hemmings, not individuals. There is still room for a little Christian charity. On that I have always insisted."

The man coughed once more as he finished speaking. He sat down hesitantly on the chair by Tom's desk, perhaps fearful that he would wrinkle his pants. Chester's eyes fell guiltily upon the newspaper article. "A betrayal no worse than my own," he said. His chin jerked reflexively towards the headline. "But I've had even shoddier fantasies."

"And what would they be?" Tom asked, a question he knew to be redundant. The issue, one of equity, was being championed to death by not only the inmates but the employee unions as well, the small clouds of self-important men who passed out literature in the parking lot each morning. Tom's recent flirtation with the largest of these groups, the red-jacketed United Auto Workers, had in fact earned him an expense paid weekend at a training retreat in Black Lake, Michigan.

Chester winked slyly. "The bull of the boonies, sir. The banking conspiracy, for one. And the government plot to steal back our land. Utter nonsense, to be sure. But when folks are disillusioned, a preacher must offer them myths."

"We all want a stake in the country." Tom said. He was all too familiar with the conceit—had in fact championed it during the Vietnam War when he had spent his seven years in Australia in defiance of the draft. Having made peace with his draft board twenty-six years ago, a truce sealed by the peacetime enlistment he had served after coming home, he had attained the myth of closure. It was within his vanity to believe his small rebellion had been equal to the task—that the business of taking back the country, for all-important purposes, was now over and done with.

"*Count time.*"

The call, a precedent to the noon meal, had come from the control desk in the dormitory. Through the glass partition in his office, Tom watched the scramble of the inmates, the docility with which a score of men relinquished the game tables and returned to their bunks to be counted. Chester, unaffected by the order, continued to sit quietly, his eyes upon the newspaper, his fingers drumming methodically upon his knees. He spoke gently as though divulging a secret.

"It's an empty ambition, sir, to compete with Philistines. Would that I still had the foolishness for such nonsense. But sense is the tonic of age, Mr. Hemmings. I am an old dog, sir, and long only to nap on a porch."

Tom shook his head. The pretentiousness of the man, not to mention his embrace of both jingoism and literature, was a little exasperating.

"The porch," Tom replied. "The solace of aging men." The comment, though perhaps too self-revealing, did not appear to have affected the man. It was Tom's habit, in any case, to share small intimacies with inmates, a practice discouraged by the prison administration but which he found to be not only gratifying, but prudent. In the event of an inmate rebellion, a real probability since the arrival of the Colonial Concession Company, the inmates would be his most reliable source of protection. And who better to confide in than a well-read man?

Tom cleared his throat. "The farm crew? Is that your fantasy now?"

"Now *that* would be a Godsend," Chester replied. "Particularly since beggars cannot choose. But *all* would

20

be compensated if you were to return an old hayseed to the sod."

"They'll start you at fifty cents a day," Tom said. "Top wage is a buck eighty-five."

Chester shrugged, perhaps already wise to the pay scale of inmates. "The minions of the Philistines," he said. "Is there no limit to their reach? But I have grown comfortable with servitude, sir, and will submit to a watchtower as readily as I submitted to the bank that took back my farm." Chester stroked his beard and chuckled. "What joy it is to give Caesar his due."

"The farm crew," Tom repeated, a compact rather than a statement. He did not think about the vanity of the promise, his implication that even fatalism might relocate an inmate from the tightly-fenced Hill to the relative freedom of the farming operation. Since the spousal killing several months ago, an incident that had cost two counselors their jobs, it had become difficult to place even property offenders on the farm and labor crews; the orchards and cornfields were mostly unattended while close to a thousand inmates were inactive on the Hill, their idleness assured by a watertight classification system and the concertina wire of the perimeter fence. Perhaps Etta Johnson, the Farm's new superintendent, had a plan to relieve the congestion on the Hill, but he rather doubted it: Etta, the first woman to be put in charge of the facility, still needed to ingratiate herself to the rank and file. Tom therefore conceded that it was a personal failing, his enduring need to rebel, that made him decide to fulfill Chester's request.

"The farm crew," Chester replied. "Assign me there, *please*."

There was new movement in the dormitory, a spontaneous scramble as a hundred inmates, many of them on idle status, crowded near the door to await a final signal from the desk officer. Chester, having gained his objective, rose tactfully to his feet, a concession to not only good manners, but to his duty of the moment. It was feeding time, after all, and Chester the Molester would soon be needed in the serving line.

21

November 23, 2000
10:15 a.m.

The Main Gate hummed shut, sealing Tom suddenly within the inner prison. His palms were damp, his breathing shallow, and his Second Chance vest itched beneath his shirt. He clipped the spit shield back onto his helmet and squinted at the smoke-filled compound. It seemed strange that the inmates had asked for a meeting: the unearthliness of the laundry dorm, still wavering behind the haze, made it seem impenetrable. He turned up the volume on his hand radio and awaited his signal from the Control Unit—his go-ahead to approach the final check-point, a tiny guard shack near the inmate hospital. It was only a one-minute walk from the gate, but it seemed to be a mile away.

The plan was a deviation from standard hostage protocol. He would meet directly with the leaders of the insurrection, record their demands, and acquire from them a gesture of good faith, hopefully the release of another hostage or two. The distress signal—"It's game time"—was to be radioed to the Control Unit only in the event that his life or the lives of the hostages were threatened. At that point, he was to trust in the accuracy of the first tear gas canisters and the efficiency with which the Point Squad could storm the dormitory. As plans went, it was not a bad one; his basic concern was with the encumbrances it placed on the emergency squads: an obligation to do battle for faceless conspiracies and to perceive him as someone worthy of quick rescue. Regardless, he had to enter the dormitory—the inmates wanted *him* and *him* alone.

Tom had realized his expendability only five days ago: a reminder he owed to a Sunday morning phone call. It was an unlikely time for introspection; he had been brewing coffee in his trailer, a one-bedroom double-wide he had rented from the prison, and planning the simple distractions of his day. The morning, brisk and bright, provided no hint of karma: the air was too crisp, the ground frost too chaste, and the fruits of

22

complacency too rich to ignore. He would start his day with a five-mile run, a jog that would take him past farm ponds and cornfields to the southernmost watchtowers of the facility. Later, he would fish the South Ranch Lake, a parkland basin near Highway 40 where prison employees were allowed to cast for stripers and channel cats. Finally, he would cruise the singles bars in Indianapolis, dimly lit meat markets that further invigorated his sporting instincts. The Penal Farm, faintly visible through his trailer window, therefore struck him as fortifying—not forbidding—as though the fifty-foot watchtowers and the chain link fence had been placed there to insulate him from intrusions. Even the road gang, a crew of inmates in orange blazers picking up trash near Highway 40, seemed to have been put there not to elevate his attention but to rescue him from the final vestiges of clutter. And so when the phone rang, he answered it leisurely, holding the receiver to his ear as though it were a shell in which he might hear the ocean.

"*Hemmings.*"

It was Brewer. He paused, suspecting what the message would be—knowing he did not wish to hear it.

"*Hemmings,*" the voice repeated. "You're playing in traffic, Hemmings. That means that *no one* will cover your ass—not until you put your John Hancock on the petition." The remark was a response to a message he had sent the man on Friday: a request that he find room on the farm crew for another tractor driver. Clearly, the operation of the farm was secondary to the Governor's memo—the directive, long overdue, that prison employees be tested for drug use.

"I'll sign it," Tom said, "when the trafficking stops." Accustomed to irony, it did not surprise him that a memo meant for his security had instead become a liability to him. According to Brewer, nearly a hundred prison guards had already placed their signatures on the petition to halt the drug testing.

Brewer snorted. "You *need* to sign it either way. Why'd you go to Black Lake if you're gonna slack off on the *union?*"

Brewer spoke the word union too bitterly, as though alluding to a partnership he had long grown weary of. The

23

man's liaison with the United Auto Workers had begun almost a decade before his arrival at the Farm, originating at a Pontiac Plant in Kokomo and enduring even after the factory had relocated to Juarez, Mexico, ten years ago. Although Brewer claimed no animosity towards the North American Free Trade Agreement—"I always preferred farmin' anyhow"—his stewardship seemed sated at best, as though he were a cuckold hoping a change of climate might revitalize a dead marriage.

"I *wanted* to slack off," Tom said. "Just like those shirkers you've got in the union. How'd they ever make it as auto workers?"

"You think I don't *know* the union is full of fuck-offs?" Brewer yelled.

Tom eased the receiver away from his ear. He felt his jaw tighten. "I doubt it."

"Well this much I *do* know. There's *shirkers* and there's *traitors*. Now the union don't care if you goof off or even if you traffic with the inmates. Just don't be cheapening your union colors. Do that and *no one* will do you any favors."

Tom knew that Brewer was right. An overtime grievance, a spat with a supervisor, a challenge to a policy deemed arbitrary—these were the evils best vindicated by prison employees, the matters least likely to set him adrift.

Tom feigned indignation. "I don't *need* any favors from *you*. Not if it cheapens my signature."

Brewer chuckled hollowly. "Okay, Hemmings. Leave your hand on your *cock*—that's where it *belongs*. You ain't married, you live like a monk, and you got no vices worth braggin' about. I doubt that you could handle a *real* favor."

"I *could* handle a little etiquette."

Brewer was silent, a somber reminder that even shirkers had standards. And then his voice became a growl.

"Hemmings," he said. "This ain't the *time* for etiquette. Not when they're makin' us pee into cups."

Tom remembered Brewer's warning as he watched the compound. The bodies now struck him as merely lethargic as though they had been lulled to sleep by the singsong garbling on the radio at his hip. The sight seemed a mockery—yet another reminder that his anthem, for want of a better word, could resonate only in a void. And yet the veiled bodies continued to pulse, a mirage so convincing that he was almost fearful of awakening them. But the sight was just one of the host of seductions: seductions he had *failed* to appraise adequately—seductions that had led him to this particular moment in time. And now, in his heightened state of awareness, he was determined to relive them all.

Tom drew a slow breath, muted his radio, and walked towards the checkpoint.

November 23, 2000
10:20 a.m.

The hospital checkpoint was the point of no return, the location where he was to be received by the inmate envoy that would escort him the remaining fifty yards to the dormitory under siege. Though no larger than an outhouse, the miniature building provided cover to two point sharpshooters and a communications officer. Lieutenant Omar Perkins, the communications officer, was holding a telephone in his plump hands, examining the touch dial as though it were a puzzle he was attempting to solve. The receiver, a direct line to the laundry dorm, seemed an embarrassment to the man and he quickly hung it up when he noticed Tom. He spoke apologetically— "They're not answerin'"—a comment that renewed Tom's hope for retreat. Tom knelt behind the checkpoint door, opened wide to provide maximum concealment to the point sharpshooters, and studied the laundry dorm through the crack. The ethereal appearance of the building was deceptive, since he believed that a few of the inmates had guns.

Would his life end today? Surely it would—probably with a shot from the dormitory or a stray bullet from one of the sharpshooters on the roof of the administration building. Why else was his memory so alive, his thoughts so invasive, his life so determined to flash before his eyes? But why was his memory recycling toxins—moments as acidic to him as the smoke? If these flashbacks bore any solace, any promise of closure, he was unable to see it. Suppressing his fear, he continued to watch the dormitory. A void, a fathomless void, was about to swallow him up.

Was it only three days since he had chaired the Conduct Adjustment Board? He was not a disciple of disciplinary hearings—kangaroo justice the inmates called them—but he did enjoy sitting on the Conduct Adjustment Board. The structure it provided him, along with the opportunity to get out of the laundry dorm every Monday and Wednesday, were invigorating. Not even a flux in cases, most of them disputes between inmates and commissary staff, diminished the patience he brought to the Board nor was he particularly distracted by the personalities of his co-members: Captain Harold Hawkins, by now his most consistent critic, and Bret Brewer, who only wanted justice for his union. This time, however, the specter of order had not refreshed him. Instead, it had provided Tom with his first clear glimpse of the shadowland he would soon enter. It was unnerving that so stark a revelation was trumpeted not by thunder—not even by the bark of shotguns—but by a few stale conversations in a carpeted room. But that was the moment Tom knew hell was coming. That was the moment he first glimpsed the void, a chasm that was yawning before him like a monster from the deep.

The board room, a carpeted chamber at the hub of the Special Housing Unit, had at first seemed a harmless location in which to continue his dispute with Brewer, a distraction he rather welcomed since the ongoing lockdown suggested it would be at least a half hour before the witnesses could be assembled. He was glad that only one case had been scheduled: a charge of battery against a kitchen inmate who had beaten up a skinhead in the Dining Hall. The accused, a towering drag queen named Trinsea, had been fetched from her cell row and placed in a holding tank next to the boardroom. Since she had requested The Deacon to be her inmate lawyer, Tom had sent a pass to the

Porter Line—a request that Chester himself be brought to the hearing.

Feeling impetuous, Tom asked Brewer if he had taken the piss grievance to Etta Johnson, the new Superintendent. It was unfair to include Etta in a gathering storm, but her response was necessary if the guards were to avoid pissing into cups. Once the grievance cleared Etta, it would probably proceed to the state appeals board and then to arbitration.

"Fuck her," Brewer snapped. "What's she got to do with it anyhow? Last month she was an ombudsman at Central Office."

"We *need* a watchdog. Just to keep things plugged up around here."

Hawkins cursed and then slapped his forehead. He spoke as though Tom had grabbed his balls. "*Bend over*, Hemmings, if it's *dogs* you're partial to. Let's see you spread them cheeks."

"I was talking about Etta Johnson."

"Fuck her, Hemmings. We already got us one drag queen too many."

Interlacing his fingers into the shape of a bunker, the captain continued speaking. "Hemmings," he said. "I've been here all my life—that's *twenty years longer* than you. I've seen seven riots, a dozen killings, even a couple of fires. I've seen the place change from a flophouse for drunks to a *real* prison. But I ain't seen nothing like what may be comin' down—not if my snitches can be believed. The anarchists here are just waitin' to pounce and if they *do* the buzzards are gonna pick our bones."

"That's why we need new management."

Hawkins clenched his fists. "What we *need* is a hundred more officers. What we *need* is twice as many segregation cells. What we *need* is a searchlight in every tower. And what they've given us is a *whore*." Hawkins frowned deeply and shook his head. "If things keep slidin' the way they've been doin', the Devil himself is gonna screw us."

"The *whore* wouldn't mind it," Brewer said. He laughed evilly and shook his head. "Since her husband died last year she can't get *enough* cock."

Hawkins, nodding reverently, positioned his thumbs into the effigy of a steeple. He spoke as though delivering a eulogy. "We got us a *prison* to bottle down, Hemmings. But we're turning it into a *brothel* instead. No wonder the inmates are about to take it over."

Brewer swore softly, "The inmates can *have* it. At least that'll stop the Governor from bottlin' our piss."

Tom had made no further comment. He was bone-weary of the conspiracy theories—conceits better suited to backwoods survivalists than protectors of the state. This was not because such theories ridiculed the social comedy, but because they complimented it too much, endowing it with powers that could only be superhuman. Preferring to view politics as a circus of errors, he had welcomed a message recently posted upon one of the bulletin boards, a comment about the redundancy of the new employee gymnasium. *Close it down*, the message read. *We're getting enough exercise already. What with jumping on bandwagons, rushing to judgment, and leaping to conclusions, we'll all be in shape by Christmas.*

"Who wrote the report on *this* queen?" Brewer snapped, as he rattled the papers before him. The reference was not to Etta, but to the business at hand: *drag queen mischief*—mischief that had at least been mundane enough to document.

"Yoakum," Tom said.

He anticipated only silence at the mention of Yoakum, a man whose notoriety could only have been forged in darkness. Brewer sighed loudly. "*Tear it up. H*e's still with AFSCME."

This mention of the American Federation of State, County, and Municipal Employees—a suck-ass clique according to the more ambitious unions—did not seem excessive under the circumstances. With union elections pending in less than a month, additional battle lines were about to be drawn.

It therefore seemed irresponsible to allow an adversary, a yeoman of a rival union, to increase his credibility.

Tom remembered the three sharp knocks that forecasted yet another showdown. He remembered the door to the boardroom creaking open, revealing the macabre presence of Henry Yoakum. He was a fleshless officer, wiry and short, and his face looked like wax that had been melted, set, and then scarred with an ice pick, the result of shrapnel he had caught in Vietnam. His bearing was humble but his eyes were astute: Yoakum knew already that he—a stooge to the lowliest of the unions—would be the real target of the Board. Yoakum lowered his head when he stepped into the room to testify. And when he lifted it, he resembled a turkey vulture sipping from a well.

Tom remembered the hearing as a blur of hazy testimonies—a blur that had lasted a full hour before the issue of inmate firepower arose. The fact that a storm was approaching—that things were seriously out of whack—was well indicated by the evasiveness of Yoakum's testimony. "All was going well," Yoakum kept muttering "They was entering the mess hall as calm as you please—causin' no problems at all. Then this fag jumped the serving line and all hell broke loose." "Did she *start* the fight?" Tom had asked him. "Can't tell ya for certain, Mr. Hemmings. All I know is everything was goin' well. They was marchin' in as calm as you please. Then this fag jumped the serving line and all hell broke loose." It was ultimately Trinsea, not Yoakum, who boldly confirmed that a standoff was coming. Her commitment to payback, crucial if the charge was to stick, was evident from the self-righteousness with which she marched into the room. Her chains seemed to rattle like the ghost of Marley.

"Was it over a debt?" Tom inquired.

She stood ramrod straight, like a sentry about to relieve him. "Honey, I ain't sayin' nothin' about that. A little chump tried to shank me—that's *all* you need to know. If you think I'm cookin' up lies, Mr. Hemmings, you can just take it up with the *Deacon*."

Tom felt his pulse leap. The tranny's fearless defiance of authority—a specter of the radical sixties—was somehow irresistible. He looked at her enviously, suppressing his sense of nostalgia—his inborn need to rebel himself. For how much longer could he continue hiding behind the law?

He drew a slow breath then he lowered his eyes. "Very well," he replied. "Let's wait for the Deacon to arrive."

November 23, 2000
10:30 a.m.

Tom knew he would die at the checkpoint—of that he was absolutely certain. The wavering compound, the pulsating bodies, the stone silence of the dormitory could only be a prelude to oblivion. But what else could he do when no options were left, when lives were on the line, when the inmates wanted him and only him to negotiate the siege? He had flaunted too many rules in his life, broken too many covenants, forged too many forbidden allegiances. And he had gotten away with it every time. But now—*now*— his bill was due. *Now*, he would have to pay the piper.

Probably, he would die within the hour, and so he was grateful for his retrospections: senseless though they were, they were his final glimpses of this world. A few hazy thoughts and then a hero's death—that would be his legacy. And so he was touched by the memory of Chester—the little man's heartening presence before the Conduct Adjustment Board three days ago. The encounter, an otherwise sordid affair, was made precious by its finality.

Sitting in front of the board members, staring at them from across the table, Chester had resembled a statue in a museum: his face was composed, his eyes impassive, his gaze as steady as an eagle's. For all true purposes, he might have been a judge in a court of Heaven.

Tom remembered that Chester had broken the silence, that his voice was as dry as powder, that he showed no concern that his client, a creature less eloquent than himself, had been returned prematurely to her cell. "We meet again, Mr. Hemmings," Chester said, inclining his head toward Tom.

Tom had felt his palms dampen. "You're on my agenda," he replied.

Chester chuckled. "There are better investments than *me*, Mr. Hemmings. You must truly be overextended, sir."

"I am. Consider it the toll of winter."

Chester shook his head. "A good day for dropping a dime, so to speak. And yet the morning is still bright. Isn't it a blessing, sir, that the sun cannot expose our true thoughts?"

"So what do you have for us?"

"*Much*, Mr. Hemmings. But scraps are all you require of me."

"A little information—that's *all* that we need today."

"Then that you shall have. But *this* time return me the favor. When you get what you want, gentlemen, you *forget* about Old Chester."

"I'm working on your transfer," Tom replied. "It *is* my first priority. One I haven't forgotten."

The little man nodded then cleared his throat. "Bless you, Mr. Hemmings. I am always grateful for noble intentions. Remember, good sir, that Rome first collapsed from within."

"I *said* it's my *first* priority."

"Please hurry then, sir. The Disciples are *also* expeditious—the rascals who suspect me of colluding with staff. I'm not worried about their animosity, sir, so much as the dispatch with which they might act upon it."

"A shank?" Tom asked.

"A *pistol*," Chester said. "A special import you might call it. One of several has been smuggled onto the grounds and hidden near the dairy. At least that's what I've overheard. What a shame it would be, not to mention an embarrassment to all concerned, if Old Chester was to be done in by a pistol."

The mention of the weapon produced a pregnant hush over the Board members. This was not because the inmates were now stocking firearms, but because the issue of gun control, a plank in the Gore presidential campaign, had become a sensitive topic at the facility, so much so that it was the subject of yet another flier. *First they ship off our jobs*, the flier read. *Next they confiscate our piss. Now they want to take away our guns. At this rate, we may just as well let them shoot us in the streets.*

"Where?" Tom asked.

"I would need to do a bit of sleuthing, sir. It is a role for which I am rather poorly equipped, but I would be willing to make the sacrifice for my peace of mind and the safety of others."

"I'll mention it to the investigation officer." Tom said. He had spoken hopefully, perhaps still a convert to the powers of fiction. It was his suspicion that Chester's story, rather than the weight of his recommendation, would be ultimately responsible for relocating the little man to the security of the farming operation.

"So what was the fight over?"

"A fee," Chester said, his tone growing sharper. "For services rendered—if I may use such language in reference to a blow job. An unsightly business, I assure you gentlemen, but it was a contract nonetheless. She wouldn't stand for it when her fee was delayed and beat the young rascal within an inch of his life. I daresay that he deserved it too, if only for bargaining with a *prostitute*."

"Did she stage the attack?" Tom asked, a suspicion he had been unable to shake. It made too little sense that the altercation had taken place in full view of Yoakum and his staff.

Chester sighed. "I'm sure that she did, sir. The Hill is restless, as you well know. Should it fall under new management, the harlots will lose their protection. I daresay the rabble will rape her bowlegged."

The matter, at that moment, had been patently concluded, the disclosures of a tested informant having more credibility than the ramblings of a wary officer or the artless evasions of the accused. Still, as Tom recorded the vote on the disposition form—a two to one verdict of guilty—Tom made mention of due process protocols, suggesting to the others that Trinsea, a creature whose innocence rivaled his own, had been duped into placing unwarranted trust in a rogue preacher. But although he had wanted to find her not guilty, he rather welcomed the reprisal he received from Hawkins: a reminder that the facility would be defenseless if it failed to protect its informants.

"Hemmings," Hawkins snapped. "Don't *you* be a woman too."

Tom kept a straight face. "Why not?"

"'Cause this boardroom's a safe place to meet with our snitches. You wanna blow Chester's cover?"

Tom egged him on. "Aren't we here to dispense justice?"

Harold slammed the table. "Not if it means outin' Chester, we ain't. Now he's much too good a snitch to be wasted on a queen."

November 23, 2000
11:00 a.m.

The checkpoint door jerked before Tom heard the shot, but he knew instantly that someone had fired a gun in his direction. He resisted the trembling in his bowels: it was time to let his training take over. *Suspend your imagination. Appraise objectively.* He repeated this mantra to himself and, after a moment, the blow to the door seemed harmless enough: as though someone had walloped it with a rock. The shooter was probably an upstart, an inmate destined for quick disciplining by the inmate leaders, and so it seemed absurd that the point sharpshooters were returning fire, peppering the dorm with volley after volley from their Mini-14s. Clearly, a lot of ammunition was going to waste.

"So much for shakedowns," he muttered to Perkins. The lieutenant blushed as though accused of selling contraband to the inmates. Squatting beneath the window of the shack, Perkins was once again punching the buttons on the telephone, an effort so obviously futile that Tom felt guilty for having bullied him. Tom actually approved of the shakedowns, not because they were particularly productive but because they usually allowed him the privilege of solitude, an opportunity to seek order through the more formidable power of the pen.

Tom had acquired, at the age of fifty-two, a fascination with the written word, a sense of aesthetics that had earned him a sound reputation as a writer of killer memos. He had therefore been grateful, upon entering his dormitory after the Conduct Board hearing, to see that the shakedowns were still in progress. He remembered the rows of inmates sitting mutely upon their bunks while teams of officers combed methodically through their mattresses and footlockers: an ironclad assurance that he would have the rest of the day to meditate and write. He was comforted by the memory of his quiet office—it seemed as though he were being personally protected by the German Shepherds squatting beside their handlers in the bed pods.

Tom had written the first of his memos to Etta Johnson, taking care to frame the issue, the fallouts of privatization, as concisely as possible. He did not share in the general opinion of Etta: a large sturdy woman with a direct manner, she struck him as a doubtful beneficiary of sexual politics. He had therefore seen no good reason to antagonize her, particularly when the pending riot was a problem she had only recently inherited.

He wrote:

November 20, 2000
Mrs. Johnson:

> *This morning the Conduct Adjustment Board sentenced Torrance "Trixie" Washington, DOC 981223, to a year of segregation for punching Cecil Hopper, DOC 991112. The incident, which took place during noon feeding, might have led to a gang fight had either participant been connected to one of the inmate cliques. Fortunately, no gang*

34

members got involved and Officer Yoakum and his staff were able to contain the incident.

According to a reliable informant, the cause of the assault was a debt owed by Mr. Hopper to Mr. Washington. Since Mr. Hopper is not a well-connected inmate, the implication is that he did not receive his commissary order in time to pay the debt. This delay seems due to the policies of Colonial Concession Inc. with whom we have contracted commissary services since May. Please note that Colonial requires an inmate requesting commissary to complete a standardized order form (copy attached) citing eight pieces of personal data in addition to an inventory of the goods he wants to purchase. Since the forms are machine-processed in Houston, a single miscalculation or digital error will deny an inmate his commissary until the following week. On top of that, the commissary items are of marginal quality and do not seem worth the aggravation it takes to order them.

To deal with the problem, I would suggest we consider a policy revision regarding commissary services. This proposal could be drafted at a meeting attended by myself and a few of the dorm officers. It is the line staff, after all, who will take the hit if the worst-case scenario should come to pass.

> *Respectfully,*
> *Tom Hemmings*
> *Counselor, Dormitory 7*

He reread the memo slowly then signed it with a flourish. The use of hyperbole seemed only slightly excessive to him since he had intervened in a similar altercation earlier that day—a standoff involving a pair of skinheads, spindly teenagers whose sunken chests and pipe stem arms belied their claims to racial superiority. He had in fact sensed gratitude, not defiance, after ordering them to sit on their bunks, an attitude confirmed by the remark that had floated through the dorm as he closed his office door: "Beau's lucky the Hog broke it up, I tell ya! I'd a kicked his happy ass for sure!" He had not bothered to inquire into the reason for the fight since he knew that the cause would be tritely familiar: an unpaid football bet or a loan collectable at a banker's rate of three dollars for one.

The second of the memos he addressed to the Classification Committee, a three-member board that met weekly to determine the placement of inmates within the institution. Since the matter required an exception to the facility's strict criteria for farm workers, he made several drafts of the memo, taking care to include his suspicion that a handgun had been stashed near the dairy. He disclosed this bit of information in a moment of naïveté, a myopic's belief that the means, on occasion, might support rather than contaminate, the ends. When he had completed the memo he held it at eye level, inspecting it as though it were a painting.

TO: Classification Committee
FROM: Tom Hemmings, Counselor, Dormitory 7
RE: Chester Herbert Mahoney, DOC 990624

The above-named inmate has requested relocation from the kitchen to the Farm Line. Although he is technically ineligible for the transfer, he qualifies on a special case basis since he has been here over a year without a disciplinary report. It should also be considered that, though charged with fondling a female of fifteen, Mr. Mahoney was convicted of the lesser-included offense of felony battery and is serving only five years.

Mr. Mahoney has been a model inmate since his arrival at this facility on June

24, 1999. Not only have his performance evaluations been consistently superior, but he has demonstrated a conservative regard for the safety and security of this facility. Our Investigations Office, for example, credits Mr. Mahoney with having provided several valuable tips regarding gang activity and dangerous contraband. At this moment, he is helping us locate a firearm that an inmate has reportedly stashed near the dairy.

Mr. Mahoney impresses, all in all, as an aging pedophile who tried to seduce a young member of his church. He has no prior criminal history, however, and once made a living as a corn and soybean farmer. Presently, he is disenfranchised both socially and financially, which makes the cult status cited in his pre-sentence report seem exaggerated. Nonetheless, he claims to preside over the American Gospel Party, a pseudo religious organization of about five hundred members that expounds the usual antigovernment rhetoric. Should this be the case, he could possibly influence some of the younger white inmates in the dormitory and provide the Aryan Brotherhood with a wider recruitment base.

In summation, the facility would be better off in many ways if Mr. Mahoney were transferred to a line more consistent with his working background. On this basis, I am recommending that he be placed on the farm crew.

> *Respectfully,*
> *Tom Hemmings*
> *Counselor, Dormitory 7*

He studied the memo with excessive satisfaction, forcing himself to set it aside when he heard the knock upon his office door. The door opened slowly, gradually, as though yielding to the ethereal: the intruder, however, was not the Muse, awakened by the spell of his words, but a *real* woman. It was Sarah Baumgardner, one of the officers assigned to the dorm, a plain-looking female of forty with disheveled blond hair. Although short and girlishly slender, her sharp chin and quick temper had acquired her the nickname 'Mother' among the inmates. He waited impassively for her to speak, not because he suspected her business would be minor, but because he had come to regard her as a symbol rather than an individual. Divorced with two children and nagging car payments, her story could have been that of any of the thirty female officers employed at the facility.

"We could use you, skipper," she said. "If you're not too *busy*, that is."

He nodded guiltily, slipping the memos into his desk drawer. "They find much?"

She shrugged. "Nuthin' to write home about, sir. A bunch of pills and some crumb-bum Nazi literature. The usual junk is what I'd call it."

The information did not surprise him, nor did it seem reason for further comment. The shakedowns, performed at predictable intervals, were a thorny issue among the officers, a gripe to the effect that they served only to aggravate the least stable of the inmates, thereby creating needless risks for staff. Yoakum, describing yet another spat with a queen, had summed up the matter perhaps too succinctly at a recent debate between the UAW and AFSCME.

"Had to fight her for that hairpin, I did. And she only got a week in the hole for it. Hells bells, I say! They don't *pay* me enough to fight those AIDS-carryin' motherfuckers!"

Tom had carelessly objected to Yoakum's comment, perhaps too reflexive in his aversion to blanket statements. After being shouted down by several officers, he had realized that the fear, if taken as a whole, was probably not as unreasonable as Yoakum had made it seem. The threat of AIDS was certainly a reality in the Special Housing Unit where segregated inmates would rake their gums with their fingers then spit blood at passing officers.

Sarah, uncharacteristically patient, continued to stand in his doorway. It was only the lines around her eyes and the pout of her mouth that mitigated her sternness. And so he detested the errand awaiting him, the stacks of confiscation forms to be filled out and then forwarded to the Screening Office. Although counselors were expected to assist with shakedowns, he avoided the duty whenever he could, considering it an insult to his many years of administrative experience and his master's degree in criminology. He had even gone so far as to share the matter with Brewer, attaching, for a moment at least, an unprecedented value to the farm foreman's opinion.

"Put it in writing," Brewer had told him. "And give me a copy. That'll give the brass something *else* to think about when they're lookin' at a contract."

Sarah, still waiting for his reply, had begun to shuffle from one tiny foot to the other. He wondered if it would help his cause to ask her out, a date he could always break if she continued to insist that he join the shakedowns. His past couplings with female officers, after all, had been hasty, rather unsatisfying affairs, perhaps because they had smacked vaguely of incest. Her eyes, to his relief, remained cool, extending only an impersonal invitation, and he felt a slight burning in his cheeks as he waited for her to speak. "She *is* with AFSCME," he recalled Brewer telling him, a damper to any further thoughts of seduction. "Best little spitfire they got. So you don't need to be gettin' involved with her none."

It was Sarah who ended the stalemate, addressing him finally in a tone so apathetic that he instinctively knew he was not a match for her—that his feeble plotting could not even afford him a respectable listing in her gallery of die-hards, ranks that surely included angry UAW members, groping sergeants, and an ex-husband late with his child support payments.

"Mr. Hemmings," she drawled finally, her voice as dull as lead. "Isn't it time you was helpin' us take inventory?"

November 23, 2000
11:30 a.m

"We have contact," Perkins said, beaming triumphantly as he extended the phone receiver to Tom. Tom accepted the receiver grudgingly, wiping off Perkins' perspiration with his shirtsleeve before holding it to his ear. He had hoped the point sharpshooters would continue firing, thereby eliminating the need for negotiations, but their rifles had fallen silent and he could hear a sound at the other end of the line: first a breathing, quick and irregular, and then the petty complaint of an inmate.

"They stole my *soup*, Jackson!"

"Gabriel?" Tom said, recognizing the inmate by the eccentricity of his speech, his habit of addressing everyone as Jackson. Gabriel Grant, a bony African American with no protective alliance, had been the subject of a memo Tom had written two months ago: a recommendation for work release that had cleared the Classification Committee and was waiting approval at the Central Office level. The man's crime struck him as laughable: he had stolen a case of vodka from a liquor store in South Bend, stashing it in an alley where another tramp had eventually made off with it. After calling the police himself to report the loss, Gabriel had been quickly copped for petty larceny with a prior and sent to the Department of Correction on a four-year stint.

"They stole my *soup*, Jackson! You hear what I'm *sayin'*? It was *chicken* soup."

"Let it go, Gabriel," Tom replied. "Don't be getting yourself in any trouble over it."

"Okay, Jackson, okay."

"And I'll need to speak to your shepherd. Is the Deacon *available*?"

"Okay, Jackson, okay."

40

A loud rattle suggested the phone had been dropped. Perhaps it had been forgotten as well: he could hear only disharmony—shouts, footsteps, the blare of a television set—noises more suggestive of a bus depot than an organized insurrection. It was several minutes before the racket was interrupted by the silky voice of his informant.

"Is it you *once again*, Mr. Hemmings?"

The voice was excessively reassuring, indicating not a relationship of convenience but a familiarity born of years. Perhaps this was attributable to Tom's baptism of fire or to the licentious thrill of the void, but he felt no hesitation to talk to the man. Tom did not doubt that Chester, who now struck him as a man of many faces, was as wary a champion as he. He spoke freely as though addressing an old friend.

"You're slow for a spokesman, Chester."

"A role I had nearly disposed of, sir, until you succeeded in calling me to the forefront."

Tom's heart skipped a beat. "I'm envious," he said. "How did you nearly dispose of your fate?"

"I told the Muslims I had fallen out of favor with the administration. In times of anarchy, sir, grace is better assured by casting off yokes."

"Perhaps you can rid me of mine," Tom replied. "Is the shooter still in business?"

"Sadly, no. That might have spared us both."

"What stole our salvation?"

"My own rash judgment, sir. I asked the Muslims to disarm him. But it was an act of desperation, sir—not leadership. Unfortunately, I'm as likely a target as you."

"Who was it?"

"Hopper, sir. The boy Trixie cold-cocked. His real lover died in yesterday's manhunt and he was beside himself with grief."

Tom felt a chill spreading over his spine. The manhunt, which Tom had been part of, was something he wanted desperately to forget. "I thought Hopper was in the Special Housing Unit."

"He was, Mr. Hemmings. But they let him out of segregation last night and put him on dorm watch. They let

41

out Trixie too. There are worse scamps around here than Hopper and Trixie. The facility needed their cells."

"So Hopper was trying to buy the farm? Death by sharp-shooter?"

"It was a bid to be sure. You may take him off our hands if you wish. And his pistol. I assure you he acted entirely on his own ..."

The voice was suddenly buried in static. Tom shook the receiver irritably, attempting to recover their conversation, but the line continued to crackle. The news—that the shooter was only a punk with a death wish—could probably be taken at face value. But the thought of this only renewed Tom's reluctance; he did not wish to be reminded that his compass, his sense of direction, had fallen into the hands of a child molester with a personal agenda. His sole consolation was the bedrock validity that Chester was acquiring in his eyes, a trust that had been practically etched in stone by his third encounter with the man.

Tom remembered the aftermath of the shakedown three days ago. He had remained in his office, not to complete paperwork, the mound of confiscation forms Sarah had dumped on his desk, but because he had realized that he had misplaced his institutional keys. The loss, though a serious one, had not caused him to panic right away, perhaps because he viewed the matter as metaphorical rather than as an issue that might earn him a three-day suspension. He had even informed one of the second shift dorm officers about it, and had stood by passively while the man unlocked his office door for him. After thoroughly searching his desk drawers, however, and probing repeatedly into the crease in his chair, Tom had decided that his situation was irredeemable and had begun to look forward to a short vacation. He was in fact expecting an inquisition, not a visitor, when he answered a rap on his door. He was not entirely surprised when he discovered Chester rather than a group of sergeants standing outside.

The little man had nodded. "A moment, good sir." His face was flushed, his eyes evasive; Chester looked like an embarrassed butler.

"Why aren't you in the *mess hall*?" Tom blurted.

Chester bowed. "It's my day off, sir. How fortunate if that should provide me with the feast of your company."

Tom shook his head. "Please cut the crap, Chester. *May I help you*?"

"Only if I might return the favor," Chester said. "Or would a Samaritan be meat to the Philistines?"

Tom shrugged, allowing Chester to close the door behind him. He waited for the little man to be seated before reclining once more in his chair.

"A favor, no," Tom replied. "But an exchange of services might keep the wolves from my door. What scrap of information have you brought me this time? A hit or a plant?"

"Neither," Chester said. "It doesn't suit you, Mr. Hemmings, to bargain with the likes of me. The scraps, good sir, I reserve for vulgarians."

Tom suppressed a smirk. "I've been told that I qualify."

"Not so," Chester replied. "If that were the case, I daresay you would have been promoted long ago."

"An oversight," Tom said. A wry smile spread across his face. "Or an unanswered prayer. Both can be payback, I suppose."

"Consider it a blessing instead, Mr. Hemmings. An opportunity to nurture your flock. But nurture it with humility, good sir. The dispensation of charity is not your privilege alone."

The man's small fist was hovering over his desk. As the fingers relaxed, a lump hit the desktop with a metallic jingle.

"I found them behind the officers' desk. I thought they might be yours."

Tom looked passively at the keys, unable at first to recognize them as his own. That a felon could have the impact of an angel was too thorough a distraction to him.

Tom felt his skin burn. "I suppose I now owe you."

Chester shook his head. "How can you owe what you have freely given? Your pledge of assistance and the gift of intelligent conversation. No, Mr. Hemmings, the obligation is thankfully mine. God, in his discretion, has provided me with an opportunity to reward you."

"Discretion," Tom said. "You don't strike me as a beneficiary of discretion. A *lack* of discretion is why you're in prison."

Chester's voice cracked. "I'm an old sinner, sir. It would insult us both if I were to represent myself otherwise. I am fortunate indeed that the Lord has not punished me according to my deserts."

"Your *plea bargain* was responsible for that."

The little man shrugged. He dropped his eyes, looking studiously at the floor. "My sentence, you mean. I'm sure I've done *something* to deserve it, sir. I would be a mighty rascal indeed to quarrel with God's judgment. Sadly, I was less enlightened when I was in the boonies, that backwoods place where the ladies flower a bit too early. I have seen mothers at the age of twelve—grandmothers at thirty. If you *must* know, Mr. Hemmings, I was not even her first suitor."

"If this is the least of your sins," Tom replied, "you must truly be a scoundrel."

"I am indeed," Chester said. "But more for the sin of omission than lust. Unlike you, Mr. Hemmings, I have broken from my covenant and slighted my flock. I have even slandered the Book of Joshua, the assurance of the Lord that the land should be a bosom to its children and not the spoils of Hittites. Is it any wonder, sir, that I am looking for a porch—a place where I might hide and lick my wounds?"

"Consider it done," Tom said. He handed Chester the memo he had written to the Classification Committee. He waited proudly as Chester slowly read it.

"Bless you," Chester said at last. "An inspired jewel, if you don't mind my saying so. Even the fib is a clever one."

"I am not your equal with fibs," Tom said. "Could you tell me what you mean?"

"You call me a conservative, sir. But doesn't that describe you?"

"*Count time.*"

The cry, a perennial distraction, once more enlivened the dormitory. As he watched the inmates return to their bed pods, Tom briefly remembered his training. The warning, *Don't become friends with them*, had been the foundation of his orientation twenty years ago, an assurance that collusion, not control, would surely result if a staff member failed to keep his distance from an inmate. He was grateful, at that moment, for his indoctrination. Myopic charters, even the bleak monopoly of the Colonial Concession Company, were somehow preferable to anarchy.

"Shall I call you a patriot instead?" Tom snapped. "What better refuge for a scoundrel?"

"You overrate my perversity, Mr. Hemmings. Be assured, sir, that a porch is all I am interested in. My sins have never extended to ingratitude."

The jangle of the desk officers' telephone, the call-out for the evening meal, seemed uncommonly loud as it resonated throughout the dorm. Clearly, the sound of the phone had been accentuated by the stone silence of the inmates—not the acoustics of the building. Only a few of them had gathered near the doorway to be called out for dinner, a sight so rare that Tom's pulse missed a beat. He looked at Chester and their eyes met.

"So when will it happen?" Tom whispered.

"In a day or two," Chester replied. "A week at most."

"The ringleaders?"

"Several members of the Brotherhood. Most of them boys like Hopper. But the Muslims are also involved. Those rascals who call themselves political prisoners."

"The demands?"

"Now those keep changing. Yesterday, the whites wanted to watch the Country Music Channel on television. That almost brought the lot of them to blows, I tell you. But all of them agree on the disagreeable food, not to mention the deadly hospital services. And Colonial Concessions will have to go."

"Hostages?"

"Cavanaugh for one. Yoakum if they can grab him. Baumgardner they want nothing to do with. She's a bit too mouthy, they tell me. And you they will also release, but that's so you'll come back and speak to the negotiator."

"And who might that be?"

"That cross is mine to bear, sir. But how can I barter with a gentleman? For the sake of our relationship, Mr. Hemmings, it's best I have nothing to do with this matter."

"For your sake as well," Tom replied.

He felt obliged to suppress his irritation, a sense of infringement that would have otherwise become the burden of the messenger. Tom did not wish to think about the mounds of paperwork that were bound to precede the insurrection: the inevitable requests for dorm and institutional transfers as well as the bogus disciplinary reports generated by the inmates seeking asylum in the Special Housing Unit. He paused a long moment, distancing himself from his anger before speaking to Chester once again.

"You'll have your deliverance," he promised. "The Classification Committee meets tomorrow. They won't begrudge you a favor you have sweated bullets for."

The little man sighed. He rose stiffly from the chair, intuitively aware that he had overstayed his welcome. "Deliverance," he said. "You are a trooper, Mr. Hemmings, to suppose it could be earned by the sweat of an old scoundrel. How about the blood of patriots and tyrants? I would hold that to be true, sir, if the words of our third president are to be believed."

Tom buried a chuckle. "Not to mention the American Gospel Party."

Chester nodded thoughtfully. "You speak facetiously of course, sir. But perhaps that is *your* deliverance."

"If you want sincerity, speak to the Teamsters. But they're gun fanatics, you know. They'll chew you out for trying to confiscate a pistol."

"A brash lot," Chester said. "But I cannot hold that against them. Even the *real* Disciples were rogues and illiterates, were they not? Without the deployment of sinners, sir, God's work would never get done."

Chester moved slowly to the door, a calculated gesture since their conversation had not quite ended. He paused before touching the handle.

"I'll close it behind you," Tom said to him finally. "And Chester?" The little man turned and blinked his pink-rimmed eyes. "Thank you for the keys."

November 23, 2000
Noon

"We have terms," Chester said, speaking to him once again over the telephone in the hospital checkpoint. Perkins sat quietly, his face now composed, while the point sharpshooters kept their rifles trained upon the dormitory.

Tom held the phone receiver tightly. "What are they?" he asked.

"A pittance, sir. They're requesting more time on the basketball courts. An hour a day. They want fresh fruit with dinner—less fried pork ..." The voice faded momentarily, suggesting that the restoration of phone contact would only be temporary.

"The fruit may be negotiable, sir ..."

"Sounds like a vocal minority."

"The Muslims, to be sure. But their price is cheap enough. Throw the mongrels some scraps, I say, and let's be done with this whole dreary business."

Tom licked his dry lips. "And the brokers their meat."

"Caesar's share, you mean. I prefer a humbler repose, Mr. Hemmings. Reward me with crackers on a porch and I will be content."

Slowly, Tom put down the phone, reluctant to relay the fruits of his efforts—an admission to the brass that the inmate demands were indicative of only a petty piracy. Removing his hand radio from its sheath, he depressed the squelch button.

"190. Control."

"Control. Over."

"Sounds like more Bermuda shorts. You may as well strike them while they're disorganized."

A long pause followed, indicating the message was too minimal for the Control officer to digest. Minutes later, he heard Hawkins' excited bark.

"You're not gettin' off that easy, Hemmings. Etta Johnson wants terms we can work with."

"They don't seem to have any."

"Then make some up for 'em. They may just be lookin' for an out. Play it right, Hemmings, and we might get 'em to surrender for a meal."

Tom returned the radio to its sheath wondering, as he did so, if any of the inmates in the dorm had managed to acquire hand radios. Perhaps it did not matter since Captain Hawkins was considered a "bitch" by most of the offender population—a creature whose moods were governed by the moon and were not to be taken seriously. Still, he had carelessly broken a rule: *Say nothing in public,* his instructor at the academy had stressed, *that you don't want the inmates to know instantly.* His hand shook as he lifted the phone receiver and spoke to Chester once again.

"How about tossing it in for a meal? Fresh fruit included."

Chester's voice faltered. "Are you suggesting a last supper, sir? It would surely be mine if I offered them no more than that."

"Just think of the martyrdom to be gained."

"Martyrdom is for saints, sir. *I* am unworthy of such a privilege. But I shall endeavor to do what I can."

The phone, thoroughly lubricated by the dampness of his palm, seemed determined to elude Tom's grasp, but he held it to his ear even after the conversation ended. A half-hour passed before he again heard Chester's voice.

"A meal will suffice, sir, but only to get the talks started. And only if *we* may host it."

"I'll call off the mongrels," Tom replied.

He nodded to Perkins and was for once grateful for the Pavlovian efficiency of the man. Already, the lieutenant was chatting into his hand radio, stalling the riflemen on the roof with a quick series of codes. The inmates' capitulation seemed surreal nonetheless—a deceptive web that had probably been spun by Chester's gift of gab—and so Tom was totally surprised when the door to the dormitory actually opened. A small group of inmates, obscured by the haze, was strolling in his direction.

November 23, 2000
12:45 p.m.

Tom did not hear the second shot at all. He heard only the ricochet on the pavement, the wallop on the checkpoint door, and then he was deafened by the rifles of the point sharpshooters. The inmates, unhurt, were dashing like greyhounds back towards the dormitory It was several seconds before Tom realized that the sharpshooters were aiming at the gymnasium, the apparent location of the second gunman.

"We lack a consensus," Tom muttered to Perkins. The lieutenant, now deaf to his sarcasm, was peering through the crack of the doorway, a sliver so narrow that it mocked the heavy set of binoculars he was holding to his eyes.

"We do have a sniper," Perkins said. "Or a wannabe, anyhow."

"How can you tell?"

"Sounded like a squirrel gun."

"A Mini-14?"

The lieutenant shrugged, jiggling his binoculars as he did so.

"How did they steal a Mini-14?"

"I have no idea, Mr. Hemmings."

The lieutenant pressed his hand radio to his ear, a gesture of frustration—not resolve. The moment, for that matter, held only one certainty—that Tom's mission had consigned him to a virtual no-man's-land, an enforced state of limbo in which he would surely perish while the riflemen on the rooftop scrambled for new positions. He felt especially vulnerable now, not to the accuracy of the inmate shooter but to the deadlier precision of his memories: memories that could only thrive within a vacuum. His recollections of the past week—assaults among staff members, parking lot demonstrations, even the rowdy union forum he had attended two days ago—would return him to the real travesty of his position: his suspicion that the facility, a place truly destined to fold from within, did not merit his heroics.

It was not until the rifles fell silent, an interlude more ominous than the storm, that Tom grew aware of the rhythmic bleating of the telephone. Slowly, as though handling a grenade, he guided the receiver to his ear. He recognized Chester's polite cough.

"Are *these* our fruits?" Tom snapped.

"Deserts, Mr. Hemmings. From a Disciple no less. A few of them are bunkered in the gym."

"Where'd they get that rifle?"

"I cannot say, sir. But I believe it's one of yours."

"Have they terms?"

"I daresay they do. They want to be flown to Africa. It seems, Mr. Hemmings, that beggars are choosers after all."

"It also appears that we're both off the hook. At least for as long as those idiots are armed."

"Thankfully so, Mr. Hemmings. But come back another day, sir, when the spirit of Job is upon us. The home fire is burning and I assure you that you will be as welcome as the prodigal son."

Without further comment, Tom returned the receiver to its jack, convinced, by the synthetic warmth of Chester's invitation, that his limbo would be a mighty one. The prospect of a long wait at the checkpoint, an enduring reprieve from the blindness of the campaign, had suddenly become appealing to him. He set the telephone aside, drew a slow breath, and waited for the rifles to resume barking.

Was it only three days ago that he had composed the memos? At least it had not been a shock to discover that the Classification Committee had suspended its weekly meeting. Given an abundance of snitches within the facility, informants less discriminating than Chester, the institution could not help but be aware of the budding insurrection. The signs of the pending riot were in fact becoming redundant: a clog of transfer requests in his mailbox, a bumper crop of cases before the Conduct Adjustment Board, and an uncommon run on commissary orders, probably because the inmates were stockpiling food in their footlockers.

The forewarnings extended to even the exercise yard where he had noticed an unusual stiffness in the basketball players, a hint that their shirts were stuffed with magazines, newspapers, or any other padding that might deflect a blade. And everywhere—the dining hall, the dormitory, the vocational shops—he had noticed a subservience to inmate conversation; it had in fact become almost a monotone, the cheery expletive "motherfucker" omitted from each and every exchange. He felt, for these reasons, a small swell of urgency when he received and read a personal memo from Etta Johnson, not a direct accommodation to his proposal but a promise at least that his fears would be addressed at the monthly forum held in the visiting room.

November 21, 2000
Dear Mr. Hemmings:

> *Thank you so much for your observations and concerns. Be sure to bring them up at our meeting with the unions this afternoon. They will receive my fullest attention.*
>
> *Appreciatively,*
> *Etta Johnson, Superintendant*

The tone of the memo—insular but self-assured— had been something of a relief to him, perhaps because it underscored the fallibility of human perception, not merely his own, his growing tendency to spot mutineers in the woodwork, but that of the inmates as well. Even the Muslims, though complimentary of the new superintendent, seemed no less helpless in their ability to accurately call a shot. *Mrs.*

Jackson's gonna wise up to you, he had heard one of them remark to another. *And when she does she's gonna punch you in the balls. See if that don't knock some sense into you, brother.* It was therefore with a sense of anticipation, hope that he had exaggerated the entire matter, that Tom reported to the visiting room later that day.

November 23, 2000
1:15 p.m.

As Tom watched the gymnasium, waiting for the rifles to resume barking, memories of the forum shanghaied his thoughts: flashbacks so stale, so utterly generic, that his pending demise could in no way sanctify them. Reliving the incidents—the loud accusations, the shopworn rhetoric, the hollow threats—he in fact wished that death would hurry up and claim him. The forum had been a joke, an insult to his mission, yet every detail of it exploded from his memory like a flock of angry birds.

His first impression, upon entering the cavernous visiting room two days ago, was that his sense of injury amounted to a small and personal pique, a matter so incidental that it would have to wait its turn while larger powers clashed. The aura of combat was in fact so strong that it amounted to parody, scrimmages all but predetermined by the team uniforms of the players: the bloated black jackets of Teamster thugs, lurking like hoodlums near the entranceway, the lime-green cardigans of the AFSMCE members, who were sitting stiffly in the center of the room, and the bright red parkas of the UAW, his personal contingent. Occupying several rows of chairs at the front of the room, where they faced a small table of poker-faced supervisors, his homeboys resembled a platoon of redcoats awaiting an order to advance. It therefore seemed odd that it was Sarah Baumgardner, clad only in her correctional officer blues, who was doing the speaking, her voice a lowly drawl amongst the loud buzz of conversation.

"Ladies and gentlemen, please!"

The plea, distorted only slightly by a chirp from a microphone, had come from Etta Johnson. The only supervisor at the table standing, she was observing the competing groups with the stoic gaze of a matriarch. Her pose was so regal that Tom grew suddenly ashamed of the secret fantasy she had conjured in his mind: a rendezvous that included palm trees, a flowered sarong, and the throbbing of distant drums. *A damn fine piece of ass*, he thought.

"Ladies and gentlemen. Respect the speaker, please!"

It was perhaps her very stature that was prolonging the chaos in the room. Statuesque in her dignity, she seemed to dwarf the rest of the supervisors, so much so that it appeared as though she were standing there alone. Still, Tom had developed a grudging respect for at least one other person at the table: Claude Adkins, the Departmental Commissioner, an erudite man with a premature stoop who had invited him to his downtown office a year ago, not to discuss the proposal he had sent in to salvage the Work Release program, but to explain the necessity of suspending it indefinitely. *Mr. Hemmings*, the Commissioner had said to him flatly. *I admire the work you have done with community integration. But please understand my position, sir. If I try to keep your inmates happy, I may lose that program entirely … Don't frown at me, please, Mr. Hemmings. Shall we use an analogy, sir. Sometimes, we must cut off a leg to save the heart.* Tom had answered the Commissioner sharply, irritated by the irresistible pragmatism of the man's argument. *Mr. Adkins*, he had snapped. *Why cut off a leg? The heart stopped beating long ago.*

The voice of Sarah Baumgardner was now completely audible, a tribute to the charisma of Etta rather than the relevancy of the topic, not the fallouts of privatization—not even the daily challenges of overseeing the laundry dorm—but the expense she was facing in acquiring a babysitter for her children. Tom suspected her dilemma had been self-generated since her transfer to the third shift, announced at roll call that morning, had followed an altercation she had

had with a hospital nurse, a spat Tom had witnessed the day of the shakedown. *You're gonna see this bozo*, she had snarled over the telephone, a reference to an elderly Muslim standing before her desk who had failed to sign up for morning sick call. *If you don't call him out, M'am, I'm going to get on my radio and tell it to the whole damn prison.* Since the nurse had capitulated and the matter had turned out to be minor—the inmate had only required medication for an ulcer—Sarah's outburst could be legitimately viewed as a violation of protocol and the reaction of the facility as justifiable, perhaps even a kindness since the graveyard shift was so undemanding that it had become a haven for senior officers biding their time until retirement.

Etta coughed crisply and finally spoke. Her voice, soft and throaty, was almost like a melody. "Mrs. Baumgardner, weren't you transferred for a *reason*?"

"Don't wanna *hear* no reason," Sarah snapped. "An inmate *did* die last month, you know. The nurse wouldn't see him when Cavanaugh called it in and the crumb bum went and croaked on him. Cost Cavanaugh a shit load of paperwork, it did. Would have cost him his *job* if he hadn't put it down in the log book."

Etta stood quietly, cupping the microphone in her hands. Her face was so tender and composed that it looked as though she were mothering a child. Even her hair, falling down to her shoulders, seemed to frame the face of a fleshy Madonna. She seemed almost resigned to the weight of her empathy—a commodity that might easily have placed her at a disadvantage.

"Mrs. Baumgardner," she said. "We *are* dealing with that nurse. And as a widow with four children, I *know* how difficult it is to get reliable childcare. Please come to my office on Monday. I'm sure we can find a solution to your problem."

Sarah nodded woodenly before walking back to her seat. The neutrality of her expression suggested that her victory was premature—that she would have far preferred a quarrel to a concession. But the floor had been vacated and a sense of opportunity, a hope for conciliations more sweeping than childcare, pervaded the room. The illusion persisted even as Bret Brewer rose ominously from his chair.

November 23, 2000
1:45 p.m.

Another shot. The door of the checkpoint banged harmlessly against Tom's shoulder. Again, the rifles of the sharpshooters spoke and, again, he could hear the distant drumming of the slugs as they struck the gymnasium. He was neither irritated nor surprised by the continuing firefight; he felt instead a growing indifference— an excuse to retreat into the comedy of his recollections. But what clue to his worth—the value of his mission—could reside in such nonsense?

"*Commish.*"

Etta had arched her eyebrows, a gesture that froze the softness in her face. She placed her hand on her hip, teapot-style. "We recognize Mr. Brewer, steward of the United Auto Workers."

"Commish," the big man repeated. "Hope you enjoyed them farm fresh catfish."

The Commissioner smiled, a hasty, rather patented expression. As an African-American, he could not have been immune to so condescending a gift. He cleared his throat. "Delectable, Mr. Brewer. Thank you so much for your thoughtfulness."

"Thank *you* for eatin' 'em," Brewer said. "My pond's overstocked with 'em as it is. A bag of dog food a day and them bottom feeders grow like crazy."

The Commissioner squinted and shook his head; his embarrassment had been compounded even further by this information. "Mr. Brewer," he snapped. "What can I do for you, sir?"

"Last Sunday," Brewer said, "my wife took me to church. Now the preacher there kept talkin' 'bout the Messiah— 'bout how he kept askin' the Almighty to take away a cup. You see where I'm goin' with this, Commish?"

"I believe I do, Mr. Brewer."

"Well then," Brewer said, "I won't say no more. If the man who *first* multiplied fishes didn't want no cups, what makes you think *we're* going to stand for 'em?"

The Commissioner smiled again and rubbed his hands together. He seemed grateful for the self-righteousness in Brewer's voice.

"Mr. Brewer," he said. "Those tests were ordered by the Governor, not me. I have the greatest respect for your faith, sir, but I am powerless to take away the cup."

Brewer rocked slowly from foot to foot as though testing the thickness of a frozen pond. His demeanor remained one of moral authority, a bastion against the forces of irreligion.

"Ain't askin' ya to presume nothing, Commish. Just askin' ya to take the cup away. We're all Christian folk here and you're wantin' us to commit blasphemy."

"Not so, Mr. Brewer," the Commissioner replied. "You can abide by departmental orders, sir, and still remain good Christians. Remember that Jesus *accepted* the cup."

The Commissioner looked pensively around the room, as though hoping to spot an angel in the crowd. His eyes softed as a soldierly figure arose from a chair, a plump officer with wire spectacles whose face resembled that of a determined cherub. *He was right*, Tom thought, remembering one of the union lecturers he had heard at Black Lake. *Attack!* the man had blurted, *and others will come to your aid*. Until that moment, it had not quite occurred to Tom that the bounties of courage might also be available to corporate marionettes.

"Commissioner, sir," the plump officer said.

The Commissioner squinted. "We recognize Lieutenant Perkins."

Perkins coughed softly, timidly, but a yellowing bruise on the point of his jaw suggested that he had already been battle-tested. "May I present the other side of the issue?"

"You may, sir."

The lieutenant coughed again then began his speech. His delivery was pedantic, overly rehearsed, and it failed to disguise the tremor in his voice.

"Last month, Mr. Adkins, we confiscated forty bottles of vodka. Found 'em in the water treatment reservoirs, but we couldn't hold no one accountable. Didn't know who put 'em there. We also inventoried two hundred rocks of crack cocaine, most of 'em taken from the furniture factory. Now with figures like that, sir, there's got to be someone bringin' the stuff in regular. Like maybe Watkins—an officer who crashed his car last week after finishing his shift. When the hospital tested his blood they found ninety milligrams of meth in it." The lieutenant belched loudly then stared at the ceiling. He seemed to be hobbled by the weight of his speech and his tone dropped an octave as he continued. "So it don't make no sense, sir, for the union people to be talkin' like they was church folk. *Not* when a bunch of bootleggers are runnin' this place. And *not* when knives come up missin' from the kitchen. It's a burden to us all, sir, especially the *good* officers who want to do their jobs and go home in one piece."

"*Lieutenant.*"

The voice stopped Perkins cold. Like a martyr in need of a blindfold, he gazed stoically at the ceiling. "I hear you Mr. Brewer," he said, squinting over the heads of those seated around him.

Brewer's tone was like thunder. "You listen up, Perkins. Wasn't it you who assigned Watkins that double shift? Third one you gave him this month, wasn't it now?"

"Yes, Mr. Brewer. But that goes with the job. He agreed to work overtime when he hired on."

"Third one you gave him this month," Brewer sneered. "And you expected him to work it without poppin' hisself a little No Doze? Don't that make you a bit of an asshole, Perkins?"

Brewer had stepped from his seat to the aisle and was approaching the lieutenant like a lynx on the hunt. His pace was slow, almost sensual, as though he were luxuriating in the short space still separating them.

"Mr. Brewer," the lieutenant replied. "He told me he had a new baby to support. So I gave him the overtime at *his* request. But that didn't allow him to swallow no drugs. That was outside the terms of our bargain."

"Well then," Brewer said, "don't offer me no bargains, Perkins. Maybe we should take somethin' *else* outside as well."

Brewer's lunge was quickly blocked by a pair of officers standing near the lieutenant. As the officers pushed Brewer back into the aisle, he offered no resistance, but they continued to clutch him, one on either side, like a pair of bouncers restraining a large drunk. Heaving his shoulders, Brewer slipped free of them, leaving only his union jacket in their hands. He seemed satisfied that he had made a strategic exchange.

"My apologies, Commish," Brewer said. "But Perkins here don't have no business runnin' down folks' religion. Not when *he's* the biggest bullshitter in the place."

The Commissioner, who had watched the incident without comment, nodded politely. "Can you *qualify* that, Mr. Brewer?"

"Last week, Perkins came into the kitchen where my boy works. He accused my boy of losing them knives just 'cause the inmates like to steal 'em. Later, he accused my boy of beating him up."

"That's a serious accusation, sir."

"*Bullshit* is what it is," Brewer bellowed. "He said my boy snuck up behind him at the Holiday Inn when all my boy was doin' was attendin' a union lunch. He said my boy cold-cocked him by the urinal. But he hadda be lying."

"How so, Mr. Brewer?"

"When the cops showed up, Perkins was out cold on the bathroom floor. And his pecker was still in his *pants*. Now if *that* don't prove he's a liar, what *does*?"

The Commissioner lowered his eyes to the table. He looked like a shopkeeper recording stock. "We need to move on, Mr. Brewer," he said. "In the interests of *time*, sir, we need to move on."

Tom, still standing near the entranceway, had not been surprised when the big man returned meekly to his chair. He was somewhat disappointed that fisticuffs had not actually taken place, so much so that Brewer's red jacket, still clutched by one of the officers, impressed him as a flag of surrender. *Will we lose the rest of him, too?* Tom wondered, He was perhaps too intrigued by the vacuum that would arise if Brewer were exposed as a paper tiger. It was as if to address this question that an opaque figure detached itself suddenly from the back of the room and then drifted like a phantom in the direction of the supervisors' table.

Yoakum, Tom realized after a moment; it was Yoakum, his pea green cardigan replaced by a rubbery jacket belonging to the Teamsters. As though wearing a life vest, the man seemed to float, his stride so buoyant that a current might have been carrying him. Yoakum took a full minute to reach the table and when he halted it was with an air of proprietorship, the attitude of a landlord whose rent was overdue.

November 23, 2000
2:00 p.m.

It was not until a third bullet hammered the roof, rattling the checkpoint to its foundation, that Tom remembered that Yoakum was reported to be among the hostages. Since the rogue officer was likely to be executed by the inmates, he hoped that this bit of information would prove to be part of the rumor mill. This was not because the death of an officer would hopelessly deadlock negotiations, but because Tom had managed to acquire an unexpected affection for the pock-faced man.

Tom covered his head with his arms, pressing his cheek to the pavement. He felt like a mole burrowing into the ground as the guns of the checkpoint sharpshooters spoke.

As Tom had stood in the visiting room, waiting for Yoakum to speak, he remembered how their friendship had developed. Their bond had begun several months ago when Yoakum guided him through the dorm training he would need to resume a counselor's duties. Thanks to Yoakum, he had been able to rekindle his sense of self-preservation, a quality he had let slip during the eight years he had run the Work Release program from the safety of the Administration Building. His resurrection had begun during the first of the evening counts when he had overlooked part of his post orders, a mandate that he go to the window of each bed pod and test the bars with a baton.

Pretend to be doin it, Yoakum had cautioned him. *Bang 'em like a two bit whore. There's sergeants watchin' you from the quad outside and some of 'em don't mind extra paperwork. They'll put you on report in a second if they don't see you bangin' away.*

Tom's embarrassment had only caused Yoakum to smirk. *Remember one thing more, Mr. Hemmings. The sergeants here ain't the only ones who can write reports. Now if ya see one of 'em noddin' off at his desk, write it down. Ya see any of 'em bird doggin' Baumgardner, write it down. Ya see one of 'em looped in a tavern, write it down. It's a pain in the ass, but sooner or later you'll be needin' that information. Now I been here twenty-one years, Mr. Hemmings, an' they ain't managed to stick it to me yet.*

Tom had acted surprised. He said, *Twenty-one years. And you spent it all stalking the brass? Where's the percentage in that?*

Yoakum had cackled merrily. *Hell's bells, Mr. Hemmings. Where else will they pay a man to sit around on his butt all day? If I went anyplace else I'd have to work for a livin'.*

Yoakum grinned like a possum as he stood in front of the Commissioner. As he watched the man gloat, Tom remembered a recent disclosure from Brewer—that the UAW, in a quest for more supporters, would be merging with the Teamsters. But he had not expected the mix to include Yoakum.

When Yoakum finally spoke, his voice filled the room. "Guv'nor," he said. "Henry Yoakum here. And I'm askin' permission to speak out of turn."

The Commissioner winced as though struck by a rock. He bowed his head humbly. "Say it quickly, sir."

Emboldened, the pock-faced man rocked on his heels, surveying those around him in the manner of a visiting delegate. It seemed callous for Yoakum to establish his dominion any further, but he cleared his throat theatrically before beginning to speak.

"Guv'nor," he said. "We just been wastin' our time here—what with talkin' 'bout catfish and Jesus and all. Now the Department ain't in the business of dispensin' charity and everyone here ought to *know* it." Yoakum smiled tightly, repressing a chuckle as he looked once again around the room. The timing of the pause was so impeccable that he appeared to be a paid barrister rather than an outlaw in a black windbreaker.

Yoakum smirked and continued to speak. "Now there *is* a fish here worth fryin', Gov'nor. But it ain't got nothing to do with babysittin' and Bibles. I don't mean to be interruptin' a good donnybrook, sir, but it's time we had ourselves a *talk*."

The silence in the room had become almost lethal, a hush so pervasive that it promised only chaos. It would have in fact seemed folly for either party to break it, and so it amounted to a tactical ploy, rather than a show of manners, that Yoakum stood waiting for the Commissioner to reply.

"Go on, Mr. Yoakum," the Commissioner said at last. "Is it a wage increase, sir?"

Yoakum shook his head. "It's best you don't talk about raises," he said. "We had us one in August, sir. Dollar an hour. But when they kicked up our health insurance we was takin' home less than when we started. So best you don't talk about raises. We can't *afford* no more of 'em."

The Commissioner frowned, probably because the matter was one of many beyond his control. By union estimates, his daily mail included thirty unrelated grievances a week. He spoke like a man impatient to board a plane.

"Promotions?" he asked.

Yoakum again shook his head. "Ain't no percentage in those either," he said. "They once *made* me a sergeant, sir, but I asked 'em to bust me back down. It kept me from gettin' overtime for one. On top of that, there's no one around here who'll back a sergeant up. Not even them that promoted him in the first place." Yoakum folded his arms as though attempting to hoard his breath. When he again spoke, his voice was even louder. "As I see it, sir, there ain't no *sense* in promotions. Now you won't be a boss and you won't be a flunkey. But you *will* be your boss's flunkey."

A musketry of applause floated through the room. The momentum clearly belonged to Yoakum.

"What *do* you want?" the Commissioner asked.

"Concessions," Yoakum said.

"What are you suggesting, sir?"

"Concessions," Yoakum repeated. "That commissary outfit—they gotta be makin' a killin' here, Guv'nor. Have you seen what they been unloadin' on these bojacks? Month old cookies, soggy sandwiches, an' potato chips that turn to powder by the time they get carried back to the dorms. The bojacks are madder 'an hornets about it, not that I have any sympathy for 'em. Scum suckers don't *deserve* no better."

"Mr. Yoakum," the Commissioner replied. "Our contract with Colonial is renewable annually. If the services do not improve, and improve very quickly, I assure you it will be terminated."

"Guv'nor," Yoakum said. "You're missin' the point here. I ain't *askin* ya to do away with the contract. What I'm sayin' is to let us in on it. With the killin' they're makin' there's got to be a shitload of profits to be spreadin' around. Now we don't mind bustin' the heads for ya, Guv'nor, but give us a bit of the action as well. Fair's fair after all."

Yoakum, his speech now finished, gazed mischievously about him. It was impossible to gauge the intent of his statement—whether it amounted to a serious proposal or the bullying of an administrator who was out of his depth. In all probability, Yoakum's sincerity did not matter: contempt for authority was so much in season that the unions could afford to be careless in their recruitment.

The Commissioner gazed wisely around the room. To deny a corporate coup would only earn him hoots of derision while it would be no less fatal for him to respond seriously to Yoakum's proposal. He sighed stoically.

"Mr. Yoakum," he said. "I have *not* missed the point. I am well aware of the shitload, sir."

Tom remembered the comment with which the Commissioner had ended their private conference a year ago—a reference not to his proposal to save a program but to the UAW pin which he had forgotten to remove from his shirt pocket. *Keep away from the unions*, the Commissioner had advised him. *They're for underachievers, sir, not the discerning or quick of mind. You will climb more quickly without their empty promises.* Tom had answered him angrily. *They're for slow climbers too. Like the counselors you fired after that woman got murdered last year. If they hadn't had a union lawyer, they would never have gotten their jobs back.* The Commissioner had only laughed. *And that won you over, Mr. Hemmings? Very well, sir, but remember the words of Nietzsche. If you stare into a void, the void will stare back into you. And if you have a weakness, the void will quickly find it.*

He remembered the final minutes of the union forum— the exhausted expression on the Commissioner's face. It impressed him that the man had ignored his own advice and come to the prison at all. Had he forgotten the covenants of office—he was after all his boss' flunky—or had he simply underestimated the power of the void? That he would not be back soon seemed a given and so, as the room began to empty, Tom seized the moment to make a proposal.

"Another speech, Mr. Hemmings?" the Commissioner asked him. The man did not seem surprised that Tom had placed himself alongside Yoakum.

"Nothing so ambitious," Tom replied. "A suggestion is all I can handle today."

"What have you in mind?"

"Colonial Concessions," he said. "If they're going to go on fleecing these bojacks, at least let them do it expeditiously.

That would cut down on some of the flak around here—maybe even keep a few of us from getting hurt."

"What do you propose?"

"A new form for ordering commissary items. Something the inmates can handle. Something that will let them pay off their goddamn debts and not get shanked."

"Very good, Mr. Hemmings. See what you can come up with. I will expect the proposal on my desk in a week."

As Tom walked from the visiting room, it irritated him that the Commissioner had snapped up his suggestion so quickly. He felt that he had been thrown a scrap—a tidbit to shut him up.

Why do you keep working here? Brewer had asked him afterwards. *You have two college degrees and they got ya doin' scut work. That's okay for slobs like me, but you don't have to put up with it, Hemmings.*

Tom had let the question rest, offering not even a quip since to do so would have seemed plagiaristic. Yoakum, after all, had said it better than he and he saw little purpose in seeking a more charitable explanation for his paralysis. Whether born of complacency or fatigue, the fruits of his career were irrefutable: he had played the game poorly, empowered the incidental, and had bottomed out finally in a laundry dorm. It therefore seemed little more than an irony to him when he discovered, later that afternoon, that Chester was in the hole.

November 23, 2000
2:15 p.m.

The gymnasium was silent. The rifles of the sharpshooters were silent. Soon, the rifles would bark again and a bullet would probably find him. But all Tom could think about, as he waited for the firefight to resume, was Chester's internment in the hole.

He learned of Chester's segregation shortly after the union forum had ended—when he returned to his office and scanned the disciplinary logbook. To his utter surprise, Chester was among the inmates pending Conduct Adjustment Board hearings the following day. He deemed the matter a mistake until later that afternoon when he opened his dormitory mailbox. Among the request slips, near the bottom of the pile, was a neatly written note from his informant.

November 21, 2000
Mr. Hemmings,

>*You may recall my mentioning the mercy of the Lord, his refusal to punish me according to my deserts. Well it seems that he has taken a stricter measure of my sins. Still, I go willingly to my exile, secure in the knowledge that he is a fair God after all. But do not think me so stoic that I would refuse a visit from you. Even Jonah, deep in the belly of the monster fish, was allowed an occasional glimpse of sunlight.*

>*Yours faithfully,*
>*C. Mahoney*
>*DOC-990624*

The first shift was ending when he retrieved the disciplinary write-ups from the Screening Office and studied the conduct report on Chester. The charge, *Inciting a Riot*, seemed excessive in view of the material the little man had been accused of circulating: a single page torn from *The New World Order*, the unofficial Bible of the Christian Coalition. The underlined quote, a Pat Robertson staple, in fact struck him as mainstay rather than radical and he wondered if Chester had somehow acquired it from a member of the UAW. The quote bored him in any case and he read it with cynical detachment, suppressing, as he did so, a mounting disappointment in the little man.

65

Have any of us been told that the Secretaries of State, the Secretaries of the Treasury, the heads of the CIA, the heads of the National Security Council, the heads of the Federal Reserve Board and countless others are in agreement that American Sovereignty is to be "eroded piece by piece"? When has there ever been a referendum for all the people to decide whether they want to discard our Constitution in favor of a one-world government? The answer is "never."

He suspected, as he re-read the disciplinary report, that Chester's violation was too conspicuous to be genuine—that the incident was a ploy the little man had orchestrated to escape the responsibilities of an inmate negotiator. After all, Chester had given the page to a skinhead right in front of the desk officer and had then waited passively on his bunk while the extraction team was summoned. Even the delivery of the page seemed ambiguous—it had simply fallen from Chester's hand to the floor—so it was probable that he expected to minimize the charge when faced with the Conduct Adjustment Board. Still, he did owe Chester a favor and he felt the pang of his debt as he made plans to visit him in the hole.

November 23, 2000
2:30 p.m.

As Tom squatted behind the checkpoint door, half hoping a bullet would end his anguish, he remembered a startling event—an event so genuine that it in no way constituted smoke. It had occurred in the visiting room a few hours before the union forum started, and it had affected him profoundly. He had gone there to check the visitor log, a chore necessary to diminish the smuggling of contraband into his dorm, and was surprised to see Chester sitting at one of the tables. It was 7:00 a.m., an unusual time for visits, and so he looked curiously at the little man's visitor, a matronly woman in her sixties with a cross of Jesus hanging from her thin neck. The woman was a missionary, but her expression was so dour, her manner so stern, that she was probably more interested in the prospect of another convert than in the unique personality of her host. But it was the woman's companion, a girl of about ten with dark braided hair, that held Tom's interest: squirming bare-legged on her chair, the child seemed too bored, too naturally precocious, to allow the dowager to focus upon her crusade. Tom paused only briefly at the table, accepting perfunctory introductions from Chester before hurrying to the officers' perch to review the weekly list of visitors. Suddenly, he knew that he would be acquiring his first unvarnished glimpse of the man.

Tom completed his work quickly, visitation having been low that week, but the job still irritated him and so he took comfort in the modulation of Chester's voice, a low seductive rhythm that mitigated the terse monotone of the woman and the guttural whining of the child. But Chester was awaiting him at the porter room door when he quit the officer's perch; the man's face, thoroughly flushed, suggested he was desperate to end the visit before his allotted ninety minutes were up. "This visit," he told Tom flatly, "will be the death of me, sir."

"Death by platitudes?" Tom replied.

Chester shook his head. "No, Mr. Hemmings. But certainly an abundance of gas." He slapped his stomach as though he were punishing it. "We had biscuits and gravy this morning, sir. And gravy has never agreed with me."

Tom wished, at that particular moment, that his instincts were less acute, his temper less controlled, his powers of observation less honed. It was obvious, from the flush of Chester's face, that the child had excited him. But for Tom to have alluded to the matter, even in the most general of terms, would have seriously breached their mutual sense of etiquette, an embarrassment he could not afford if he were to retain the man as an ally and informant. In any case, Chester had ended the visit himself, a gesture that suggested that his better angels were in charge. And so Tom responded charitably—"Better gravy than the grave"— and held the door open, allowing Chester to pass before him into the porter room. He even nodded to the porter room officer, implying that the little man was truly sick and in need of a concession. The nod, though a lie, kept Chester from being strip searched.

The Special Housing Unit, a starfish-shaped bunker near the southeast tower of the compound, struck Tom as a haven—an airtight retreat too snug to resist even though the union forum had ended hours ago. It was dinnertime when he arrived at the building and so he waited an hour in the control module while the inmate trustees wheeled the dinner carts to the ranges. The portal to C-Range, the gallery where Chester was housed, looked fragile, probably because the Plexiglas panels were still spider-cracked from a recent rampage—an incident that had happened a week ago when one of the residents had pounded on the door with an iron bar taken from the weight lifting room. Though the range had been easily recaptured—the emergency squad had simply waited for the inmate to fall asleep—the matter had resulted in a prolonged query from the Investigation Office and a suspension of all exercise privileges for the inmates on C-Range. The C-Range internees were now known as "dandies"—an understatement since most were gang members that had been delivered from the state reformatory due to a recent rash of stabbings at that facility.

When the portal finally rolled open, Tom suppressed a familiar swell of panic then, abandoning the security of the control module, walked through the opening. Entering the range, he was greeted by a wall of sound—transistor radios blasting, voices calling out to one another—noises that seemed ghostly since the residents were not immediately visible to him behind the heavily barred doorways. Only as he strolled the range did they become conspicuous: young men appearing one-after-another, some doing pushups, some dozing, some sitting on toilets—sociopaths, according to Hawkins, who would take his life if they had the opportunity to do so and believed that his death might benefit them. He walked quickly along the freeway, avoiding eye contact, his tie, a potential noose if left around his neck, tucked into his pants pocket. It was a relief to him when the procession of sullen faces was interrupted by the sight of the genial con man sitting upon his bunk. Chester was wearing a red jump suit in place of his starched prison whites.

A circuit hummed, the thick bars parted, and Tom ducked his head as he entered the six-by-nine foot chamber. As the current reversed, locking the heavy door behind him, he was seized by the fatuity of trying to conduct a visit under such circumstances. The acoustics of the range remained overwhelming and the cell, an echo chamber, contained only a small mattress to absorb the sound.

"Some tea, Mr. Hemmings?"

Tom shook his head, not in refusal but because he was startled by the incongruity of the remark. He slowly sat down upon the far end of the mattress.

"The trustees provide it," Chester said. "Hot tea on the line—a solace within the belly of the whale. I believe they brew it from pilfered tea bags, but they are charitable in their mischief, sir. A piping hot cup costs no more than a cigarette or two."

"I don't care for any, thank you," Tom said. He felt uncivil refusing the little man's hospitality.

"You have mischief of your own to account for," Tom went on. "Hawkins won't believe you dropped that page by accident. He's been through too many free-for-alls to give you the benefit of the doubt. So your ploy may not work, not if you're banking on a short stay in here."

Chester, his hands folded loosely on his lap, seemed to be nursing an invisible smoking pipe. He looked curiously at his visitor as though studying him through a cloud of haze. "A ploy, Mr. Hemmings?" he said at last. "Might we call it something nobler? A final act of gumption from a rascal who has long ago squandered his cause? Would that I still had my faith, Mr. Hemmings. I might now have the dignity of a monk."

Tom shook his head, unimpressed by the confession. The echoing shouts, now a cover to their conversation, continued to bounce off the metal and brick.

"Railing against the void," Tom remarked.

"As futile a pastime as any," Chester said. "Still, it is consoling to do so now and again. Silence can be crueler than noise, Mr. Hemmings, and also more deafening."

"But why Pat Robertson?"

Chester shrugged. His hands, rubbing one against the other, appeared to be rolling the pipe back and forth. "It's a measure of my poverty, sir—the bane of a rootless man. Had I not lost the farm, I might have seeded a garden of my own."

"And not fifteen-year-old girls."

Chester sighed, dropping the pipe. His hands rested firmly upon his knees. "You think too highly of me, Mr. Hemmings," he said. "I am impotent to even the Jezebels, sir, the lowliest sirens in the void. Do you know she is trying to tempt me still? Every month she shows up in the visiting room and asks the officer to call me down. But I have spurned her advances, sir—for her sake as well as my own. I prefer now the comforts of the porch. Give me a restful sunset instead and the memory of my good wife."

"Not to mention the abuse of trust. The inmates *trusted* you to be their spokesman."

Chester shrugged. He folded his hands. "Chicanery, Mr. Hemmings, is the only vice of which I am still capable. And it's a sensible one at that. Sir, what can I possibly accomplish without faith? I have no proverbial tea to dump."

"Nor the originality to even coin a phrase."

"You recognize it?" Chester pouted his bottom lip.

"Proverbial tea? Wasn't that coined by an Oklahoma bomber?"

Chester nodded. "Ten years ago," he sighed. "In a letter he wrote to the Union Sun and Journal. Yes, Mr. Hemmings, we read such trash in the boonies."

"An educated man like you?" Tom crossed his arms across his chest. "Wouldn't the *Bard* be better reading?"

"He would," Chester replied. "So you see now, sir, the extent of my poverty. My pockets are so empty I have solicited the Devil himself."

Chester rose slowly from the bed, stretching as he did so, and shuffled over to the metal sink. He washed his hands lovingly, as though ridding them of an earthly contaminant. "But the truest of beggars can *count* their wealth, sir. Once I was even poorer than I am today."

"And when was that?"

"When I owned a farm—or believed that I did, having paid for it at least once. Imagine my relief, sir, when the bank took it anyway. Suddenly, I was as free as the birds in the field."

He dried his hands meticulously with a state-issued towel, a gesture too theatrical to be convincing. Given the aplomb of the man, the poise of a consummate actor, it seemed doubtful that he had ever had much calling to farm.

Slowly, fastidiously, Chester hung the towel from the edge of the sink. He seemed anxious to watch it dry. "All is vanity, Mr. Hemmings, if you will permit me to steal from the *Bible*—a fruitless pursuit of the wind." Shaking his head, he returned to the bunk. "May I give you some advice?"

Tom raised an eyebrow. "And what would that be?"

"Forsake the tempest, sir," Chester drawled.

"In other words hide in a hole."

Chester's laugh was high, almost like a girl's. "The wind can howl *without* us, sir. I am an old man and prefer a gentler summons."

"Like the memory of your wife."

"Yes, Mr. Hemmings. The memory of my wife. Every now and again I can hear her whispering to me."

The little man sighed. He sat down stiffly. When he again spoke, his voice bore a trace of unfamiliar timber. "She might not have passed had we kept the farm. But Heaven would be poorer without her, sir."

"I'm sure you must miss her."

"I do, Mr. Hemmings. Mine was the harsher liberation by far, an opportunity not for solace but pitiful mischief. Still, my romp is over now and I have welcomed my punishment. I shall try, from here on out, to pay her memory the homage it deserves." Chester closed his eyes prayerfully. He lowered his head. His hands again held the invisible pipe.

"Are you serving her memory by sitting in the hole? You're not exactly easing a debt in here."

"A debt?" Chester said. "Sir, my pockets are bare. How could I settle a debt?"

"By saving some lives. By talking the inmates out of rioting. You could *start* with the Devil's Disciples."

Chester sighed weakly. His face morphed to the color of tallow. "Again, sir, you are overrating me."

"*Am* I?" Tom's voice rose. "You speak like an angel and you know it. Your words have the power to ease a storm. But instead you hide out in the hole."

The little man coughed. He squeezed his hands tightly together as though attempting to warm them with the pipe. "There are *limits* to my ambition, Mr. Hemmings. Perhaps the storm *should* blow. Perhaps it is God's own storm and not to be trifled with by an old shirker." Chester lowered his head and studied the floor. "But at least I'm a foil to the brass, Mr. Hemmings. Fibbers and scamps for the most part, but they haven't forgotten Old Chester quite yet. That's probably because I'm not asking them for much."

Tom shook his head. "Certainly not for redemption."

"No, Mr. Hemmings. A patch of dirt will do me far better—a place where I might sit and watch the sunrise. Grant me that escape and I will help you stop another."

"Okay," Tom whispered. "Who?"

"Two kitchen boys. They're planning to make a run. Ordinarily, I would be happy to see them go. The fresh air might restore the color to their cheeks. But they know where the pistol is hidden."

Tom raised his eyebrows. "Your worthiest theft by far," he muttered. "That is, if you manage to steal it."

"I am still *awaiting* the chance," Chester said. "Abstinence is a tonic to the soul, sir, but there is deliverance to be found in *some deeds* at least. But the window of opportunity is narrow. I will have to act quickly or not at all."

"How long will the window stay open?"

"A day perhaps—maybe two. I tried to talk the boys out of it, but they are hopeless romantics. As flighty a pair as you could hope to find though at least they've kept loyal to one another."

"Their names?"

"Hopper is one. But let's keep that between ourselves, Mr. Hemmings."

Startled, Tom lowered his voice. "He's short on time for a runner. Hopper gets out next March."

"That's just the problem, sir. He doesn't wish to leave here without his lover."

Tom shook his head. "I'll tell Hawkins you'll give him the details in exchange for a transfer. But that may not be enough to get you out of the hole."

Chester nodded solemnly. Slowly, his face lit up. "What if I steal the pistol in the dairy? Surely, that would earn me a bit of porch."

Tom shrugged. "That might tip the scales. I'll see what he says. But you'll have to beat this *incitement* charge if you want to get out of here and join the farm crew. You'll have to *impress* the Conduct Adjustment Board."

"*That* will be easy," Chester said. "I have never stood long upon principle, sir. I will hang my head, like a mongrel dog, and offer my sincerest apology."

November 23, 2000
3:15 p.m

Why was he still alive? Why had a bullet not found him? Why were the snipers *still* scrambling about on the rooftop of the administrative building? Tom shook his head, weary and disappointed. And his thoughts returned slowly to what he *did* know.

The first shift had long since ended when Tom left the Special Housing Unit after visiting Chester. The delay was not caused by the quality of his conversation with the little man, but by the inattention of the control room sergeant. Preoccupied with delivering mail to the cells, the sergeant had simply forgotten that Tom was on the range, and so it was an hour before he was sprung from Chester's cell. He left the building reluctantly, preoccupied by the news of the pending escape, a matter that had awoken in him not the vigilance of a centurion, but a rather pitiable pang of envy.

He had been less impressed by the rest of his informant's observations—*Chesterisms* he called them now, perhaps because this placed them at a safe distance. It was their enduring triteness, after all, that made them susceptible to time and tide. *The shrub must not whither*, the little man had remarked, yet another reference to the tree of liberty. *And so the torrents must rise. Defy the storm, sir, and only marshland will water it*. When Tom told him of a tidier liberation, the removal of Sarah from the first shift, Chester had simply bowed his head as though saddened by an inevitability. *It is man's nature to assert, Mr. Hemmings, while woman's is to cope. That is a premise established not only by the immortal Bard but by the very nature of their genitalia. Reverse the order, sir, and we can only have bedlam.*

Finally, Tom had mentioned the U.S. Presidential election, a topic forced upon them by the boom of the radios in the adjourning cells. And Chester had nodded vigorously, perhaps remembering a bet he had placed with one of the bookmakers on the range. *Can it matter, Mr. Hemmings, which rascal prevails? It's of no concern to the Hittites, I assure you. But I will say they're getting rather arrogant. Never have their puppets looked more wooden.*

Tom remembered approaching the West Gate after abandoning Chester in the hole. He listened to the lively palaver from the off-Hill pistol range, a crackle so festive that it undermined the sight of two-dozen German Shepherds posted with their handlers alongside the edges of the promenade. Through this staggered gauntlet, the fish line was trudging in double file towards the dining hall, a sight that implied intimidation although the controlled movement, a safeguard introduced that morning by Etta Johnson, had in fact been welcomed by many of the inmates in his dorm. *'Bout time they tightened things up a bit, sir,* one of the Muslims had remarked to him. *Mrs. Johnson got the touch, I'll tell you that right now. Don't have to watch your back so much with that bitch in charge.* Yoakum, however, had only shaken his head when advised of this new restriction. *Oughta leave things how they was,* Yoakum had spat. *As long as the scum buckets are fightin' with each other they won't have no time to be plottin' against us. 'Sides, Mr. Hemmings, with most of the officers stuck up on the Hill it's you an' me who'll be chasin' down the rabbits.*

Tom waited patiently for the inmate movement to end and the West Gate to roll open for him, unconcerned with the delay since he could see a staff demonstration taking place in the parking lot beyond the gate. A loose horde of men wearing green had settled like a flock of parrots upon the steps of the Administration Building while thirty yards away from them, sheltered beneath the roof of the state garage, he could make out a small red cloud of homeboys. Although the demonstrations seemed directed at the Commissioner—his insistence at the union forum that the piss tests would continue—the sight of a police car parked near the Administration Building suggested that the matter had disintegrated into yet another brawl between the unions.

When the West Gate lurched open, allowing Tom a body width of space through which to pass, he strolled slowly towards the garage. He was glad he had been delayed on the lockup range since the donnybrook appeared to have only just ended. The sight of Bret Brewer, standing by himself at the entrance to the garage, relieved him further. The big man looked mellow as though lulled by the static hum of the electrical garage gate, and his hands were tucked harmlessly into the pockets of his pants.

"Did your son start *this fight* too?" Tom asked.

The big man nodded proudly. "Hats off to Brewer Junior," he said. "He beat up another toady."

"Who?"

Brewer grinned broadly. "One of Perkins' boys, I think. Don't matter much who. They're all fair game when they're wearin' puke green."

"What was it over this time?"

"Cartoons," Brewer said. He withdrew his right hand from his pants, displaying a crumpled leaflet. The drawing, two fat politicians smoking cigars over a pot of gold, was notable not for its artfulness so much as the swiftness with which it had been produced. The alliance between the UAW and the Teamsters' Union had been announced only minutes before the union forum had ended.

Brewer covered his mouth, attempting not to laugh out loud, but the drawing, particularly its hardy caption, *SELLOUT*, seemed highly amusing to him. He looked as though he had just made love.

"Fightin' words," Brewer said. "Particularly when comin' from an AFSME scab. The crud had no business stickin' it in my boy's face."

Tom frowned and shook his head. "How badly did your boy bust him?"

"Not badly enough to be copped," Brewer said. "He knocked out a couple of teeth, that's all. I doubt that the fucker will miss 'em—they're a toothless bunch anyway."

Tom glared at Brewer and shook his head. "Strong words from a man with religion."

Brewer laughed. He spat cautiously as though fearful of hitting his shoes. "Don't give me no crap about fishes and loaves," he said. "It's as good a crock as any. Don't hurt to conjure up a rainbow or two if it helps you kick some butt."

Tom had to laugh. "The Deacon would agree."

"The fucker in the hole?" The big man grunted loudly. His eyes remained fixed on the AFSMCE crowd. "You're much too patient with these bojacks, Hemmings. And I ain't sure that's such a good thing. If you let 'em, they'll have you thinkin' water runs uphill."

"What can that matter? They're all doing time."

"Well, the Deacon ain't doing *enough* time. Not for the crime *he* committed. He must've jerked off the judge to get only five years for it."

A stone struck the pavement beside them. A burst of marching music erupted from a cassette player near the Administration Building, an anthem that further demonstrated the bedrock self-righteousness of the unions. The sound grew louder as the police car, its business apparently over, pulled away from the curb and drifted in the direction of the arch tower.

"I hope they throw another," Brewer said. "Give us an excuse to beat up a few more of 'em. There won't be no payback from the brass if it was them that started it."

The boast seemed improbable, not because of Brewer's expression, the indifference with which he had watched the stone fall, but because of his posture, his heroic immobility as he kept his eyes on the Administration Building. He seemed, at that moment, to be an edifice rather than a leader—a stone general posing safely in a park.

"You'll be beating them up on faith," Tom said, "if you don't think there'll be payback."

Brewer shrugged. He continued to stare towards the Administration Building.

Tom raised his voice—the music was growing even louder. "Or are you counting on that cherry union of ours to bail you out of jail?"

A bottle exploded harmlessly near their feet. The big man shrugged as though suddenly vindicated. "Faith don't got nothing to do with it," Brewer said. "We been put in charge of men we don't trust. And we're answerin' to men we don't trust."

"So you're conjuring up rainbows."

"I may as well, Hemmings. Colors is all we *got*."

As a final stone bounced off the wall of the garage, Brewer placed his hands contemptuously upon his hips. The bombardment had become irrelevant: the AFSMCE crowd had assembled into small clots that were beginning to move away from the Administration Building. In twos and threes they were drifting through the arch and heading in the direction of the stone quarry, a trek that would take them alongside Highway 40, where news media had probably assembled, and then to the staff parking lot situated to the west of the quarry.

"Looks like *your* colors have been stolen," Tom said. He was speaking literally, having finally noticed the stiff article hovering above the demonstrators: It was Brewer's red jacket, the same jacket that had been taken from him during the union forum. An effigy now, probably stuffed with newspapers, it seemed destined for a ceremonial burning when the marchers reached the parking lot.

"Egg suckin' dogs," Brewer muttered. The big man's eyes remained fixed upon the demonstrators as they continued to file past the garage. With his hands upon his hips, he appeared to be offering them a challenge, but the drift of the marchers implied that there would be no takers that afternoon. Soon even the music had begun to fade, its cadence replaced the hum of the gate and the insular crackle from the pistol range.

November 23, 2000
4:30 PM

Perkins grunted. The high-velocity slug had penetrated his boot before tumbling through his thigh, creating an exit wound that resembled the mouth of a clubbed catfish. The lieutenant seemed relieved—not shaken—as though he had been anticipating something worse. Already, he had opened a First Aid kit and was beginning to bandage his wound. He worked carefully, as though wrapping a gift, while the checkpoint sharpshooters took pot shots at the gymnasium.

When the shooting stopped, Tom turned his attention to Perkins. He suddenly felt sick to his stomach. "You're going to get sick leave," he muttered, lamely.

Perkins waived Tom away as he tried to assist him. His manner was impatient. "I could *use* a goddamn vacation," he said.

"Talk to Brewer," Tom murmured: he could not take his eyes off the gaping wound. "He'll show you how to milk it. You ought to be good for six months leave."

The phone, as though wise to their conspiracy, was ringing in Tom's lap like an alarm clock. Slowly, he lifted the receiver, unsure as to how much to disclose to his informant. To reveal, even in confidence, that an officer was down would be a criminal thing to do; the stakes would only climb if the hostage takers acquired this information, perhaps placing a bloodless resolution to the takeover completely out of reach.

"Tom's Bait Shack," he murmured.

"Mr. Hemmings, is it?" It was Yoakum, of all people.

"What are *you* doing on the phone?"

"I'm a *hostage*, sir. I thought ya knew that."

"And they're letting you use the phone?" Tom couldn't hold back his dismay.

"I've been politickin', Mr. Hemmings. Makes for uncommon bedfellows, don't it."

Tom rested his shoulder against the back of the door. "The *Teamsters* were bad enough."

Yoakum's chuckle rattled emptily through the receiver, much like an echo from a cave. "I've been *conscripted*, sir. They asked me to take out the sniper for 'em. If I get that accomplished, they'll let me go free."

"How do you propose to do *that*?"

"Same as we did it on the manhunt, sir. You create the diversion. Meanwhile, I'll be sneakin' into the gym through the back door."

Tom felt his heart kick. "Have they *got* a phone in the gym?"

"There's one in the recreation director's office, sir. Call those bojacks up after dark and I'll do the rest."

The plan, a not unforeseeable twist of fate, was too much for Tom to consider at the moment, not because of its ramifications—a wholesale allegiance with rogues—so much as the suddenness with which it had been sprung upon him. Given his fatigue, the vulnerability of his position, and the increasing accuracy of the inmate sniper, he was unprepared to feel so devilishly empowered. Tom rubbed his head and spoke softly.

"So they gave you Hopper's pistol?"

"Except for the hollow points, sir. They don't trust me as far as all that. But a .38 Smith & Wesson don't *need* to be loaded. It *still* oughta get me the bluff on the bastards."

"All right then," Tom answered. "I'll call the recreation office. It's as good a place as any for a diversion."

Tom let the receiver roll from his hand, sighing softly as it interlocked with the cradle. It would be another hour or two until nightfall, enough time for the manhunt to seep back into his consciousness. He hoped Yoakum's plan would spare him a comparable trauma—that it would somehow keep him out of that dormitory. He concealed his envy as he looked at Perkins, a damn lucky man if his wound were as superficial as it appeared to be.

"Yoakum will capture the shooters this evening. They've given him Hopper's pistol."

Perkins nodded, accepting this bit of information without comment. It was the encroaching darkness, after all, that would allow him to retreat from the heat of dubious battle to the safety of a hospital bed. Perkins pressed the squelch button on his radio and paused, perhaps searching for a code that might convey to the control officer the ingenuity of Yoakum's plan.

Perkins' bloody hand trembled as he muttered into the radio. "Don't turn on the street lights," he said.

November 23, 2000
5:00 p.m.

Tom remembered the manhunt, a victory less than a final concession to smoke. Yet the manhunt was the *least* confounding of his memories: if nothing else, it offered him some linkage to the firefight. And so it seemed fitting to relive the manhunt—relive it in its *entirety*—before he died.

The manhunt had happened only yesterday, the morning following the union forum. It had rained early that morning and a cottony fog had settled over the leafless forest surrounding the prison. Awaiting the employee shuttle bus, he had found himself missing the fall foliage: the blush of the leaves was a gentler sight than the yellowing leaflets that were now blowing about in the parking lot, the sheets displaying the two fat politicians in collusion and some NRA fliers of a hillbilly holding a shotgun. The testy caption—"You're taking *whose* guns?!"—seemed too dreary a complement to the approach of winter and the ever-present turkey vultures that were still visible above the quarry. The hovering birds were reminder enough that expectations were at hand. But of the promises that had been made at the union forum—higher wages, cheaper insurance, a revived grievance system—only one, Henry Yoakum's caustic prediction, appeared to have come about. *Rest assured, Mr. Hemmings,* the pock-faced man had told him before they left the visiting room, *it's you an' me who'll be baggin' the rabbits.*

The escape was evident to Tom the moment he stepped off the bus that morning. The K-9 Unit, a score of dogs and their handlers, had already assembled beneath the Central Watchtower while a dozen line officers, all carrying shotguns, were pairing up in front of the Administration Building. The shotguns winked, deflecting the sun, as the men tightened the slings and adjusted the bills of their field caps.

Walking towards the administrative building, Tom felt a shiver of anticipation. He hoped the adventure would not exclude him and he felt relieved when he spotted Yoakum on the front steps of the building. The pock-faced man was holding two shotguns, one of which he handed to Tom.

"You're my road partner, sir. And you just have time to change yer clothes."

Tom sighed gratefully, accepting the gift. The weapon, a Remington 870 pump, was not unfamiliar to him. It had been only a month since he had practiced skip shooting buckshot at the pistol range.

"Kitchen workers?"

Yoakum nodded. "Couple of fairies is all. We ain't even supposed to dust 'em. Not unless they're armed."

That Chester had again been right, only added to Tom's anticipation. It did not concern him that the escape may have been preventable—that Hawkins had been unwise when he had refused to barter with the little man. Two lovers in white, callow boys who thought with their genitals, seemed as compatible a quarry as he could hope for.

"They may have *rods* on 'em, sir. That's what *I* heard anyhow." Yoakum smirked impishly, relishing his own joke as he adjusted the cartridge belt at his waist. He seemed more like a bounty hunter than an officer assigned to a field unit. "Won't know for sure till we flush 'em, Mr. Hemmings. So don't be allowin' 'em no slack."

November 23, 2000
5:15 p.m.

Tom had learned too much on the manhunt: opaque lessons that now seemed consistent with the bareness of the compound and the enduring silence of the radios and the phone. Even the sharpshooters on the roof seemed bloodless—as inanimate as gargoyles cemented to the arches of a church. Only Perkins, muttering faintly as he applied a compress to his still seeping wound, challenged the stillness of the moment—a reprieve that offered neither rest nor contemplation, only a prelude to the logistics of nightfall. What affected Tom, however, was not the innocence the manhunt had cost him that day, but the darker suspicion that he had in fact been liberated. Without the forfeiture of his innocence, the desecration of his standards, he would not be equipped to survive the void.

Later yesterday morning, once he had slipped into some boots and a pair of field pants, he stood passively by the water treatment plant to await his instructions. The tactics of the manhunt, announced earlier at roll call, consisted of the classic hammer and anvil maneuver. The dog handlers were to follow Sugar Creek, the main waterway on the property, sticking to its southernmost bank while half a dozen two-man shotgun teams kept pace with them on the opposite shore. The course seemed nearly inaccessible since the stream meandered over several miles of rugged brush and heavily wooded terrain, but it was believed to be the route chosen by the escapees.

"A no-brainer," Yoakum scoffed, once the two of them were headed towards the woods. "The fuckers will do anything to shake loose the dogs."

Tom and Yokum were strolling beside a cornfield—an inhibiting sight since the stalks, rigid and shoulder-high, looked like troops awaiting inspection. The corn seemed to mock the noisy movements of the other officers, most of whom had melted among the sycamores, yet could still be heard crashing awkwardly about. Only a Canada goose, a fierce clumsy bird that was hissing suspiciously as they approached it, suggested real vigilance—a reminder to Tom that he was performing serious business and not taking a vacation from the stressful demands of a laundry dorm. Tucking the stock of the shotgun beneath his armpit, checking the safety as he did so, he took comfort in the unfocussed barking of the dogs on the opposite side of the creek.

"Redcoats," Tom joked, ridiculing the other shotgun teams. Most of the officers he recognized as belonging to the UAW.

Yoakum spat. "Don't know why you keep messin' with them unions, Mr. Hemmings. They're all jack and no jizz if ya ask *me*. You oughta *know* that by now, sir."

"So what were you doing in that Teamster jacket?"

His companion laughed mirthlessly. "Suckin' up is what," he said. "An' I wanted to take a poke at that Commissioner fella—let him know we ain't *all* as stupid as he thinks. Figgered I'd better do it before Brewer climbs into the same bed as him." Yoakum tapped his temple with a forefinger then he spat once again. The man's candor was refreshing.

"Brewer," he went on, "knows the score as well as I do. He just don't have the balls to come out an' say so. Figgers he's better off playin' their game. Well that ain't the case with Henry Yoakum. I'll have left 'em high and dry long before they try slippin' the shaft to me."

They were climbing into the fog bank. The cornfield, a quarter mile behind them now, had already become a blur while above them the boughs of the sycamores were barely visible. Tom wondered if he would soon lose sight of Yoakum as well: his companion was gliding before him with the stealth of a bobcat, a stride so graceful that not even the swaying of a branch or the snapping of a twig betrayed his movements. It was finally the squawk of Yoakum's hand radio, a sound so remote as to seem otherworldly, that enabled Tom to locate him. The pock-faced man was waiting for him at the top of the hill, sitting upon a log and leisurely smoking a cigarette. His face looked macabre in the smoky half-light, as though it had been clawed by the talons of an eagle.

"V'et Nam taught me well," Yoakum remarked. "Must've kilt a dozen of the little yellow fuckers. And the place was a fuckin' *gold* mine"

"Nam's a good *place* for a shaft," Tom grumbled. He was hot underneath his Second Chance vest and his skin was beginning to itch. He sat down gingerly upon the log.

Yoakum shrugged. He squinted, as though measuring a target in the haze, then spat once again. "Their ghosts never bothered me none, Mr. Hemmings. Guess I must've kilt them too. 'Sides," he said, chuckling, "It's the ones left alive I feel sorry for—sittin' around in dirty huts, missin' an arm or a leg, while their leaders break bread with foreign cap'lists. By now they must be wonderin' what the war was all about." Yoakum laughed dryly and lifted the cigarette. The red eye expanded between his fingers. "But you're right about the shaft, Mr. Hemmings. Ol' Henry Yoakum struck pay dirt in the end. Mailed home a fortune, I did. I made out of black market commissary and the gold I pulled from the teeth of them fuckers we shot dead."

A hollow boom interrupted the conversation. The sound was remote—barely audible—as though the fog had cushioned it. Yoakum shook his head and slipped his radio from its leather sheath. Depressing the squelch button, he spoke softly into the receiver. Not waiting for a reply, he plunged the radio back into its sheath.

"It was one of *our* guns," he announced. "I'm bettin' that fucker was shootin' at a deer."

"You sure of that?"

Yoakum nodded. "It ain't likely we're gonna flush 'em this side of the dam." He rose lightly to his feet, surveying the woods as he did so. A gray squirrel scrambling among the boughs caught his eye momentarily before vanishing into the mist. Yoakum sighed, relaxed his shoulders, and checked the safety on his shotgun.

"Let's get outta range a friendly fire," he said.

It was midmorning before the two of them stopped to rest. It seemed as though they had been hiking forever, perhaps because the ground rose sharply and Yoakum had set a brisk pace. As they sat on a fallen maple, Tom gazed around uneasily. It was unclear to him what the haste was all about; he could not be sure whether Yoakum was seriously bent upon catching the escapees or simply wanted to keep out of range of the other shotgun teams. In any case, Tom needed a rest—and so he welcomed the wintry air and the perpetual laughter of the creek. Not even when he studied the terrain below, observing the fog-shrouded prison in the distance, was he able to recover his sense of mission. The buildings seemed as remote as passing ships.

"What if we *do* catch up with them?" Tom asked, a prospect he had only begun to consider. He could hear a sound like distant thunder, a hint that the dam was not far away.

Yoakum shrugged and lit another cigarette. "Ya ever *dusted* yerself a bunny, Mr. Hemmings?"

"I'm not that good a shot," Tom confessed.

"Shoot at the ground in front of 'em. Like they showed ya on the range. That'll spread out the shot some and throw it smack into 'em."

Tom felt his scalp prickle. "What if they're unarmed?"

Yoakum chuckled. He lifted a pant leg, exposing what at first appeared to be a toy pistol strapped to his shin. It was a nine-millimeter Glock.

"Ain't no way they can trace it, Mr. Hemmings. The serial number's been filed to the quick."

"A throw-down?" Tom said. He was somehow not surprised.

"An equalizer, *I* call it. We ain't supposed to carry 'em, but the brass don't bother checkin' you out. An' I'll be damned if I'll chase down their hares without a little insurance. They'll hang ya good and proper if the shoot ain't up to standard."

Yoakum wagged his foot. The Glock glittered like ice.

"Rules of engagement they call it," Yoakum said. "'Cept that they make the rules while we do the engagin'."

Another boom rebounded faintly in the woods below them—an indication that they were at least a mile ahead of the other shotgun teams. Yoakum lifted his radio to his ear and listened carefully to the garbled messages. His face was expressionless when he returned the radio to its sheath, confirming another false alarm.

"Once I brought it out barkin'," he remarked. "Happened six years ago. Baumgardner and I was workin' third shift in the kitchen dorm when this nut case with a Smith & Wesson got the drop on us. He must've snuck it through the Main Gate when he was returnin' from a work detail." Yoakum frowned and lifted his hand. The eye of the cigarette glowed like a coal. "It was cold clear thinkin' that got me out of it," he went on. "The bojack said he was gonna waste me and keep Baumgardner. Said he didn't have no use for *two* hostages. Told me I had it comin' anyhow so I asked him if I could take a few minutes to pray. Said I wanted to confess my sins to Jesus 'fore meetin' my maker an' all."

Yoakum laughed then shook his head. His hand stroked his shin. "Well, the fucker was a Muslim so he hadda respect religion. He told me to take a few minutes an' I closed my eyes on him. When I opened 'em five minutes later he was lookin' away so I hit the light switch and rolled. Now the dorm went blacker 'an pitch, but by then my eyes had adjusted to the dark. I could see that fucker, clear as day—stumblin' around like a blind man. Put four slugs into his chest before he even knew what was happinin'."

Yoakum dropped the cigarette, chuckling before crushing it out beneath his boot heel. "It don't *hurt* a man to see clear in the dark."

"What about the inquest?"

"I told 'em the bojack had *two* rods on him. Said I just took one of 'em away so I could give him what he had comin'. Now they couldn't prove nothin' else 'cause there weren't no witnesses. I took care a that when I turned off the lights."

"And that's what it took? Killing the lights?"

"Fooled 'em all but Perkins," Yoakum said. "He came around later and tried to pin me down. Said, 'Ahem, Mr. Yoakum. You know there's rules about carryin' weapons into the dorms?' Well, I just stared back at him, like I was lookin' at a piece of shit, and I said, 'Mr. Perkins. Are them rules as important to you as yer life?' Well Perkins goes redder 'an a beet an says, 'Is that a threat, Mr. Yoakum?' but I just kept starin' him down and I said, 'I repeat, Mr. Perkins. Are them rules as important to you as yer life? If it is you'll go on with yer questionin'.' Well, off he goes, madder 'an sin and promisin' to put me on report. But that's the last I ever heard about it."

Yoakum shook his head, cackled, then unsheathed his radio. The static coughed feebly, a sound too anemic to compete with the distant rumble of the falls. Yoakum called in their coordinates then muted the volume. A smile sliced his face as he rose to his feet. "'Bout time we caught us some rabbits."

November 23, 2000
6:00 p.m.

The phone in the hospital checkpoint shack rang, distracting Tom from his reverie but committing him only briefly to the comedy of action. He did not even bother to brace himself as he lifted the receiver to his ear. His fatigue had mercifully taken over, so much so that it no longer concerned him which scoundrel he should happen to talk to.

"The feast is prepared, sir." It was Chester's voice.

"Surely, you exaggerate the Devil's bounty," Tom replied.

"Am I still soliciting the Devil, Mr. Hemmings?"

"If you're in cahoots with Yoakum, it sure looks that way."

"Then I shall consider myself honored, sir. Given the competition, it is rare that a pauper has the privilege to do so."

"Not only that, you've *armed* that motherfucker."

"Does that not please you, sir? As a minion to the Philistines, I should think that it would."

"Is Yoakum carrying slugs? I need to know that much."

"I honestly cannot say, Mr. Hemmings. Thankfully, sir, I do not seek to know too much. I am better off preparing for your arrival—an occasion for which we have already killed the fatted calf."

"Give me an hour," Tom muttered.

Tom returned the phone to the cradle and continued to watch the gymnasium through the doorway crack. The windows were aglow and the long bulky building had come to resemble a ship at dusk. He welcomed the cloak of evening if only for the opportunity it would give him to part company with Perkins. The lieutenant, as though energized by his wound, was writing furiously on a pad of paper and it was Tom's suspicion that he was recording the conversation for a report. *I hate that snitching fucker*, was the only reaction Tom could feel at that moment, a contempt he could not blame upon his fatigue or even the heat of the moment so much as the defining incident of the manhunt.

Tom had felt his pulse hammer as the two of them descended the knoll. The falls were now louder—like an approaching freight train—and the fog was so thick that he could have traced out his name in it. Walking behind Yoakum was like following a shadow: the man appeared and vanished so subtly that it was difficult to tell him apart from the trees. Tom wondered if Yoakum was trying to outpace him. If this were the case, he could not fault the man. Tom, with his heavy stride and callow sense of ethics, could only be a liability to a phantom. He felt suddenly amiss, like a thief in a church, a guilt that persisted even after he spotted Yoakum once again. His partner, crouched on a high bluff, appeared to have turned into stone.

Tom froze, his hands tight on the shotgun. He did not draw a breath until Yoakum signaled him to come forward.

"We'll be spottin' 'em eventually," the pock-faced man said, an observation that seemed to have been founded upon faith alone. Below them the creek was bellowing, a current too furious for anyone to traverse, while the brush alongside of it, a thicket of wild raspberry bushes, looked totally impenetrable.

"When you see one of 'em," Yoakum said, "make sure to shoot twice. If yer first load hits pay dirt send the second one high."

"You're speaking to the converted," Tom said, already a believer in the warning shot. His plan, for that matter, was to make sure both his shots missed.

Yoakum spat disdainfully. "The bojacks won't hear ya shootin' at 'em—loud as that creek is. But ya still can't be droppin' 'em without etiquette."

"The Redcoats tell you that?"

Yoakum laughed, a sunless croak that complemented the lifelessness in his eyes. "Wouldn't pay 'em no mind if they *had*, Mr. Hemmings. Ya shoulda heard Brewer's bunch after the union forum. Bitchin' 'bout this and that, they was. 'Bout how the Gov'ment was takin' away their jobs and their guns an' all that malarkey. Bitchin' and moanin'—that's all they're good for. No wonder the auto plants took off for Mexico."

Tom had to agree. "No wonder the unions can't jack."

Yoakum shrugged. "Who wants to *sweat* for a livin' anyhow? There's better ways 'an that to turn a dollar!"

"Trafficking?" Tom guessed.

Yoakum nodded. "An' I wanta thank you for the opportunity, Mr. Hemmings. You remember that grievance you filed last year? 'Bout how the tobacco in the dorm kept stinkin' up your office an all? Well, ya did a good job stickin' that one, sir. Since they stopped sellin' cigarettes in the commissary, the price of 'em has shot through the roof. Fifty dollars a pack—that's what the bojacks are payin' me for 'em. An' that's just for Winstons and Salems."

"Isn't it rather risky?"

Yoakum smirked. "A bit," he replied. "But I sell 'em through my snitches so I got my ass covered. They know I'll rat 'em out to the rest of the dorm if they drop a dime on me.

"Anyhow," he went on, "it's all peanuts compared to what they're makin' downstate. Must've takin' a *ton* of smoke for ol' *Colonial* to get through the door. A week's suspension—that's all they're likely to give me for creatin' a market of my own. An' I could use me a vacation anyhow."

Yoakum gestured with his chin, a motion that stopped their conversation cold. As Tom looked towards the opposite bank of the creek, he suddenly felt blessed by their high elevation and the prohibitive snarl of the water below them. The movement, a stirring among the bushes, was so quick and illusive that it took away his breath. It had to have been caused by the escapees.

Tom's thumb freed the safety on his shotgun. The branches grew still.

"They was lookin' to ford it," Yoakum whispered.

Shortly before noon, they spotted the inmates. Predictably, Yoakum saw them first. Clutching Tom's sleeve, as though protecting him from a fall, he pointed to the bottom of a hollow ravine. The two boys had managed to ford the creek.

Were it not for a pocket of sinewy smoke, a drift rising lazily from a campfire, Tom would have felt that he was looking at a painting. The inmates, lying motionless beside the blaze, looked small and defeated, more like lepers than the stealthy adversaries Tom had imagined them to be. They were probably exhausted—pummeled into submission by the brambles and the bog—and were waiting for a search party to come and find them. The plume, bleeding gently into the fog, looked like a signal of distress.

Tom nodded to Yoakum, a prearranged signal, and took his position behind a sagging oak. It would take Yoakum ten minutes to position himself on the northernmost lip of the gully, ample time for Tom to muster up the courage to squeeze off a round. With their movement impeded by the creek, the inmates would be easily intercepted by Yoakum if they chose to flee the warning shot.

Tom waited and watched, convinced he was invisible. The fogbank was particularly thick within the gully, filling it like soup in a bowl, and the inmates appeared to be turning into mist. They were as impalpable as wraiths and for this reason Tom grew less reluctant to shoot in their direction.

A bough above him snapped and then teetered. He did not hear the pop—the bark of a light caliber handgun—until a second later. The sound seemed as impotent as a firecracker, so it surprised him when the bough came crashing down. Only then did he notice the glint of metal in the gully below. Had the weapon been discharged in his direction?

He fired too quickly, failing to brace the stock of the shotgun against his shoulder, and he lost his balance when the butt kicked his chest. A rock struck his head—he swore someone had flung it—but no one approached as he lay semiconscious on the ground. Only darkness assailed him— darkness and a distant booming that sounded like an echo. It was a second boom, sharper than the first, that convinced him that Yoakum was shooting at the inmates.

The darkness dissolved as Tom's senses recovered. Slowly, painfully, he rose to his feet. His shotgun, half buried by dead leaves, seemed as foreign as an amputated limb, and he picked it up slowly before peering through the branches of the oak. The sight in the gully was the same: the fog lay like soup, the plume climbed feebly from the campfire, and the two boys still appeared to be asleep. Only the sight of Yoakum, crab crawling down the slope, suggested that anything had changed.

He kept his eyes on Yoakum now; the movement of the man, quick and precise, was in sharp contrast to the lazy trajectory of the smoke. When Yoakum finally waved to him,

Tom chambered a round and set the safety on his shotgun. Dead branches pawed at him, scratching his face, as he abandoned his position behind the oak. Stepping into the clearing, he began the descent to the bottom of the ravine. A minute later, he was standing in front of the campfire.

The inmates lay slack-jawed and peaceful upon the ground. They looked like children napping, a sight that belied their crank-rotted teeth and the dark blue swastikas printed upon their wrists and biceps. Obscured by a membrane of watery heat, they had retained their ethereality and Tom gazed upon them as though they were sacred. Not even the odor of shit diminished the sanctity of the moment.

"One of 'em crapped his pants," Yoakum said.

"Are they dead?"

Yoakum gestured toward one of the bodies. "*Hopper* ain't. The fucker fainted before I had the chance to plug him too."

As he spoke, Yoakum cracked the pump-action on his shotgun. His face was like stone and he looked coldly at the surviving inmate. After a moment he shook his head then slipped the safety into place.

"He'll squeal on us for sure, Mr. Hemmings. Try an' pack us in. But it's his word against ours, ain't it, sir?"

Tom shook his head. "How much punch can he pack? It was a clean shoot."

Only then did Yoakum point, calling Tom's attention to a shiny object, the thing he had seen while behind the dead oak. Tom's heart sank like lead when he saw what it was. It was not a .38 pistol—not even a knife—but a small can of Pork-'n'-Beans.

"That's just the problem, sir," Yoakum said. "The fuckers *weren't* packin'. We dusted ourselves a clean bunny."

Tom looked at the can and saw only reflection, a heatless flutter of flame upon metal. That the can was unopened seemed also prophetic—an indication that his future, or whatever remained of it, was sealed as compactly as the beans. He suddenly felt the weight of the Devil's wages. Could Chester have misinformed him about the pistol?

Tom spoke lamely. "How *could* we have known?"

"It won't matter at the inquisition, sir. They'll make us out to be child killers. That'll be certain if Perkins has his way." Yoakum coughed—his lungs rattling crisply—but when he spoke again his voice was sharp and clear. "We may as well beat 'em to the punch, sir."

A murmur, cold and disembodied, interrupted their conversation. Yoakum unsheathed his radio, muted the sound, then reported their coordinates with a quick series of codes. He sighed before returning the radio to its sheath.

"Let's get down to business," he said at last.

Yoakum slipped his hand into his pocket, removing the Glock and a large dirty handkerchef. For a moment he fumbled with the gun, stroking it with the cloth as though burnishing a jewel. He then pressed the cloth to the dead boy's fingers. "Gotta get gun powder on 'em," he said.

Finishing his work, Yoakum pocketed the handkerchef. The gun he placed in the dead boy's hand.

November 23, 2000
6:30 p.m.

Inside the gymnasium, a gun barked three times. The reports were so steady that they seemed to be keeping time with the distant pulsing of the telephone in the athletic office. Tom replaced the receiver and the pulsing stopped. He nodded to the checkpoint sharpshooters. "It's over," he said. That Yoakum had executed the Disciples brought him neither regret nor emancipation—only the numbing embrace of the familiar. Deliverance, if such a word were applicable, lay only in the ingenuity of his judgment—his willingness to invest in his own gullibility. Fortunately, Yoakum had told him no more than he had needed to know.

His own telephone rang. Tom paused and then answered it, knowing already that Yoakum was on the line.

"Still politicking?" Tom said. He heard Yoakum chuckle.

"Like I said, Mr. Hemmings, it makes for uncommon bedfellows."

Yoakum's jest seemed excessive, forced—like the humor of death row inmates. Tom felt as though he were talking to an imposter. "You'll sleep alone on this one."

"The sandman willing and the creek don't rise, I will. Ain't sure I can *do* that much sleepin' right now."

"Is the sandman out of dust?" Tom joked. He was desperate for more humor.

"He's gotta be, sir. The fuckers in here are nappin' permanent."

"You *might* have let them live."

Yoakum groaned. "Like we done with Hopper on the manhunt? I'll keep that in mind, sir. Ya got any *more* good advice?"

"Did they give you much choice?"

"Put it this way, sir. It was either dust' 'em or pack 'em off to Africa. So I'm thankin' ya for your help."

Tom drew a slow breath. "So what happens now?" It was a question he did not want answered.

"An investigation, I guess. But fuck 'em. We don't even *need* insurance this time."

"The investigation *is* our insurance," Tom snapped. "It'll prove you saved Perkins' life. He was hit by a slug and he's lost a lot of blood. So you *needed* to take out that sniper."

He heard Yoakum sigh, a sound like an inner tube losing air. "Is *Perkins* there with ya? You should have told me that, sir. I'd a waited for the fucker to kick off on us first."

Tom lowered the phone, taking a moment to assess the situation. It was evening and the street lamps were off, but an unearthly sheen still pervaded the compound, a glow emanating from a harvest moon and the jack-o-lantern lights from the dormitory. The sharpshooters beside him, taciturn men who thought with their reflexes, had already found their element in the half-light. Wearing night vision goggles, they looked like aliens as they watched the compound for signs of movement. Only Perkins, who was napping at the back of the shack, was oblivious to the pregnancy of the moment.

Tom gripped the receiver. "So what happens now?"

"Don't know about you, sir, but I'm stayin' put. The *inmates* may be outa shooters, but there's no point temptin' *friendly* fire."

"I suppose not," Tom replied. He pressed the buttons on the cradle, killing their connection at least symbolically. What he needed could not come from Yoakum. What he needed was an honest appraisal of his soul—an assessment that exceeded his guilt obsession or the sterile evaluation of an investigator. He released the buttons then dialed the dormitory. It consoled him when he heard the gentle voice of his informant.

"Is it over, Mr. Hemmings?" Chester asked.

"Yoakum shot the Disciples. Does that make it over?"

"It does, sir, if it spares the lives of nobler men. The Muslims will not mourn them, I assure you. Nor will the Aryan Brotherhood."

"How about Moses?"

"Is it absolution you wish, Mr. Hemmings? I cannot help you there. That is beyond the power of an old sinner."

"Okay, Chester. So what happens next? Are we done? Are the inmates going to surrender?"

"Come to the dorm, sir, and broker the truce. It is safe now, I assure you. And there *is* some distraction to be found in deeds."

"Is the meal still ready?"

"That it is, sir, humble though it be."

"Send me an escort. That will show the brass that you're sincere. Meanwhile, I call off our snipers."

Tom unsheathed his hand radio—quickly, as though drawing a sword, then spoke to the control officer. "It's over," he announced. "I'm going in." He stepped through the door of the shack without waiting to hear back from Captain Hawkins. He knew that his small mutiny was hollow, but he was still determined to begin the talks. Had his bridge not been burned, had his shock not begun to thaw, he would have returned to the parking lot with Perkins, but his complicity in a triple homicide—whether real or imagined—demanded a darker retreat. Salvation—as compelling an illusion as any—could only await him in the dormitory. He would have to go in there. He would have to set things right.

Yet how could he possibly set things right? He could see the three Disciples, their lives snuffed out by Yoakum, lurking in the shadow of the gymnasium.

Tom sensed a supportive presence behind him. He turned his head slowly, reluctantly, and confirmed that it was Perkins. The proximity of the man was both a comfort and an irritation to him, and so he chose to say nothing. Perkins broke the silence.

"Were you talking to Yoakum?" The lieutenant's voice was sleepy, as though he had awoken from a long nap.

Tom nodded, offering no elaboration. He returned his gaze to the dormitory. "How bad is the leg?"

Perkins grimaced. "Not bad. But I *could* use a stool."

"Talk to Brewer," Tom replied. "He'll help you pad that sick leave."

"Obliged," Perkins said then he said nothing more. A sliver of sharp light had emerged from the entrance to the dormitory, teasing them like foxfire before vanishing as quickly as it had appeared. A bed sheet, distinguishable in the moonlight, seemed a further parody of phantom hope, but Tom watched with interest as it waived lazily back and forth. He did not see its bearer until almost a full minute later: a leisurely manifestation which, when finally visible, seemed to complete the comedy.

Gabriel Grant was strolling towards him.

II
VAGRANTS

You said you'd never compromise
With the mystery tramp, but now you realize ...
—Bob Dylan

November 23, 2000
7:00 p.m.

T om folded his arms. "You the best they could do?"

Gabriel shrugged. He was a slim but ungainly individual with narrow eyes and spatula-shaped fingers. He looked at Tom eagerly, as though anticipating a tip for the service he was providing. When none was forthcoming, he lowered the truce flag. The bed sheet slipped off the handle and he was left holding a naked broom.

"The Deacon been messin' with childrens!" Gabriel said finally.

Tom shook his head. It was the first disparaging thing he had heard a resident say about Chester Mahoney. Misogynistic remarks—such as "hand in the cookie jar" or "caught pokin' jail bait"—were more typically used by the inmates when describing Chester's offense.

"Let it go, Gabriel," he said. "He *is* more saint than sinner. And you need him as a spokesman."

Gabriel snorted. "Ain't *lettin'* it go, Jackson. The dude ain't *speakin'* for me. He done been messin' with *childrens.*"

Tom's radio coughed and he muted the static. Gabriel, still clutching the broom, looked at him thoughtfully. "They sendin' us to Africer, Jackson?"

"That's improbable right now."

"Don't wanna to be sent to no Africer, Jackson. Got nothin *comin'* in Africer. And the elephants be *steppin'* on ya."

"At least you can *hunt* them in Africa," Tom replied. "Here, they hunt *you.*"

Tom's attempt at political sarcasm was obviously lost upon Gabriel. Embarrassed, he looked away from the man. Tom now noticed that the moon was brighter, that Perkins had disappeared, and that there were more sharpshooters

99

on the roof of the Administration Building. Without a doubt, Gabriel was in the crosshairs of several rifles.

Tom said, "Drop the broom. They might think it's a weapon."

Gabriel snorted but complied, tossing away the broom with an awkward movement of his wrist.

"You gonna get my soup back, Jackson?"

"Not if it's in a can," Tom snapped.

Tom eased the radio slowly from its sheath, restoring the volume as he lifted it to his lips. His announcement—that he was about to enter the dormitory—seemed merely a gesture, a claim so lacking in spontaneity that he suddenly felt ashamed. Only the ache of physical hunger provided him with an immediate motivation to enter the damn place.

The control officer spoke. "Hold for Hawkins, sir."

"Fuck him," Tom said, returning the radio to its sheath. He looked at his escort. "Is it suppertime, Gabriel?"

"Gotta be, Jackson. They stole all my soup."

"For a poacher's banquet?"

Gabriel nodded. "The Deacon done set you a place."

November 23, 2000
7:30 p.m.

Tom had not prepared himself for the total familiarity of the dormitory—a sight so mundane that he may as well have been arriving for an evening of paperwork in his office. A large group of inmates, most of them pimply adolescents, were sitting as usual in the television area while the Muslims, a score of African Americans wearing skull caps, had assembled in one of the bed pods for their evening prayer. Curled into small inauspicious bundles, they looked as though they were attempting to perform somersaults.

He looked cautiously about, then stepped past the doorway as Gabriel made his way toward the television. The dormitory, perhaps because of its enormity, seemed entirely too normal. His informant, for one, was nowhere to be seen while most of the hostages were sitting unguarded at one of the game tables. The hostages—third shift officers—were not familiar to him. Playing cards while sipping coffee, they looked like pensioners contentedly passing the time. They smiled and nodded at him, but didn't move from the table; apparently, they were well briefed in hostage protocol. So peaceful were the sights around him, so contrary to his expectations, that he was not surprised when he saw Sarah Baumgardner walking towards him. It somehow comforted him that Sarah too was a captive—that she was no longer empowered to take inventory and count heads. *She can't nag me now*, he thought.

Although a prisoner, Sarah did not seem inhibited in the least, an indication that she had fallen under the protection of the Muslims. This was probably the result of her recent spat with the nurse—her untimely insistence that an aging Muslim be escorted to the hospital for treatment. Clearly, this breach of rules—the incident that had resulted in her transfer to the third shift—had given her special status and the run of the dorm.

"They fixed you a spread, skipper."

"Ahhh, the fatted calf?"

Sarah glared at him. "Don't talk fancy to me, skipper. I'm a country girl—in case you've forgotten. Born and raised in little old Rockville."

"So what are they serving tonight? Duck under glass?"

"Kool Aid and Spam sandwiches. I'm sick of 'em myself, but it's the best these bojacks can offer." She sighed, apparently relieved that the supper was not her responsibility. Tom pulled his eyes away from Sarah and looked around the dorm, half expecting a knife to be thrown at him. He realized finally that his arrival was a matter of only modest importance. Certainly, it could not compete with the ritual of prayer or the canned dialogue coming from the television set. The inmates were watching *Felicity* of all programs—a show about another novice, a provincial girl of eighteen who had left her hometown to attend an impersonal city college.

He said, "Where's the Deacon?"

Sarah shook her head. "He's got bowel trouble, skipper—or so he says. If you ask *me*, he's jerkin' off."

"He seems ill, Mr. Hemmings," a gentler voice murmured.

Tom turned, relieved to have been noticed by somebody other than Sarah. The speaker, Jamal Hassan, was a reed-thin African American with a seductive tone of voice. His ever-present bodyguard was standing alongside him, a muscular dwarf whose nickname, Short Dog, suggested that he had yet to earn his Muslim identity. Tom knew little about Hassan—whether he was an orthodox Muslim, as many of the inmates were, or a member of the more radical Nation of Islam. If the latter were true, it seemed vaguely ironical that he was standing in Chester's place. The Nation's first prophet, according to his training literature, was also a sexual miscreant with a quick and flowery tongue.

"That's a shame," Tom replied. "He invited me to dinner."

The thin man bowed. He motioned towards the game area. One of the tables had been covered with a brown Army blanket in lieu of a tablecloth.

"Pork sandwiches?"

Again the man bowed.

"A strange offering—isn't it?" Tom said. "Considering you want no more pork products."

"Just sit, Mr. Hemmings," the thin man murmured. His voice was soft and conciliatory, like that of a servant.

Slowly, self-consciously, Tom sat at the game table, taking a final look around the dorm. The Muslims, for the most part, were continuing with their prayers while the rest of the inmates—those not assembled in the television area—were reclining on their bunks, some in bathrobes, others in socks and underwear. The sight was so provincial that he was almost relieved when he noticed that Hopper lay tied to one of the bunks—probably so he could not commit suicide and join his lover. With his hands above his head—his boney wrists strapped securely to the bed bar—he appeared to have attained for himself the facsimile of a crucifixion. The cup of all fantasts, Tom thought to himself, unconcerned that he was probably over-dramatizing the matter. That boy was a pariah—not a martyr.

Sarah, to his surprise, seated herself beside him, and he noticed with regret that her nails looked bitten. He was still grateful to have her near him, and suspected that she would accompany him when he left the dorm. He did not attribute this to the Code of Islam—its reluctance to wage war upon women—nor to his skills as a negotiator, but to her notable reputation as a complainer. Over the last two days, she had probably been a heavy burden to her captors.

It was Short Dog who served him the feast—the inevitable pitcher of grape Kool Aid along with a plate of sandwiches. Tom was wary of Short Dog, if nobody else. A compact mute with the mind of a child, he was too easy a target for manipulation. *Beware of the true believers,* his instructor at the academy had emphasized time and again. *They'll take out the Commissioner if ordered to.* Tom had chuckled at this bit of hyperbole, not considering the Commissioner an inestimable loss, but had otherwise respected the information.

Slowly, his eyes upon Hassan, he selected one of the sandwiches. Embarrassed by the man's disapproval of pork products, he nibbled it tentatively at first, but his appetite soon took control of him and he began to eat ravenously. He had consumed three of the sandwiches, along with a mug of Kool Aid, before he felt ashamed enough to push the plate to one side. He felt even more conspicuous when he finally spotted his informant; Chester, his bowels apparently relieved, was now shuffling in his direction.

The little man looked uncommonly pale. At first this seemed due to an accident of lighting, but his face remained pasty even after he had bowed to Hassan and taken his place on the opposite side of the table. His face was so wan, his expression so fixed, that he appeared to have been carved out of soap.

"The blood of Christ, Mr. Hemmings," Chester remarked dryly. "Drink deep of it, sir." Chester pushed the pitcher of Kool Aid towards him. His remark, an obvious effort to placate an ally, suggested that Hassan was a zealot after

103

all and would prove to be the wild card in the negotiations. To the best of Tom's knowledge, the Nation was the only denomination of Islam that considered Christ to be a black prophet.

Hassan, his expression noncommittal, remained standing while Chester sat. He seemed content to let Chester do the talking, a tactic, Tom suspected, rather than a courtesy. With the Muslims in control of the dormitory, it would be to Hassan's advantage to remain as inconspicuous as possible to the authorities. The man's silence was still infectious: the only noise in the dormitory was now coming from the television set.

Chester, his eyes distracted by the television, finally broke the silence. "*Philistine rot,*" he spat. "Have you *seen* the program, Mr. Hemmings?"

Tom nodded.

"*Female masturbation, adolescent bed-hopping, homo-sexual marriages. What* makes them think we will *stand* for such filth?"

The remark, even if calculated, seemed sincere and Tom wondered if he was again witnessing the essence of the man. Unfortunately, it was Tom who felt exposed: the program was among his favorites, and he would probably be watching it in his trailer, if left to his own resources. He changed the subject.

"Aren't we here to discuss terms?"

The question was no less rhetorical than Chester's and probably a redundancy as well. Tom already knew what the terms would be: better hospital treatment, a select pampering of the Muslims, and no more rip-off commissary services. The grievances were so easy for him to anticipate that he suspected he could have drafted them on his own and saved himself the trip to the dormitory.

"We have a precondition," Chester said.

"What is it?"

The little man sighed. He looked critically at the table as though noticing the crumbs on the blanket. "That we be treated according to our deserts, sir, and not the mischief of others. I'm speaking of the murder, sir. To my mind it has already been avenged."

"The murder of the Disciples?"

"The murder of Lieutenant Perkins."

The news should have stunned him, but Tom felt no capacity for further shock. Instead, he looked mutely at his informant, aware only that the stakes had been seriously raised. Was his reaction legitimate under the circumstances—the only response he could afford—or genuine antipathy towards an officer he regarded as a snitch and an ideologue? He looked at Sarah, hoping for sympathy, but she seemed to be preoccupied. Her expression was like that of a commuter impatient to board a train.

He turned towards Chester. "When did it happen?"

"This evening, sir. It was on the television. They said he was shot by a Disciple and died sometime later."

Tom felt his voice catch. "*Perkins*," he stammered. "He was *standing* behind me ten minutes ago. He was as healthy as a horse."

Chester reached across the table and patted Tom's wrist. "Could that have been his spirit, Mr. Hemmings? The TV reporter was very clear—we saw the news broadcast just minutes ago."

Tom let his jaw tighten, his dismay giving way to anger. Whatever the time and circumstances of Perkins' passing, he had surely been the last to learn about it. But the blame—should the negotiations fail—would surely fall on him. The knot in his stomach tightened.

Chester, noticing Tom's panic, patted his wrist again. "Please don't mourn him by his merit, Mr. Hemmings. Grief must have limits, sir, if we are to get on with the toils of the living. But let it be said that he was a model among officers—a fair and consistent man. His loss is a harsh lesson to us all."

Sarah groaned and scrunched closer to Tom—he could feel her hair tickling his neck. Her proximity, along with the huskiness of her voice, was an utter distraction to him. But she had every reason to groan. Were it not for the tenacity of Perkins—his by-the-book persistence—she would have probably never been placed on the graveyard shift. Nor would she have become a hostage.

"He was *consistent* all right," Sarah muttered. The comment was somehow reassuring to him.

It was probably Sarah's boldness—the impropriety of a woman speaking out of turn—that prompted Hassan to lower his guard. With his arms folded, his head still bowed, Hassan spoke in a firm but compassionate tone.

"A mighty angel will take his soul."

Tom shook his head, impressed by Hassan's gallantry. *That tall drink of milk is probably the self-educated leader of a lost nation*, he thought. *A fucking Malcolm X.* The observation only made him irritable.

Tom shook his head. "Are you saying an angel is going to save an infidel?"

"I am sincere, Mr. Hemmings," Hassan replied. "And my prayers do not go out to his assassins. They were justly executed according to the Code of Islam."

"What kind of code employs Yoakum?" Tom asked, a question so careless that he was instantly embarrassed.

Hassan raised his head. His eyes were vacant—his face profoundly sad. "*All* religions use mercenaries, Mr. Hemmings," he said. "Perhaps that may free up an angel or two."

The man bowed meekly, having spoken his piece, and Tom once again grew aware of the pervading reticence of the dorm: the pod-like quality of the inmates as they knelt in prayer, sat upon their bunks, or gazed hypnotically at the television set. Had they been pummeled into submission by the Muslims or were they simply worn down from the prolonged siege? A nasal murmur, as though answering him, arose from the television area. "Nice tits!" It could only have been the voice of a heretic and Tom felt a small measure of relief. It appeared that the Muslims had their limits after all.

"So it's amnesty you want?" Tom said. It was time to get down to business.

Hassan paused before replying. "No, Mr. Hemmings. It would imply that *we* too are murderers."

"Then what?"

"A promise, sir, that we will not be punished. Not for the crimes of others. We only wanted decent care for our sick. We only wanted reasonable prices for paltry goods, so we could settle our debts among one another. We never wanted blood on our hands."

"Don't all of us pay for the crimes of assholes?"

Hassan smiled thinly. "Public servants do. But *we* are here involuntarily."

"Political prisoners," Tom said angrily, too suddenly aware that the meeting had become a sham. As a mediator, Tom knew that certain matters were to be considered nonnegotiable—the academy had made that clear enough. And foremost among them was the killing of an officer by inmates. Since immunity for Perkins' death was on the table—the talks could mean little if wholesale prosecutions were to follow—everybody in the dorm, himself included, had become a hostage. He could only go through the formalities now and hope, perhaps with a little luck, to salvage a timber from the shipwreck to come.

As he glanced at Chester, he knew without a doubt that his informant was aware of this also. The man's face was like that of a veteran poker player—an attitude so superior to the cards he was holding that it validated only the power of pretension.

Tom looked back at Hassan. "I'll take your requests to the Commissioner. But he'll want a concession before he decides anything." He was sticking too closely to the negotiator's script, but his transparency seemed irrelevant to Hassan. The man seemed eager for an opportunity to be magnanimous, an assurance of martyrdom if the worst-case scenario should come to pass.

"Take Mrs. Baumgardner with you," he said, with a slight bow. "She has been most kind."

Sarah gasped, a sound Tom at first took for an expression of relief, but when he glanced at her he saw that her face was flushed. She was looking at him so intently that he wondered if he had accidentally groped her.

"Don't make *me* your concession," she muttered. "I can't be leavin' this dorm by myself. The whole damn prison will think I'm a suck-ass. And my union won't have nothing more to do with me."

Hassan dropped his gaze. "You should be embraced, Mrs. Baumgardner—not ostracized."

"Why?" Sarah snapped. "Because I helped one of you sticky creeps? That's the dumbest thing I *ever* did. Them hostages think I'm a terrorist lover."

"But you have other considerations," Tom said. "What about your children?"

"My brats, you mean? Call 'em up and talk to 'em. Tell 'em I want 'em in school an' not sittin' around watchin' the boob tube all day. I'm stayin' in here till the end." She clenched her fists tightly as she spoke, as though she were concealing something in them, and then she looked away. Her metallic aversion to Tom's eyes convinced him that she wanted to be forced. He looked at Hassan and the thin man nodded tactfully. His face, though a mask of piety, displayed only tenderness towards the flustered woman.

"I insist you leave, Mrs. Baumgardner," Hassan said, his voice now loud enough to be overheard by the officers at the game tables. "It is not Islam to ignore a kindness."

Sarah rolled her eyes. "*Keep* your Islam. You're worse than the sergeants when it comes to puttin' down women." Her voice was sharp but her gaze remained unfocussed, as though she were scolding an uninvited solicitor over the phone. Hassan, perhaps also embarrassed, skirted the subject.

"The Disciples, Mr. Hemmings," Hassan said.

Tom stared up at Hassan. "What about them?"

"Consider their execution our concession. Mrs. Baumgardner can only be a gift."

The remark, though intended as a compliment, served only to aggravate Sarah further.

"A suck-ass ain't no good to anyone, Hassan."

Hassan dropped his gaze, and Tom knew the conversation was over. "Say what you wish, Mrs. Baumgardner. We will not hold you here any longer."

The finality in Hassan's voice seemed less poignant than resigned. It was clear that he did not feel vested in the negotiations—that his only sense of commitment was to Sarah. The canned chatter from *Felicity*, the only sound in the room, seemed to further define their circumstances. The negotiations now seemed as prepackaged as the program, extending only the illusion of vitality and embrace.

Chester brought the matter to a close. "There it is, Mr. Hemmings," he said. "We ask not for justice, sir, but merely an admission that justice has been dispensed. Since the facility is a temple to equity, this should be an easy matter to settle. I daresay I am ashamed by the meagerness of our request."

Tom sat silently for a long time. Finally, he murmured, "I'll see what I can do."

Tom glanced at Sarah, a signal that it was time for them to go. When she continued to look away from him, he felt as though he had indeed groped her. The circumstances of her rescue—the stigma she would have to endure from the rank and file—made him feel deeply sorry for her. How could she possibly face life as a suck-up, a deserter, and a Muslim collaborator? How could she possibly work without comradery? Her rescue seemed a poor substitute for a blaze of final glory or, if she managed to survive the attack, the more prosaic home fires of her union.

Carefully, Tom separated the radio from its sheath. Depressing the squelch button, he spoke. "One Ninety. Control."

"Control. Over."

"Hold your fire," he said. "We got two coming out."

November 23, 2000
8:30 p.m.

Gabriel Grant led them from the dormitory, waiving another truce flag—a T-shirt tied to a mop handle— triumphantly above his head. Sarah, looking like an adulteress about to be stoned, shuffled along behind him. She did not say a word as they walked across the compound, nor did she lift her head when a flare popped above them like a holiday rocket. The ball dropped slowly, its cold light intensifying, and their shadows preceded them as they approached the hospital checkpoint.

A figure was awaiting them there—a form so still, so seemingly impervious to them, that Tom felt a thrill of trepidation. He suppressed his panic, bracing himself for another encounter with the lieutenant's wraith, yet he somehow felt cheated when he saw Brewer standing there instead. Apparently, the big man had taken over the role of checkpoint communicator.

Tom saluted stiffly. "Waiting for a parade?"

Brewer grunted. "No way, Hemmings. There ain't nothing to *sit* on out here."

"That's what Perkins said."

Brewer chuckled. He seemed grateful for the joke. "A stool pigeon without a stool," he said. "Didn't make for much of a target, did he?"

"So how did the sniper get him?"

"He was lucky," Brewer said. "Perkins, that is. He *should* have bought it from one of his *own* men."

Brewer unsheathed his radio and called in a message to the Control Unit. He repeated the codes meticulously as though he found the codes preferable to further conversation. He did not look at Sarah at all.

Gabriel spoke. "That dude in the dorm been pimpin'."

The revelation did not surprise Tom. "Why say that, Gabriel?"

"'Cause I knowed him in East Chicago, Jackson. 'Fore he started callin' hisself Hassan. He had hisself a stable full a hos."

The disclosure, clearly more information than Tom wanted, pricked his embarrassment even further. He spoke without thinking. "Don't go back to the dorm."

Gabriel shook his head. "Ain't goin' with *you*, Jackson. They be puttin' me in the hole if I do *that*."

"That's better than getting a hole put in you."

Gabriel again shook his head. "Ain't *goin'* to no hole, Jackson. The *bitches* be messin' with ya there."

The word "bitches"—a range term for segregation officers—suggested that Gabriel was speaking from experience. Still, his infantile mind did not seem capable of anticipating the consequences of returning to the dormitory—the buckshot and heavy batons that would soon replace the promise of a settlement. Tom tried once again.

"I'll walk you through the gate myself."

Gabriel shook his head. "That dude been *pimpin'*, Jackson. *He* ain't speakin' for me neither. Ain't *goin* to no hole on his account."

Brewer returned his radio to its sheath. He then jerked his thumb towards Gabriel. "Let the fool get what's comin' to him," he muttered. "It's not like he doesn't *deserve* it."

"For being an asshole?" Tom offered.

Brewer looked contemptuously at the truce flag in Gabriel's hand. "For carryin' another man's colors," he said. He coughed, rocking slowly upon his heeals. "Hawkins wants you for a debriefing," he went on. "When they're done tearin' *Yoakum* a new asshole."

"How'd *Yoakum* get loose?"

"They took him out through the Main Gate while you were in the dorm. Snuck him alongside the fence. They also carted out three stiffs." Brewer folded his arms and continued glaring. "Word is you helped set 'em up for the kill."

Brewer's remark, the contempt with which he uttered the word "stiffs," suggested that there were others worthy of the definition. Since the shooting had been unauthorized and since Tom had managed to involve himself in it, it was suddenly evident to him that he would be needing the support of the UAW—support that he clearly had not earned. He again felt panic grip his chest.

"Are they trying to pin it on *both* of us?"

Brewer shrugged. "Maybe," he said. "And maybe they ain't. But *you* shoulda let those Disciples be, Hemmings. They was killin' off scum buckets anyhow."

Tom felt Sarah's hand burrow into his own. Her skin was soft, her grip surprisingly gentle, but when he looked at her he saw little reason for comfort. Her eyes were remote and testy like those of a jilted lover. She tugged his hand impatiently.

"We need to get *out* of here, skipper," she said. "Hawkins can't *eat* you, you know."

"I think he *can*—unlike the fatted calf."

"What are you talking about now, skipper?"

"That was picked clean long ago."

Sarah shook her head. "There ain't no fatted calf. That's just something the *Deacon* went and made up."

Brewer grunted. "Don't tell that to Colonial Concessions," he said. His eyes remained cold and contemptuous. "So how's it feel, Hemmings? Whorin' yerself for another man's colors?"

Only the faintness of the signal flare, a dying ember upon the ground, mitigated the hostility in his face. When Tom made no response, Gabriel broke the silence.

"You got yer pole out, Jackson," he said.

The remark, a reference to his flirtation with Sarah, was a welcome distraction. He feigned indignation.

"I *don't* have my pole out, Gabriel."

"Yes you do, Jackson. You be *fishin'*." Gabriel's teeth, white as piano keys, gleemed in the semi-darkness.

Brewer chuckled cruelly. He seemed more angered than amused by the artlessness of Gabriel's remark. "There *are* some largemouths worth mounting, Hemmings. But *she* ain't one of 'em. Remember what God told Eve."

"And what was that?"

"Get outa the stream, Woman. Now *all* the fish will be smellin' that way."

The big man's face was now covered in shadow. The compound was also dark and the sheen had vanished from the rifles of the checkpoint sharpshooters.

Sarah again tugged his hand. "Let's get outa here, skipper. Before one of *our* snipers starts shootin' blind. I ain't wearin' no Second Chance vest."

Tom stared at the silhouette of Gabriel and spoke.

"You *have* one last chance." He heard no response.

They parted company with Gabriel at the checkpoint.

November 23, 2000
9:00 p.m.

Leaving Brewer at the checkpoint, Tom hurried Sarah towards the West Gate. But the gate did not open—not even after Tom radioed the control officer, advising him he had returned from the dormitory with one of the hostages. It seemed as though the gate were welded shut—a reminder to Tom that he had gone too far. He now knew that Brewer was right—that Hawkins was angry with him for conspiring with Yoakum.

He muttered to Sarah, "You see how we rate?"

Sarah stood stoically. Waiting for the gate to open, she gazed at the watchtower beyond the wire mesh. The pallid light from the tower cast a fishnet pattern upon her face.

Her voice was apathetic. "Have we *got* something coming?"

"Why not a parade?"

Sarah groaned. "If *that's* the case we shoulda invited Brewer."

When the gate finally budged, allowing them a shoulder-width opening, he let Sarah slip out ahead of him. The parking lot was empty so there would probably be no attack that evening; the E-squads, in all probability, were now quartered in the Administration Building where they were on a standby status. He could see only a deserted ambulance, its lights rotating rhythmically as though attempting to awake three frozen bundles that had been discarded upon the pavement. He looked at the lifeless Disciples, then quickly looked away. They seemed as claylike as manikins, but their pulpy brows and uninhabited faces assured him that he had not been misled. All three of them had been shot in the back of the head.

Slowly, with Sarah alongside of him, he climbed the northern steps of the Administration Building. Pushing open the doorway, he hesitated, again allowing Sarah the opportunity to pass before him. This was not a gesture of chivalry, but a concession to nerves: the hallway, like the parking lot, was totally abandoned, a haunting sight since he could hear voices floating from the officers' dining hall at the far end of the corridor. He stood as though shackled while Sarah eased by him, grateful for the brush of her soft body against his own. Once Sarah was in the building, he followed after her.

As he pulled the door shut, the jamb clicked hollowly. Sarah's face, mellowed by the dim lighting of the hall, now seemed a pleasant enigma. Although her eyes were too cool to imply indebtedness, the ironic pout of her mouth suggested that she was not without pity for him. Shaking her head, she again took his hand, squeezing his fingers as she did so. The press of her palm seemed more charitable than intimate, but he welcomed her touch anyway.

"Put your pole away, skipper," she said. "I'm easy to screw—everyone will tell you that. You wanna keep *on* takin' advantage of me?"

"What's in it for me if I don't?"

Sarah smirked. "A swollen head in your pants, I guess. And you already got one on your shoulders."

"Then perhaps we should negotiate."

She chuckled then brushed a stray lock of hair from her eyes. "I'd only get the better of you, skipper. 'Cause you *obviously* ain't too good at it. You're worse than the Deacon when it comes to slingin' shit."

Tom smiled down at her. "*You're* better off now."

She squeezed his fingers harder, causing them to ache. "You think so, skipper? You saw how he treated me, didn't you?"

"Brewer?"

"Like I wasn't even there. Like I was some kinda spook. And you know what makes it worse? The crumb bum is right."

"So why *did* you come with me?"

She looked at him angrily. "You want me to paint you a *picture*, skipper?"

The injury in her voice made him feel like a novice. Again, he had overestimated his training, having entrusted to the canons of his instructor what he should have invested in empathy. Not even projection—the patented assumption

114

that Sarah was suffering from survivor's guilt—could alleviate his shame. He spoke woodenly.

"Think of it as a sacrifice," he murmured. "That might make it easier."

"What for?" Her voice was wholly despondent.

"For the *big* picture. For a bloodless resolution to this mess."

Sarah shook her head. "You really *believe* your crap, don't you, skipper?"

"If my crap stops a massacre, why not believe it?"

"Why bother *stoppin'* it? Some of them bojacks are *better off* dead. You'd know that if you'd ever actually *worked* a dorm."

"Bloodshed isn't acceptable," Tom snapped. "I saw Perkins' ghost, you know."

She sighed, relaxing her grip on his fingers. The sag of her face, the hollow pouches beneath her eyes, made his pep talk seem ridiculous. Clearly, she had too little left in reserve to have made a legitimate sacrifice.

"*I* ain't acceptable either," she said. "So it wouldn't hurt none if we had a few more spooks around. They might just give me a bit of company."

He walked Sarah to the officers' dining hall at the end of the hallway. There was visible activity in the dining hall: two members of the Critical Incident Stress Team, a lanky nurse and an obese psychologist, were conversing with several correctional officers. The officers, small wiry men, wore the pop-eyed look of sharpshooters who had been staring too long through telescopic rifle sights. He had once been a member of the stress team and considered its work indispensable. His own guilt-obsession, not to mention Sarah's voluble state, seemed textbook examples of trauma displacement.

He looked hopefully at Sarah. "These people can help you recover."

"Recover what?" she snapped. "Recover what you took from me?"

"No. But they *can* help you suspend judgment."

Sarah shrugged. "I'd just as soon *not*."

"What do you mean by that?"

"I'd just as soon *stay* mad at you. It's the *one* satisfaction I still got."

"You still need to talk to them. It's procedure."

"Is that what it's called?"

"It's called a debriefing."

She looked at him coldly. "Don't be callin' it no *debriefing*, skipper—not while that head in your *pants* is swollen. That *ain't* the way to put it to me."

Tom felt his skin burn. "I won't be involved."

Sarah chuckled. "No, I don't suppose you will. 'Cause Hawkins and them will be *de-briefing* you."

Her face had lost its vulnerability and she appeared to be appraising him from a tactical distance. He looked warily at her russet-colored nails and the sharp rise of her cheekbones.

"Just get it over with," he muttered.

"Why should I? You're actin' like I *owe* you a favor."

"You owe it to yourself. *And* the facility."

Sarah shrugged and brushed back another lock of hair. "It's easier to owe *you* than the goddamn facility. But remember I ain't no whore. So quit talkin' to me like Hassan."

Tom bowed and clicked his heels. "I'll behold you with total respect."

Sarah laughed. "Then don't plan on sleepin' with me, skipper."

He frowned. "Why not?"

"Hassan *turned* me over to you—that's why. You wanna be beholdin' to a pimp?"

She gave him a gotcha' smile then turned and entered the dining hall alone. "Keep your pecker up, skipper," she joked.

Was that flirtation in her voice, Tom wondered, *or a comradery wrought from distress*? Under the circumstances, what more could they be than a couple of cave dwellers huddling from a storm? He wanted to call after her, but turned away instead and walked slowly to the superintendent's office at the northern end of the hallway.

The office was closed, but a lamp burned within it, illuminating the frosted glass panel on the door. He knocked before entering.

The room, dim and sparsely furnished, seemed more like a mortuary than an office—so much so that Harold Hawkins, sitting stiffly behind a desk, appeared to have been mummified by the cheerless gray light from the ceiling and the synthetic oak paneling on the walls. Tom was no more encouraged by the sight of Etta Johnson: the large regal woman, looking weary and self-absorbed, was practically consumed by the overstuffed leather chair in which she was lounging. Only the presence of Henry Yoakum alleviated the sterility of the chamber. Perched on a tall wooden stool, he looked as comical as a dunce in a one-room schoolhouse.

As Tom closed the door, Yoakum turned his head towards him. A mischievous grin crept over his face and he hopped lightly from the stool. He began to applaud slowly, methodically, as though proclaiming the ordination of a prince.

"And *here's* who made it all happen!" he said.

"Inadvertently," Tom admitted. He selected a swivel chair that had been parked in the corner of the room: a typing stool that seemed to have been abandoned there. He swayed back and forth after taking this seat, unprepared for the pliability of the springs. Watching the others, he tried not to react, not even when Yoakum, crossing the room, clapped him mightily on the shoulder.

"An' he's a gennelman to boot," Yoakum said. "Makes me pleased as punch to be teamed up with him. A man won't get himself dusted with *this* fella around."

Tom did not feel let down as Yoakum babbled on, perhaps because he was unduly comforted by the morgue-like quality of the room. He was also confident that Etta could see through Yoakum's manipulations. Her smile seemed to pain her, and her voice, when she finally interrupted him, had lost its modulation.

"The facts will hurt you less, Mr. Yoakum."

"Less 'an what, Miss?"

"Less than the dust you've been blowing in our eyes. You can spare us the hearts and flowers, too."

Yoakum bowed. "Then facts you shall have, Miss. The Gospel Truth. The truth is we got us the drop on the bastards and now they're sleepin' permanent. Had us some dust from the *sandman*, you might say."

Etta pinched her nose. "I can still smell flowers, Mr. Yoakum. Try to remember that three men have died. *Shot in the back of the head.*"

"Not men," Yoakum said. "Murderin' scum. Gives a man *reason* to gather up a few flowers, don't it now?"

Etta folded her massive arms. "Save us the *flowers*, Mr. Yoakum."

"I will, Miss. I'll be needin' 'em to lay on their headstones."

Etta's smiled crisply, as though she were about to close a deal with a used car salesman, but her bearing seemed forced—stagy—a demeanor better suited to the closeted dominion of a dominatrix. This was possibly due to her ascension to superintendent: a rise that suggested not vision so much as a determination to enforce rules. At least this was what Tom was determined to believe, having learned from Brewer the progressive milestones of her career: her start as a line officer at the Women's Prison, followed by meteoric promotions to lieutenant of custody, departmental ombudsman, then spokesperson for Central Office. It therefore did not displease him that Henry Yoakum was getting the better of her.

"Mr. Yoakum. *Who* armed you and why?"

Yoakum chuckled. "It was Hassan what done it," he said. "He gave me the gun and the slugs to boot. Said there weren't no *place* for them Disciples in the general mix of things."

"So it was a vendetta."

"I wouldn't call it that, Miss. Not *my* vendetta, anyhow. I'm sorry ol' Perkins is dead and all, but that fucker ain't worth no vendetta."

"Don't change the subject, sir. *Why did you shoot those Disciples?*"

Yoakum shook his head. "Some folks just *need* dustin'. You of all people oughta *know* that, Miss. Ya gotta put one *over* on 'em while ya got the chance." He grinned impishly, an indication that his confession had preceded a Miranda warning and would therefore be useless in court.

The room seemed to shrink when Etta leaned forward and pulled herself slowly to her feet. Her effort was cautious, deliberate, as though she were removing herself from a bathtub. She seemed to have recovered her stature— probably because Yoakum's clever evasions had irritated her to the point of fury."

"I believe, Mr. Yoakum, our *conversation* is over."

Yoakum beamed broadly. "And a pleasure it was talkin' to ya, Miss. You've eased a weary heart, I assure ya. An' ya can hang me for sayin' so if ya wish."

Etta stood calmly, her eyes on the door, her expression so devout that she appeared to be awaiting the tolling of a church bell. She spoke without inflection.

"If you hang, Mr. Yoakum, it will be for more than that."

The room seemed even smaller now, perhaps because Hawkins, holding a telephone receiver tightly against his ear, was arguing with his wife. Meanwhile, Etta was lounging once again in the leather chair. She seemed relieved that Yoakum had left, a sign, Tom hoped, that his personal contribution to the triple homicide had not been enough to incriminate him. Looking at Hawkins, noticing the desperation with which he was clutching the receiver, Tom felt inspired by a piece of information he had recently received from Brewer: a revelation that surely challenged Hawkins' powers of assessment. "His *first* wife ran off with an inmate," the big man had told him. "Happened twenty years back. Hawkins came home from work one afternoon and his wife and that bojack had driven off to Juarez, Mexico. At least that's what the note that she left him said." "*An inmate*," Tom had repeated, a statement—not a question. He had only been surprised that it had taken him so long to learn of this. "One of the gardeners," Brewer said. "You might say he helped the ol' boy with some prunin'. Done him a favor if you ask me. She was a lot more puss than *Hawkins* could handle."

Hawkins, his patience as fragile as his libido, was now barking into the receiver.

"*Veal,*" he spat. "*Ten o'clock sharp.* What more can I *say* about it, woman?"

The tremor in his voice was a further solace to Tom. It was good to see Hawkins lose it. The captain returned the receiver to the cradle and looked irritably in Tom's direction, apparently noticing him for the first time. He spoke as though he were expecting Tom to chastise him.

"My supper a problem to you, Hemmings?"

Tom nodded. "If it's the fatted calf, yes."

Hawkins picked up a pen. Tapping it upon the desktop, he looked at Tom impatiently.

"And what about you, Hemmings? You as poor with the facts as Yoakum?"

"Not when they deny a fiction."

"What does *that* mean, Hemmings?"

Tom leaned back in the stool and glared. "That you thought it was *safe* enough to send me into that compound. You've kept pretty good company with the sandman yourself."

"Just tell us what happened. No sermons 'bout sandmen."

Tom shrugged. "That means I'll be echoing Yoakum."

"I would *rather* you told us what happened."

"He dusted three Disciples. That's all I know and all I *want* to know."

"Why did he dust them?"

"One of them was shooting at the checkpoint."

Hawkins continued to tap with his pen, a cadence so deliberate that he appeared to be signaling in code. His tone, when he spoke again, seemed profoundly sad.

"What made you think that, Hemmings? The fuckers in the dorm?"

"The shots were enough to convince me. They were coming from the gym."

"You sure of that, Hemmings? Or were you listenin' to echoes instead of waitin' for your instructions? The echoes are *strong* in the compound, you know."

"A reliable informant convinced me. At least that's what *you* call the Deacon. But Yoakum and Hassan were of the same mind."

"I see," Hawkins said. "So *that's* who you deserted me for, Hemmings. A pervert, a back shooter, and a pimp."

Tom shrugged again. "*You sent me into that hell hole.* That pervert, that back shooter and that pimp were the best the void had to offer."

Hawkins let the pen drop and then folded his hands. He seemed heartbroken and in a hurry to leave the room.

"You shoulda *used* the Deacon, Hemmings. Forced him to con them fuckers into surrenderin'. But it looks like Chester's controlling *you*." His eyebrows rose, but the gesture lacked impact. He was as pathetic as a politician without a crowd. "And where do *I* fit in?"

"What can *you* offer?" Tom snapped.

Hawkins glared. "A *prison*—once we've taken it back. And those bojacks in the gym *were* ready to surrender!"

"Why? Were you sending them to Africa?" Tom's sarcasm, perhaps too strong for its target, made him feel suddenly like a bully.

"The *New Mexico State Penitentiary* is where we were sendin' 'em. As part of the prisoner exchange program. That woulda been a whole lot better for 'em than Africa."

"What were they giving you in exchange?"

"Trash, Hemmings. They were about to tattle on trash. Anarchists, dirty officers, Bible thumpin' perverts. I actually had a chance to clean this place up and you went and ruined it."

"By stopping some outlaws from *lying*?" Tom ran his hand across the stubble on his chin. "But you made a good deal for some fleabag prison in New Mexico, didn't you? A *hell* of a deal. It's too bad they died before you could finish gypping them."

"That ain't a hell of a bargain, Hemmings. It's a *hell* of a bargain to be screwin' with the wrong company."

Tom rocked from side to side in his chair. He spoke bitterly through the side of his mouth. "That's better than the company screwing you."

"This ain't about Colonial Concessions," Hawkins yelled. "This is about firing *you*."

"Good. Then I guess I'll be keeping my *own* company."

"A guess is what it'll be, Hemmings. And you'll keep on guessin' if it's Yoakum you're beddin' with."

"I'll be bedded *permanently* if I counted on you." Tom sat up straight in his chair and leaned in. "Should I really have taken a bullet for Colonial Concessions?"

"It's Yoakum you're takin' the bullet for, Hemmings. Cause what he was doin' was killin' off snitches. An' they weren't bearin' false witness against him either."

"How do you know that?"

"He left his calling card in the gym."

"What was that?"

"A nine-millimeter Glock. It was planted on one of the bodies. That's the only weapon we found in there."

November 23, 2000
10:00 p.m.

Walking from the superintendent's office, weighing the transparency of Yoakum's charade, Tom could scarcely remember the remainder of the meeting. To Hawkins' final question—"What are they askin' for in that dorm, Hemmings?"—he had responded with a single word: "Immunity." That its definition eluded him for the most part had not affected his sense of justice: his naïve assumption that the inmates in the dormitory should not be held accountable for the crimes of murderers.

"Immunity?" Hawkins had repeated. He seemed to be savoring a piece of sour candy in his mouth.

"For Perkins' murder," Tom had replied. "Not for the crimes that brought them here in the first place."

The predictability of Hawkins' response—"Bojacks don't *get* no immunity, Hemmings"—had been a relief to him. An attack on the dormitory somehow seemed preferable to the ploy it would take to defuse the standoff: a ploy that would only have accelerated his guilt when the inmates were finally prosecuted.

His footsteps echoed hollowly as he walked down the hallway. They seemed as hollow as the forces he was alienating: forces he no longer feared. There was little reason, after all, to suppose that the stars aligned against him would keep their pattern long enough to hold him to account. He could therefore wreck havoc, invest in the wind, and confront even Hawkins at will. Tom had, in fact, enjoyed a rather cruel fabrication of his own before leaving the room. "Captain," he had remarked. "Is framing me for murder worth your pension? Because it's *you* I'm going to sue."

"Why?" Hawkins had snapped.

Tom had smiled evilly. "For making me wear your colors."

He paused at the Key Room, a small anti-chamber near the end of the hallway, and noticed that it was empty. He pushed the door open, closing it behind him as he entered. Moving slowly, contentedly, Tom unsnapped the radio from his hip and slipped it into a charger. On impulse, he then lifted the receiver from the count phone and punch-dialed the laundry dorm. He waited. The phone in the dormitory rang, an enduring rhythm that seemed fraudulent to him since it still suggested a vital pulse. He was grateful when the pulse stopped beating, a demise accompanied by a loud and fitful grunt. Short Dog, he suspected. He did not bother asking the party to identify himself.

"The Deacon," he muttered. He waited for five minutes, savoring the delay since he could clearly hear the ten o'clock news on the television set in the dormitory. When his informant announced himself over the din, he felt as though he had been interrupted.

"Mr. Hemmings, is it?"

"The cuckold will do."

"I suspect, good sir, that you have broken bread with the Hittites." The voice, weary and rather breathless, suggested that Chester had again been summoned prematurely from the toilet. "Did they crucify Old Chester, sir? Or were the nails yours alone to bear?"

"Hawkins called you a pervert. That hardly qualifies as a crucifixion."

The sigh seemed pretentious, but well timed. "It's a blow nonetheless, sir. And to think I might have achieved eminence at the same price. After all, Mr. Hemmings, stones are cast upon scoundrels and champions alike."

"They say that you helped set me up. To instigate a triple murder."

"A ruse, Mr. Hemmings?"

"What else? Those Disciples were unarmed. Or so Hawkins says."

"How unfortunate, sir." Chester's voice was deeply saddened.

"Unfortunate for whom?" Tom snapped.

"Certainly for the cuckolds. Caesar said it well, did he not, sir? 'Surround me with men who are fat' were his words. 'Sleek-headed men who sleep soundly at night.' That, Mr. Hemmings, is the extent of my treachery. Like men who are fat, I do not seek to know too much."

Tom leaned against a locker and sighed. "You may have succeeded a little too well."

"I think not, Mr. Hemmings. Is it a triumph to be ignorant?"

"Only for a *real* champion."

"Indeed, Mr. Hemmings. But ignorant people should be less aspiring."

"Sly words for a man who claims to be fat."

"The porch, Mr. Hemmings. That is my only sanctification, sir. Perhaps there I *will* grow fat."

"You'll need to betray the inmates if you want to go to the Farm Line. You'll need to barter a piece of your soul."

"How do you propose that I do that, sir?"

"The *brass* will propose it, not me." Tom snapped. "My guess is they'll ask you to create a diversion with your gift of gab. That way the E-squads can storm the dormitory."

He heard Chester sigh. "Very well, Mr. Hemmings. Convince Hawkins to assign me to the Farm Line, sir. What a bargain that would be given the worthlessness of my soul."

The television had grown louder, a timely intrusion: the news broadcast, a belated account of Perkins' death, had been interrupted by a commercial for Target Stores. Tom paused, again suppressing his sense of irony, and then spoke softly into the receiver. "*Hawkins* won't bargain with you. But *he* won't have the last word. That will probably come from the Commissioner."

"The *last* word, Mr. Hemmings? What a godly privilege for a mere commissioner."

"The last ruse, then. Call it what you will. But selling out the dorm is your ticket to the porch."

"A Godsend would better describe it, Mr. Hemmings. Or shall we call it an ark? The refuge of a fortunate few from God's just storm?"

"Cut the bullshit, Chester. Call it whatever you want."

"An ark will do. And I hope, good sir, that you will be aboard."

"Not if I can help it," Tom muttered.

He hung up the phone without waiting for a reply then instantly regretted his callousness. Since he could not be sure where the comedy would end, or whether his role in it was something he could effectively relinquish, a cohort in crime was something to be treasured. A guilt shared, after all, was preferable to an isolated one.

As Tom walked from the Key Room, he savored the sudden lightness at his hip—a sensation that increased as he opened the door to the Administration Building and stepped once again to the porch. The lot, still deserted, seemed a haven to him now—so much so that the three dead bodies, appearing and vanishing in the red light of the ambulance, struck him as vaguely ornamental. So intimate was the silence, so pleasant the night, that it was a minute before he realized that he was not alone.

Sarah Baumgardner was waiting for him in the parking lot.

November 23, 2000
10:30 p.m.

H e sat beside Sarah as they rode the shuttle bus to
the employee parking lot. They were alone on the
bus—a novelty since the seats and isle were usually packed
with chatty officers who were between shifts. Instead, he
heard only the monotonous drone of the engine—a sound
so hollow that he felt as though he were riding in a wind
tunnel. He sat loosely in his seat, grateful whenever the bus
hit a bump and his shoulder jostled against Sarah's small
body.

Her question—"Can you take me into town, skipper?"—
was barely audible above the hum of the engine. "My
Gremlin's in the shop," she went on. "Third time this
month. So I rode in to work with Yoakum."

He nodded, ignoring the absurdity of his good fortune.
They were passing the stone quarry and he looked tactfully
through the window at her side. Though the night was like
pitch, a sprinkling of frozen starlight defined the dark water
below them.

"It's *time* they fixed it right," she murmured.

Minutes later, seated in his Volkswagen Rabbit, they
were rolling towards Castleberg, an IBM and college town
that lay ten miles south of the prison. He was taking the
service road, a blacktop route that bypassed Highway 40,
and so they remained on prison grounds, rolling alongside
barren apple orchards and rutted cornfields. He liked the
route since he rarely struck traffic on it and would usually
take it on his rare trips to Castleberg.

Sarah sat silently as he drove, her body so still that he
began to wonder if she had fallen asleep. He was tempted to
turn on the car radio, not to hear an update on the siege but
to solicit a reaction from her. His hands, however, remained
on the steering wheel, their grip so firm that he wondered
if he was suffering posttraumatic symptoms. His suspicion
was confirmed when a hare, hopping alongside the road,
caused him to flinch violently.

126

Sarah spoke. "Nervous, skipper?" Her voice was soft but weary.

He nodded.

"Don't look so surprised. You *deserve* to be spooked."

"Tell me why."

"Shit, skipper—you're stuck on yourself for one. And you've got nothing to show for it for another. Nothing but *three dead bodies*. Like Brewer says, you're wearin' the wrong colors an' lyin' through your teeth about Yoakum."

"Small sins," he replied, "compared to what I did to you."

"You fucked me good, skipper," she said. "But it's the Commissioner who's gonna make you pay."

"And *you* won't?"

She shrugged. "I *would* if I knew *how*. Tit for tat, I always say. It sure ain't because I feel *sorry* for you."

"You may just as well. Compassion might set you free."

"You *want* that I should feel sorry for you?"

"If it eases your anger, yes."

Sarah cracked her knuckles. "Don't *bet* on that. That's how the *real* shit starts. The joker I married I felt sorry for and it sure didn't set me free. Not until I kicked him out of the house."

"You talk tough for a co-dependant."

"How'd you know Harry was a boozer, skipper?"

"You're not the only one with rescue fantasies."

Sarah poked him, a sharp punch that this time suggested real anger. She was clearly not impressed by his attempt at seduction.

"*You* don't need to worry none, skipper. I don't have no goddamn calling to rescue *you*."

"Aww," he replied. "Who will if you won't?" He winked at her in the dark.

Sarah groaned. "Go an' ask Etta Johnson. She's an easy touch, they tell me. And *her* pity might do you some good."

"You couldn't think *that* highly of her. Not if you're wishing her on me."

"Put it this way, skipper. She's been rode hard and put away wet. You know what I mean by that, don't you?"

"That she's short on breath?"

"Hell, skipper," Sarah laughed, "she's short on something."

"A quality you only prefer in men?" Tom jibed. He continued to watch the road, grateful that he could not see her expression.

Again Sarah poked him. "It's *you* we're talkin' about, skipper. And what you need is a big tit to suck on. *That* ain't somethin' I can't help you with."

They were passing through the outskirts of Castleberg. The fast food outlets and trademark superstores—indistinguishable from those of most other towns in America—offered him a fleeting sense of security: an assurance that his dilemma could not be significant in the face of such overwhelming homogeneity. The superstores, a Wal-Mart and a recently constructed Target, in fact seemed like bastions to him, having diminished the town's unemployment rate after the IBM plant closed down a year ago. He was indebted to the stores, however, for the relief they gave him on his rare shopping trips to Castleberg. An advocate of no-stress shopping, he was glad to acquire the staples of his life—fishing lures, tennis balls, and condoms—in a single productive stop. He was in fact so infatuated by the stores, the quick getaways they allowed him, that he could scarcely begrudge them their rampant proliferation.

He pulled over at a small tavern near the campus. The novelty of the sign—a logo of a notorious parachutist named D.B. Cooper—suggested a college hangout, but the bar was more frequented by correctional officers getting off the evening shift. Suspecting Sarah to be a regular, he offered no explanation as he killed his headlights then slipped from behind the wheel. He opened the door on Sarah's side of the car, half expecting a rebuttal for his courtesy, but she slipped silently from her seat and coughed discretely as he closed and locked the door. As they walked towards the bar, her hand slipped into his.

"I'll take tit," he remarked.

Sarah groaned again. "Don't be jokin' about it, skipper. I'm just not that particular tonight. When a woman lies down with the Devil, she may as well finish the job."

A square of struggling light was the brightest illumination in the barroom. It was not the television, however, that forced him to think of the penal farm. This linkage was caused by the heavy parachute linen draped behind the counter. He knew little about D.B. Cooper—only that the man had robbed a commercial flight thirty years ago and, after making his jump through the passenger door, had never been heard from again. But the celebrated scandal was enough to affiliate him with the dim, dilapidated room. If nothing else, it was a reminder that he was not alone in sentimentalizing scoundrels.

Sarah, sitting on the opposite side of a booth, no longer looked like a sharp-boned woman of forty. Instead, she seemed hauntingly attractive and he waited self-consciously for her to speak. That his infatuation seemed incidental—an accident of smoke and lighting—did not make her any less desirable to him. The pout of her generous mouth and the wounded intensity of her eyes were enough to provide him with a fresh illusion: the notion that he might yet succeed in rescuing her.

Sarah, sensing his obsession, spoke flatly. "Put away your pole, skipper. I *told* you that once already."

"Where can I put it?"

"It don't matter where. You won't need no goddamn pole to get what *you're* after. Everyone knows I'm an easy lay."

He shrugged. "You're an arm's length away from me."

She narrowed her gaze. "How much closer do you *want* me? You're a one-nighter, skipper, and that's as much as I'm going to say about it. I just wish I wasn't tramp enough to *know* that for sure." Her stare was condescending but without reproach. The television, a more fickle commodity, flickered irresolutely behind her.

"Do I only deserve tramps?" he asked. He took a sip of his beer.

"I guess you do at that, skipper. Close as you are to the Deacon an' all. In fact, I'd say tramps are 'bout all you can handle."

She sipped her beer slowly, deliberately, as though she were doing him a favor. Her clear-sightedness, a necessity for a correctional officer, was disappointing to him since he

---

craved seduction over intimacy. He hoped a confession—or at least the pretense of one—would diminish his transparency to her.

"I once deserved better." His eyes strayed towards the television set.

"An' when was *that?*"

"Back when I wore my own colors," he mumbled.

"What are you talkin' about now?"

"The work release program. That was *my* release, too."

"An' what *good* was it? 'Cept for keepin' you cooped up in some office all day."

He set his beer down with a thump. "It was all that I had and they stole it away."

Sarah laughed and shook her head. "You never had nothin' worth stealin', skipper."

"No," he replied, examining the foam in his glass. "But it mattered to some of the bojacks."

"The bojacks got nothin' comin' either."

"Sure they do. Everyone deserves a chance."

"A chance at what?"

"Easy time. We all deserve that."

"There *ain't* no such thing, skipper. An' if there was, who are *you* to be dolin' it out?"

"If I don't, what's left for me? Besides a rock and a hard place?" Tom swirled his glass and the foam slowly thickened.

"That ain't for me to say. All I know is that you could be helpin' us take inventory in the *dorm* now and then."

"You've already made that clear."

Sarah smiled thinly. "I'm glad *somethin's* clear to you, skipper. They talk about you, you know. Brewer and them. About how you been to college and all and you ain't even a supervisor yet."

"It's a shame," he said softly. "But I don't play the game as well as some."

"A shame is what it *oughta* be, skipper. The *fact* is you're damn well proud of it."

He sighed and lowered his head. Her remark, although coldly accurate, would have been more effective if it had been made somewhere other than the tavern. As it was, it competed poorly with the cheap lighting and the hypnotic drone from the television: an eleven o'clock coverage of the presidential election, a contest still stalemated by the Florida vote count. The corporate-sponsored adversaries— hirelings who *were* playing their game well—did little to prick his shame.

He felt only vaguely liberated when Sarah, apparently tiring of the conversation, rose from her chair. "Gotta make a phone call."

"Your kids?"

She nodded. "They're with their grandparents. That's in *Rockville* in case you wanna know. It's too late to be fetchin' 'em home tonight."

"Not until you've paid the piper anyhow." He gave her a silly grin.

She looked at him coldly. "That won't take till *morning*, skipper. Ten minutes oughta do it."

"Tell me this," he muttered. "Why go to bed with the Devil at all?"

"A deal's a deal." Sarah drained her glass and set it down hard on the table.

Tom looked at the empty glass, reluctant to meet her gaze. "I'll free your account," he said.

Sarah shrugged and also looked away. "That won't do no good, skipper. Not when devils are all I *got* to pick from. Just be glad you're the slickest of the bunch."

November 23, 2000
11:30 p.m.

He wondered if Sarah had forgotten her promise. The thought of this caused him to feel desperate, hopefully because he was only experiencing an excess of anxiety. He could find no easy explanation, however, for the fact that she had been talking on the pay phone for nearly half an hour. The television, still locked on the presidential election, had begun to bore him, perhaps because the courtship of the voters—the high tech equivalent of a one-night stand—seemed as presumptuous to him as his pursuit of Sarah. It was finally his contempt for deception, an aversion more compelling than his need for a woman, that prompted him to slip from the booth and return on his own to the parking lot.

A scuttling sound, followed by a flash of movement, made him flinch—a reflex that embarrassed him profoundly when he noticed that it was only a rat retreating from his footsteps. The parking lot seemed otherwise deserted, and so he took comfort in the pale glow that was emanating from across the street: a jack-o-lantern flush that suggested casing rather than habitation. The light was coming from the deserted IBM factory, a ghost house as far as the town was concerned—but, although the building was empty, its light was as fetching as that of the moon. He stood in the parking lot, waiting for Sarah, and realized only gradually that he was being stalked.

The figure, short and wiry, had slipped from the cab of a pickup truck and was now walking slowly towards him. He knew it was not a patron of the bar—the stride was too easy, the footfalls too silent—and he knew also that whomever it was had been waiting for a long time. He felt reinforced as the intruder came into focus; although palpable now, the man had seemed a specter to him since early that afternoon. He nodded to Henry Yoakum.

"Evenin' to you again, sir," the pock-faced man said. His voice was as hearty as that of a toastmaster. "I noticed your car so I thought I'd stop by. I been meanin' to thank you once again."

"Do I shake your hand?" Tom replied. "Or would that be collusion as well?"

Yoakum seized his hand, clapping him on the shoulder as he did so. "Don't matter to me *what* they call it," he said. "When a man saves my crack hole I'm goin' to shake his hand."

"Crack," he replied. "is probably *all* I saved for you."

Yoakum chuckled. "You've been *listenin'* to Hawkins an' them, haven't you, sir? He tell you I been trafficking drugs?"

"That *is* the implication. He also said you were killing off snitches."

Yoakum nodded. "An' that I *was*, sir. Snitches and killers. They'd a taken me out in a second if I'd given 'em the opportunity."

"Taken you out how?"

Yoakum laughed. "They'd a put out my lights, Mr. Hemmings. They'd 'a put me to bed for keeps."

"I suspect you'd have plenty of company. Who *are* your bedfellows? Besides the Teamsters."

Yoakum shook his head. "I'll tell you who it ain't," he said. "It ain't Sarah Baumgardner an' that's for sure. It's a credit to you, sir, to be courtin' a woman like that. I rescued her myself a coupla years back but she wouldn't have nothin' to *do* with me afterwards."

Yoakum lowered his head. A match flared brightly as though challenging the pallid glow from the factory across the street. The flame, hovering between his palms, fluttered like a serpent's tongue. Yoakum tossed away the match and looked at the factory with amusement.

"They'll be rentin' it to the gooks in a month or so, sir. Accordin' to the newspaper, anyhow. A Jap'nese 'lectronics company."

Tom drew a slow breath. "Why tell me *that*?"

Yoakum shrugged. "Not everyone *minds* makin' light bulbs, sir. An' ya might be *needin'* a job when this is all over. Even if it's for coolie wages."

The joke did not amuse him. "I'm getting that much now."

Yoakum laughed. "An' some mud for yer turtle to boot, Mr. Hemmings. Thanks to a fine woman."

"Why should Sarah concern *you*?"

Yoakum spat then lifted his hand. The coal gleamed between his fingers like a cat's eye.

"*Everythin'* about you concerns me, Mr. Hemmings. You saved my neck, sir, an' that's a plain fact. It's important to me that ya be gettin' some reward for yer troubles."

"Unless you're her pimp, that's not your concern."

"Right you are, sir. But there's *one* screwin' ya *won't* be gettin', believe you me. 'Cause Ol' Henry Yoakum looks after his own."

"Just how do you intend to look after me?"

"Like a hawk, sir. I'll watch over you like a hawk in the woods."

"That sounds rather ominous," Tom murmured. He shifted his feet on the asphalt.

Yoakum winked. "Ya done a good deed, sir. That's all that need concern you. Some things a man's better off *not* knowin'."

"Like how to plant a pistol?"

Yoakum fell silent. His eyes, perhaps eager for a diversion, studied the glow from the IBM plant: a light so imperial and cold that it may as well have been coming from a monument.

"Looks kinda like foxfire, don't it, sir."

Tom dropped his gaze. "Foxfire, he muttered. "So *what*? It only shines in *rotten* wood."

Yoakum laughed, "Don't knock it, sir. Sometimes it's bright enough to read by."

Tom shook his head. He felt lonely for Sarah, an abrasive companion, perhaps, but one whom he did not find untrustworthy. "Were they armed?" Tom asked, finally.

Yoakum shook his head. "Put it this way, sir. Plantin' is one thing. An' provin's another."

November 23, 2000
Midnight

Tom's car crept through the back streets of the campus, sedate suburban lanes whose names—Longfellow Way, Tennyson Drive, Spencer Road—seemed to sanctify the pseudo Victorian homes and the beehive fraternity houses. Ignoring Sarah, who was sitting quietly beside him, he drove carefully past the ivy-strewn buildings, observing each one as though taking inventory of a personal estate.

Sarah broke the silence. "You was talkin' to Yoakum."

134

"Inadvertently," he admitted.

"What's that supposed to mean?"

"He was lying in wait for me."

Sarah snorted. "And that's reason enough to be *talkin'* to him? As far as liars go, you're better off stickin' with the Deacon."

"I *do* find Chester entertaining. As far as child molesters go."

Sarah groaned and rubbed her forehead. "That's 'cause *you've* never been *molested*."

The bitterness in her voice, the product of some girlhood trauma, made him feel sadly transparent once again. He changed the subject.

"What *did* happen in that dormitory? Before the Disciples were dusted."

Sarah paused before speaking. When she replied her tone was so soft she seemed fearful of being overheard. "The Muslims was *using* Yoakum, I think. Using him for a gang *payback*. But I don't know that for sure. Can't say I wanna know either."

"Stick to that story. It may be for the best."

Sarah covered her mouth, burying a girlish giggle. "Ain't none of this is for the *best*, skipper."

"Were the Disciples armed?"

She cracked her knuckles again. "Would it matter if they were? It's just crumb bums pickin' off crumb bums, ain't it? Kinda like a self-cleanin' oven."

They were passing the city park—a cluster of baseball diamonds, picnic tables, and tennis courts—and approaching a working class neighborhood. The prefabricated houses, square and austere, bore the stale uniformity of military barracks.

"It matters," he said, "if it leaves me up the creek."

"Shit, skipper, it don't matter *that* much. Not when you're steerin' blind, it don't. As I see it, you're no worse off *up* the creek than comin' on down it."

"And you?"

She shrugged. "What do you want me to say? You want me to make you feel better about what you did to me?"

Tom glanced at her hopefully. "If it's a cheap fix, yes."

"Well, either I'll stay at the Farm or I'll go back to workin' for Wal-Mart. That's all I can say an' that ain't sayin' much."

"You're saying *too* much if those are your only choices."

"They may as well be, skipper. Either one of 'em's more reliable than a man."

"The Farm," Tom said firmly. "It has to be better than Wal-Mart."

"Was," she replied. "I won't say that no more though. Not since the brass started piss testin' the officers and doggin' the unions. That's not much different from how they run things at Wal-Mart."

"The minions of the Philistines," Tom said. He looked at her profoundly.

Sarah snorted again. "You oughta stop hangin' with the Deacon too, skipper. You're starting to sound like him."

"Does that make him wrong?"

She chuckled harshly and shook her head. "There ain't no minions or Philistines about it. It's just bums doggin' bums."

Sarah's home, a tidy cottage with gray vinyl siding, eased into his headlights like a ghost ship. He pulled triumphantly into her driveway, invigorated at having accurately followed her directions. The house faded when he turned off his headlights and he felt the added thrill of encroachment.

Sarah patted his arm, a caress so undeserved that he knew it was conciliatory.

"This is it," she remarked. "Thanks for bringin' me home."

He followed her into a small living room, a cramped chamber filled with overstuffed furniture and hinting of a gas leak. That the room was unremarkable was a relief to him: an assurance that he would harbor no lasting references when he took his leave in the morning. Even a framed photograph on the wall, the annual picture of the Reserve Emergency Squad, contributed to the foreignness of the room. Sarah, recognizable in the photo by her disheveled blonde hair, seemed to represent a younger version of herself—a version so dated that the picture might have been taken a decade ago. He sat uncomfortably upon a tweed-covered couch. Dropping his eyes from the photo, he watched Sarah disappear into a bedroom.

He was dozing when she returned. The room, restored suddenly to his senses, was too plain to startle him; instead it was a generic reminder of other nights, other women, other small living rooms. Sarah, now clad in a loose gray sweat suit, sat down beside him on the couch. She appeared to be self-absorbed, perhaps because her hair, freshly washed and wrapped in a heavy towel, gave her an aura of regality. She was squinting, her eyes focused downward, and he noticed that she was painting her toenails.

She spoke tonelessly. "What happens now, skipper?"

He shook his head. "Hawkins said to report back to him in the morning."

"Why? So you can keep *bullshittin'* the bojacks?"

"There no point in *that*. They'll still want immunity."

"We *all* want that, skipper."

"For the murder of Perkins *and* the Disciples."

She wiggled her toes, examining her work. The blood-colored nails, although smaller than sequins, struck him as macabre.

"Hell, skipper. Even *you* ain't gettin' immunity for the Disciples."

"Don't mention that to Yoakum. His plan is to plug things up for me. Keep things buried."

"And you trust him to *do* that?"

"He says he'll cover my back."

"He once said that to *me*. A few years ago when we were both assigned to the kitchen dorm. What he ended up pluggin' was one of the dishwashers."

"A Muslim?"

"A Bozo with a beanie. He said the fool got the drop on him, but I couldn't tell *what* was goin' on. All I know is he cost me a shitload of paperwork and a week's suspension."

"Why the suspension?"

"Perkins and his spooks investigated *me*. Yoakum told 'em it was *me* who provoked the Bozo and that's why he had to shoot him. He also told 'em that women had no business in the dorms."

"That's not much of a plug."

"Maybe not, skipper. But he damn near buried me."

Capping the bottle of nail polish, she rose stiffly from the couch. A radio, perched on the end table, had caught her attention and she turned the dial methodically, pausing when it hit on a bluegrass number. The song, "Pig in a Pen," seemed to soften her mood and she smiled enigmatically as she turned down the volume. The gesture was so instinctual that she appeared to be accommodating even the scrounger on the radio: a boisterous bumpkin in search of a woman to stay home and feed his prize boar. She sat down beside him once again.

"I'm gettin' a week off work, skipper."

"Convalescent leave?"

"That's what they call it. But all I'll be doing is sittin' around watchin' the soaps."

"You could try getting out," Tom blurted. "Maybe visiting the zoo."

"And see animals in *cages*? What kind of change would *that* be?"

As her hand, soft from skin moisturizer, slipped once again into his, he listened with amusement to the Ralph Stanley number, a patronizing ditty, perhaps, but a complement at least to the reflexive tenting in his pants. She hummed along softly, her head upon his shoulder, and poked him in the ribs when the song ended.

"Ain't gonna nurse no *pig* either."

Tom felt himself shrink. "I guess that leaves me out."

"You guessed right, skipper. You'll have to take care of it yourself."

She stretched slowly, lazily, and then dropped her hand, interlocking his fingers with her own. When she turned back towards him, her sweat suit now rumpled, she seemed to have awakened from a nap and so it seemed accidental when her lips, dry and chapped, brushed softly against his own. The kiss was brief, experimental, as though she were sampling a tidbit at a buffet, and he felt that he had been objectified rather than embraced. Only the tang of her mouthwash convinced him that the peck had happened at all.

"You know what'll happen now, don't you, skipper?"

Tom felt depressed. "The pig won't get screwed?"

"That's right," she replied. "And *that's* why you need to stay out of it. Let 'em put you to pasture same as they done to me."

"How *did* you arrange it?"

"I didn't do nothin', skipper. Etta called me into her office two days ago and told me I was stressed. Next thing I knew I was workin' the graveyard shift with the geezers."

"That doesn't sound too bad. Not as far as graveyards go, anyway."

Sarah nodded. "Funny thing about it is it turned out she was right. That's what makes it so annoyin'."

"You'd have rather stayed mad?"

"I guess so. But it's *hard* to be mad in a graveyard. The spooks there are harmless and the fossils don't bother you none."

"I'll keep that in mind when they put me to pasture."

"You and your fossil both."

"Who? The Deacon?"

"You think I don't know what he's up to? He talked to me some once the shit hit the fan. When the dorm fell under *new management* as he put it. He told me to give you a message."

Tom rubbed his forehead. "Something about an ark?"

"Don't know about no ark. A storm maybe. He said the best time to storm 'em was Sunday night. That's when they'll be watchin' the football, he said."

She stretched once again then she shook her head wearily. It seemed appropriate that her sense of self-preservation, her well-honed instincts, had killed his hope of bedding her.

"You don't seem to approve," Tom said.

She shrugged. "A snitch is a snitch an' I never had no use for 'em. That's as much as I'm going to say about it."

She squeezed his thigh gently then rose from the couch. The towel, wrapped turban-style around her hair, still gave her the impregnable aplomb of a priestess. She looked down at him with sternness and pity.

"You'd best get some sleep, skipper," she said. "They're gonna be needin' you come mornin'."

It was well past midnight when she came to him—4:00 a.m. according to the red digital clock on the radio—and he realized that he had been dozing for several hours. He was awakened too suddenly by her footsteps, an intimidating cadence upon the creaky floorboards, and her body, a shadowy outline, seemed to be that of an intruder. He did not say a word when he felt the couch sag: to have done so would have probably killed their covenant—a compact assured not by friendship or fate but the lingering cover of darkness. Her hand, guiding his as he shrugged off the blanket, seemed oblivious to even the hysterectomy scar he was tracing with his fingers. The scar, though harder than rope, was his first indication that she was naked below the waist.

She sighed stoically when he reached the end of the scar, a sound he took for a critique, and he did not take credit for the slickness upon his fingers, a sensation so alien to the moment that he felt she was determined to scald him. Her lips, again brushing his, were still dry, while the flicker of her tongue seemed as tentative as the probe of a serpent. She shuddered too quickly, a sharp but personal fulfillment that contributed to his sense of subordination. Moaning generously, she removed his fingers and snuggled beside him.

"Easy, skipper," she whispered. "I'm a mess down there."

She lay beside him quietly, perhaps preoccupied by the betrayal of her body. But her breathing, sharp and rhythmic, was more distracting than erotic. He therefore failed to respond when her fingers, as though fulfilling an agenda of their own, burrowed between his legs and traced his zipper. When she spoke to him again, she sounded amused.

"You're weak there."

"Call it passive resistance."

Her fingers tightened gently. "Bullshit, skipper. You ain't resistin' nothing."

The flicker of her tongue, like warm raindrops upon his lips, was sufficient to seal her monopoly. He felt himself expanding in her hand.

"You got a rubber, skipper?"

"I'm without protection," Tom whispered.

Her breath cooled his neck as she sighed reproachfully. "*Men*," she muttered. The sofa creaked, relinquishing her weight, and he heard her footsteps fading from the room. Minutes passed but her scent remained with him, a ripe bouquet that dulled the metallic aroma of the gas leak. He lifted his fingers to his nostrils, further diminishing the smell of the gas, and then he heard her returning footsteps. The couch sagged once more but she did not touch him immediately. She was tearing something apart.

"You got your immunity now, skipper."

A sharper tearing, the descent of his zipper, accompanied her remark and he felt the caress of a wet rubber noose. He continued to expand as the noose descended, not in arousal but rebellion against the tightness of the condom. His desensitization was so complete that he could barely feel the experimental flicker of her tongue upon the stretched rubber.

He touched her once again, a quick defensive gesture that allowed him more direct contact with her fluids. She shuddered when his thumb found her clit and her tongue darted into his mouth. Her vagina, simultaneously capturing his member, offered him a duller embrace—a remote counterpoint to the warm exploration of her mouth.

She rose slowly, tentatively, as though she found the coupling unsatisfying and had decided to dislodge him. She hovered momentarily, perhaps making up her mind, then jerked her loins back into him. The movements continued, thrusts so punishing and rapid that when she froze once again her shudder seemed one of aversion. It was only her tongue, still buried in his mouth, that assured him his climax, a sharp but superficial relief since the warmth he felt was from his own discharge. She hovered above him then convulsed one more time. Releasing his member, she snuggled back down beside him.

When she spoke, she still seemed amused. "I must have been hornier than I thought."

"Does that mean you still owe me one?"

She chuckled dryly. "I suppose I do, skipper. You may as well collect it too. It's not like I have any *other* use for you."

"It's as good a use as any," he said. "And I *think* it makes us even."

"For what, skipper?"

"For pulling you out of the dorm."

She poked him in the ribs. "Don't flatter yourself none. You ain't *that* big a stud."

She circled his waist with one of her legs, a tight but comfortable embrace. He could now feel the heat of her naked thigh and the sudden novelty of her dampness as she wiggled against his hip. After a while, she kissed him gently on the mouth.

"You done all right, skipper," she said. "Only you been thinkin' with the wrong head."

November 24, 2000
7:30 a.m.

He awoke to a Ralph Stanley number, an infectious ditty whose key refrain—"Please papa don't whip little Ben"—intensified his sense of trespass. Sarah was nowhere in the house, but he suppressed his disappointment, suspecting that she had left to do a short errand before setting the radio alarm for him. The song, a plea for some potty-mouthed whippersnapper, blared plaintively as he put on his pants and was not quite over when he returned from his car with his sports bag. Discarding his pants on the couch, he slipped on a pair of shorts, a stale sweatshirt, and some Air Nike jogging shoes. His morning ritual, a three-mile run, had lost none of its sanctity to him and so he dressed quickly, intent on leaving the house before the eight o'clock news interrupted the music.

Stepping back onto the porch, he looked cautiously around the neighborhood, half expecting to see Yoakum waiting to applaud his conquest. He wanted nothing further to do with Yoakum, not because he did not feel vested, but because he regarded his night with Sarah to be a providential alignment of the planets rather than a personal triumph. She had made that clear to him before falling asleep at his side. "You're a one nighter, skipper," she had murmured softly. "But one-nighters are the best of all." He stretched his legs slowly, enjoying the gaminess of her scent, and then began jogging upon the soft shoulder of the road. His memory of her, the desperation of their coupling, assailed him like a phantom breeze.

He ran slowly, methodically, heading in the direction of the college football stadium. He knew the stadium would be empty—another blessing since he preferred the sequestration of a quiet track to barking dogs and noisy kids. The houses, barren slate-sided units, rolled past him as though carried by a current and soon he was passing the mulberry bushes and groundskeeping sheds of the city park. The downtown district, a collection of taverns and empty storefronts, took only a minute to navigate, while the campus, deserted for the Thanksgiving holiday, slipped past him so smoothly that he barely took notice of it. When the stadium appeared he felt strangely unworthy of it, a sensation that only intensified as he pushed past the turnstile and trotted onto the rubberized track. The freshly mowed football field, tangy and apple green, seemed to embrace him as an afterthought, perhaps because it had already become a retreat for some Canada geese that were resting from their southern migration.

He paused for a moment, recovering his breath, and listened to the mindless honking of the geese upon the green. A tiny graveyard, barely visible beyond the visitors' bleachers, caught his attention for the first time ever, but the sight of it did not cause him to reflect upon his mortality. Not even a twinge in his side, a superficial but lancing pain, gave him a sense of premonition; instead he felt only heightening anticipation for the moment. Ignoring the bullet-like pain in his side, he stretched his legs lazily one more time. As he started to circle the track, the stitch began to fade.

He ran on the grass with a heel-to-toe gait, scattering those geese that were sitting too close to the track. He was determined to complete twelve laps around the field, an ambitious goal since his body was already showing signs of fatigue. Still, the tugging at his lungs seemed secondary—a poor criticism of a habit that had sustained him for twenty years. He ran ploddingly, compulsively, and was gulping for air as he finished his final lap.

He rested for only a minute, enjoying the prick of the grass on his legs, and then he rose slowly and ambled towards the gate. The joy of his exertion, the utter refreshment it had given him, was almost like a drug and so he barely noticed the stout figure that was standing near the scoreboard: someone he would have mistaken for a gardener were it not for the pallid blue of a correctional officer uniform. As his distance from the man diminished, he was not surprised to discover that it was Lieutenant Perkins. This was not because he was anticipating a visitation from beyond, but because he had not really accepted the lieutenant's demise. His denial, although stubbornly irrational, was in no way challenged by the hearty corpulence of the man and the ruddy flush upon his face.

The lieutenant nodded pleasantly and spoke. "Don't forget the coleslaw," he muttered.

Tom decided not to react, a callous response to the esoteric but one that seemed valid under the circumstances. The ghost, if it could be called that, was clearly lacking an agenda and therefore seemed deserving of the snub. He would have far preferred the grisly stare of a Banquo or the haughty self-righteousness of a Marley: dispositions to which he could have at least offered an angry defense. As it was, he had glimpsed only the complacency of a stout man—a cheerful panache that promoted not cheer, not even repose, but the final inanity of the void.

He passed through the turnstile and walked from the field, pausing momentarily to retie a shoelace that had come loose. A rhythmic popping sound, somebody practicing his serve, was coming from the college tennis courts that lay behind the stadium—a noise so purposeful as to seem vaguely out-of-place. He tied the lace quickly, suppressing his nostalgia for tennis, then looked one more time at the football field. The sight of it caused him a pang of sorrow, not because he had agreed to report back to Hawkins, a total downer, but because Perkins, for some queer reason, was still standing there among the geese.

November 24, 2000
9:00 a.m.

He had showered and shaved and was starting to dress when Sarah returned to the house. He did not mention Lieutenant Perkins to her, perhaps because Sarah, wearing sandals and dressed in a light summer frock, seemed to be something of an apparition herself. Her hair, freshly cut and styled, completed the image of self-renewal and he felt a stab of lust as she kissed him dryly on the chin. He held her waist lightly, prolonging the embrace, and was disappointed when she pushed him away.

"Don't go there, skipper," she snapped. "It ain't happenin' twice. Not unless I turn into *Santa Claus*, it ain't."

He nodded and finished dressing. "It figures," he said.

"Just what do you mean by that?"

"You said it yourself. I can only handle tramps."

"Well, it explains why you're hurryin' on back to Hawkins, doesn't it?"

"I don't think so," he said. "*Hawkins* can't *handle* tramps."

"From what I heard, it's the other way around."

He laughed and shook his head. "You're right. Even tramps have standards."

"How about you, skipper?"

He lowered his head. "*I* have no choice at all."

"Well, you *could* stay for breakfast. But that ain't your style, is it?"

She had turned on the radio, a gesture that seemed automatic to her, and he could hear the beginning of the hourly news. The siege, from the broadcaster's point of view, was not going well: a fresh round of gunfire had erupted from the inmate commissary building—an attack so unexpected that the National Guard Armory in Terre Haute had now been placed on standby alert. But the Commissioner was in the process of being interviewed and his voice was a reassuring counterpoint to the tense questioning of the reporter.

Amnesty, the Commissioner declared, *will be immediately available to those inmates who surrender at once and are cleared by the investigation.*

They gave us a statement of demands, the reporter's voice said.

I have read the statement, sir. I assure you it is without foundation. For one thing, our contracts with the privateers will not be renewed. The statement, sir, is proof.

Proof of what?

That we are dealing with a handful of implacable zealots—not the cream of the inmate body. And we owe no allegiance to hooligans, sir.

Tom listened carefully as the interview continued, unaffected by the trademark buoyancy of the Commissioner or the fact that his speech had obviously been prepackaged for inmate consumption. Tom further suspected that the echoes *had* confused him—that the inmate shooter had been in the commissary all along. But would he ever really know for sure?

He looked reproachfully at Sarah. "Maybe there *is* time for breakfast," he said.

"What changed your mind?"

"The power of banality. Call it the Peter Principle."

Sarah sighed stoically. "Now what does *that* mean?"

"The cream rarely rises."

She shook her head, clearly unimpressed. "Are you referrin' to that Commissioner fella? I'd say he's more peter than principle. But I guess that describes you as well."

Tom chuckled dryly. "That's not saying much."

"I guess it isn't, skipper. Long as it took for *you* to rise."

"You told me I did all right."

"Well, I'm telling you *different* now."

She turned her back towards him, a damper to further conversation, and began occupying herself in the small kitchen adjacent to the living room. The smell of frying bacon, although it buried the scent of the gas leak, seemed a further act of retribution: a fitting disposal of pigs less fortunate than himself. Her irritability, probably the result of old baggage, was a burden he still felt obligated to bear and he sat quietly upon the couch as she finished preparing the meal. The plates clattered sharply when she set them upon the kitchen table.

"There's a *phone* message for you," she muttered.

"From Hawkins?"

"That's right. How'd he know *you* were here?"

He shrugged defiantly. "I have no idea."

"I'll *bet* you don't. You knew it was him that called?"

"Who else would *want* to get ahold of me?"

"That's a good question, skipper. Even *Hawkins* wants you buried."

"Did he say as much?"

"He told me you can *stay* gone as far as he's concerned. It's that Commissioner who's wantin' to talk to you."

"That's not much improvement."

"Shit, it ain't, skipper. He's handing out *amnesty*. That's all the improvement you need."

"Only if I con the bojacks into surrendering."

"Well, you may as well go and con 'em, skipper. You don't have no call to be hangin' around here. I already told you, it ain't gonna happen twice."

She turned up the volume of the radio, as though soliciting the voice of an ally, and looked at him guardedly. He sat down meekly at the table. The eggs were hard, the bacon overcooked, but he ate quickly, grateful for the distraction the meal provided him. He regretted her incisive intelligence, the quality that most attracted him to her, and he remembered the warning Brewer had given him a week ago. "If you're gonna fuck her, Hemmings, fuck her and be done with it. She's a funny woman from what they all say. She'll go with a man for a week or two then end up findin' fault with him."

The Commissioner's voice, a monologue now, droned on as Tom finished his breakfast—a glib but improbable assurance that there could be no bargaining with hooligans. Sarah, not eating, sat across from him, her manner so disinterested that she may as well have been listening to a wheat report. Clearly, she had no further use for the game—not because it had disinherited her but because the outcome, whichever way it went, could only amount to a victory for crumb bums. Watching her sit there, he felt both small and obtrusive—like a child who has forgotten to put away his toys.

She spoke to him finally. "You called me a *name*, skipper. Last night in the car."

"A co-dependant?" he guessed. He was beginning to sense the irony of the comment.

She nodded. "It wasn't that way though. Even if my husband is a boozer. 'Cause I was a bitch to him even when he was *sober*."

"Maybe he still deserved it," Tom muttered. "Did he gamble away your money? Did he mess around with other women?"

Sarah laughed and nodded. "I mighta loved him once. But the man I *loved* never really existed."

"So what did he do to bewitch you?"

She shrugged, displacing a shoulder strap from her dress. Reflexively, as though swiping at an insect, she brushed the strap back into place. "Nothin' *you're* capable of doin', skipper. But don't be takin' it personal."

"Why *shouldn't* I take it personal?"

"Don't," she replied tenderly. "'Cause there was a time when you might have spooked me too."

"Before you married that joker?"

She sighed. "Before I stopped trustin' in ghosts."

She rose from the table, collected their plates, and carried them over to the sink. The broadcast was over now, a dubious relief since he could hear the mocking strains of "Dueling Banjos." He listened to the accompanying tinkle of plates and cutlery as she busied herself at the sink, a noise interrupted by the periodic whir of the garbage disposal. It was surely the music, its lyrical disparity, that made him suddenly feel maudlin.

"I *could* come back," he said, hoping he didn't sound weak. "Whenever it's over. Assuming I'm not dead and buried."

Sarah's face softened. "Do that," she murmured.

November 24, 2000
10:00 a.m.

His drive back to the prison seemed shorter than usual, perhaps because he had chosen to take Highway 40 rather than the densely-wooded service route. He did not take the highway for expediency, but because he had grown weary of dead foliage. Even the few trees alongside the highway depressed him. Balding and stale, they were perhaps too reminiscent of the final words Chester had muttered to him before he had followed Sarah out of the dormitory. "Beware the daughters of Zion, sir. They are haughty and cheapened by rouge. Therefore, the Lord will smite them with a scab and lay bare their secret parts." He was not sure whom this quote alluded to, but it haunted him nonetheless. He felt only foreboding, a deep sense of doom, when the watchtowers came into view.

The sight of the shuttle bus parked beside the arch reminded him that he was technically late for work and so he drove directly to the arch, pausing only to signal to the checkpoint officer who appeared to have been expecting him. As the electronic gate parted, he turned off his car radio, aborting the country music that had accompanied him from Castleberg. Already he could see sharpshooters on the roof of the Administration Building: a spectacle that would scarcely have affected him were it not for a starker sight. An armored personnel carrier, probably from the National Guard Armory in Terre Haute, was also parked near the arch.

He drove slowly through the Arch Gate, passing the vocational shops and the school, and rolled into the administration parking lot. The lot was overcrowded with cars and pickup trucks: an indication that the kitchen duties had been taken over by prison staff members. He pulled into the only parking space available—that belonging to the recreation director—suppressing a sense of the absurd as he did so.

Despite the abundance of vehicles, the lot was practically deserted, a sight that made it appear surreal. Only the presence of Hawkins, standing like a sentry on the steps of the Administration Building, bore testament to the bluster of the preceding day. But the captain now seemed inconsequential, abandoned by even his own troops, and so he looked less like a field commander than an enduring monument to cuckoldry. Noticing Tom, Hawkins shook his head slowly, a reminder that even waifs had schedules, and so it was not the isolation of the man that impressed Tom so much as his attitude of reproach, a disapproval that was sadly merited. What was he, after all, but a failed negotiator, a penny boy to scoundrels, and a possible accessory to four homicides?

Tom shut off the motor, jerked the car door open, and slipped from behind the wheel. The smell of burnt leaves assailed him, an aroma too pleasant to add to his discouragement. He instead felt the intimacy of fall: the seductive aroma of cleansing fires. He shut the car door, locked it quickly, and walked towards Hawkins.

"You're late," Hawkins said. His voice lacked conviction.

"Is an apology in order?" Tom snapped.

"I wouldn't go *that* far, Hemmings. They just freed two more hostages. That might not have happened if you'd been here bargainin' for 'em."

"So maybe I'm better off late."

Hawkins shrugged. "Not if you're porkin' Sarah, you ain't. You shoulda left her in the dorm with the bojacks, Hemmings. You'd *both* be better off."

"Maybe I don't *want* to be better off."

"Then don't bother apologizin'. You're sorry enough as it is."

Tom folded his arms and glared. "I'm only sorry I didn't sleep with her sooner."

"If that was the case, you'd be *smarter* by now. She *is* a mistake worth makin', Hemmings, but you only want to make it *once*. Unless you're a scumbag, a woman like that has no use for you."

Tom grinned mischievously. "There's still time for me to qualify."

Hawkins chuckled. "There is at that, Hemmings. An' it shouldn't be hard with the company *you* been keepin'."

"Perverts and pimps ought to do it," Tom joked.

"Keep on lettin' them influence you," Hawkins said. "They're the only chance you *got* for hangin' onto a woman like Sarah." The captain lifted the hand radio from his girth, lowered the volume, and then muttered several codes to the Control Unit. Finishing with the message, he plunged the radio aggressively into its sheath.

"You still have time for some *real* action, Hemmings—if that's something you think you can handle. The Commissioner wants someone to create a diversion. That's so we can take 'em by surprise. And the way *I* see it you're good at diversions."

"Not *that* good," Tom replied. "Not if you ask Sarah." The confession made him feel sadly exposed.

Hawkins waddled down the stairs and clapped Tom on the shoulder. A food stain dotted his shirt. "That's 'cause a slut needs a *cocksmith*, Hemmings—not a sorry bojack like you. But consider that a silver linin'. You can forget about her and take a better offer."

"And what is that?"

"The chance to avoid another ballin' you can't handle. And maybe help us hunt down an anarchist or two."

Tom shuddered as Hawkins spoke, preparing himself for the probability of an armed attack—an assault he would have to play a role in. He had hoped the price of deliverance would be cheaper.

Tom spoke angrily. "I'm going to keep on balling her, Harold. If she'll take me back, that is. I *might* even take the day off to do it.""

Hawkins scowled. "You're screwin' up your *salvation*, Hemmings."

"A cocksmith might serve you better."

Hawkins unsheathed his radio, a gesture that suggested the conversation was over. "Don't bullshit me, Hemmings. You ain't *that* pussy whipped and you know it. An' what needs to be takin' back is a *facility*."

"Keep your shirt on, Harold. I'll help you get it back."

"We're *countin'* on that, Hemmings. So get that hussy off your mind. She's a Jezebel and a huntress of godless men."

Hawkins lifted the radio. Depressing the squelch button, he spoke. "Control. 140."

"*140. Over.*"

"It's game time," he snapped. "You can phone the commish."

November 24, 2000
11:00 a.m.

Tom could not shake his sense of finality as he mounted the stairs to the Command Center: a small conference room on the upper story of the Administration Building. Having steeped himself in the sin of four murders, he rather doubted Hawkins' promise of salvation. And so he was not particularly curious as to what the Commissioner had in store for him. Savoring his independence, he rapped boldly on the door to the conference room.

The door was opened by the Commissioner himself—a stooped but dapper man in a well-tailored suit. His narrow gaze, a tight myopic squint, suggested that he had forgotten who his visitor was. It was several seconds before the warmth of recognition softened the Commissioner's

152

face. Please excuse me, my friend," he murmured. "I *was* expecting somebody else."

"Yoakum?" Tom surmised.

"No, Mr. Hemmings. I do have my limits."

The Commissioner stepped aside, allowing Tom to enter the room, and then closed the door gently. The room was not impressive: an uncarpeted floor, a collection of hard-backed chairs, and a conference table covered with half-filled water glasses. An aerial map of the facility was spread across the table like a battle plan. The overall effect was so severe that it was not alleviated by even the Commissioner's robust smile.

Tom waited while the Commissioner seated himself at the table, then he selected a chair on the opposite side. They were the only two people in the room.

"Yoakum *did* try to help you, Mr. Hemmings."

"I imagine he did," Tom replied. "He said he would watch over me like a hawk."

The Commissioner rubbed his temples and sighed. "Are you *fond* of hawks, sir?"

"Not particularly. But I prefer them to canaries."

The Commissioner's smile grew even broader. He seemed to be genuinely amused. "Whistle blowers *can* be embarrassing," he said.

Tom's heart beat faster. "Did he threatened to drop a dime on you?"

"What *else*?"

"How did he go about it?"

"Without specifics, which a competent blackmailer must always have. When he called on me this morning, he confided very little. Only that he had some dirt on me and he'd sing if I got on your case."

"What kind of dirt?"

"My dear Mr. Hemmings, I have *no idea*."

"Well," Tom chuckled, "at least he's snitching out you and not me."

"And does that indenture you to him, sir?"

Tom shrugged. "I don't know."

"Then consider putting *me* in your debt, Mr. Hemmings."

"Will *that* require specifics?" Tom blurted.

"Yes, my good man. For starters, you will have to forsake your canary."

"Yoakum?"

"Keep away from him, Mr. Hemmings. The governor wants to protect him for now, but Yoakum is *bad news*."

"Yoakum has my back," Tom snapped.

The Commissioner shook his head, "In exchange for your silence, I presume. Are your personal secrets so severe, sir, that you would bind yourself to a man like that?"

Tom felt his skin burn, an instinctual flush that shattered his sense of immunity. The silence seemed to last for minutes.

The Commissioner blew his nose then continued talking. "Mr. Hemmings," he said. "I don't really *believe* you anticipated those murders." He smiled wearily then rested his elbows upon the table. Supporting his chin with his delicate thumbs, he seemed graceful to a fault: a man too sensitive, too uselessly wise, for the brutal job of prison command.

"So let's start with some *facts*, sir. They are tedious and not very sexy, but they are far more sobering than your secrets." The Commissioner looked down at the map that lay between them. He figited in his chair and then spoke. "There are a hundred and two inmates still quartered in the laundry dorm. We don't think they have any more firepower. A few other inmates are bunkered in the commissary—castoffs whom we believe snuck into the commissary before hostages were taken. These men have somehow acquired a rifle. One of them took a shot at the Administration Building this morning. We also believe that he may have shot Perkins yesterday."

Tom leaned forward. "Is *that* a fact too?"

The Commissioner shrugged. "About Perkins, we cannot be sure. A few of our sharpshooters think there was another rifle in the gym."

"And Yaokum may have filched it," Tom guesssed. "*After* he shot the Disciples in there." He sighed and rubbed his eyes. "Well, what about the hostages in the dorm?"

"There are still nine left. Two were released an hour ago through the sally port. The inmates exchanged them for cigarettes and food."

"From Colonial Concessions?"

"Yes."

Tom shook his head slowly. "Then you got the better of the deal."

The Commissioner's face clouded. "I *know* that the goods are inferior, Mr. Hemmings. But why should *that* be your concern?"

"Why shouldn't it? Colonial *did* anticipate a killing. A *financial* killing."

The Commissioner's eyes narrowed."Don't you think I'm aware of that, sir?" He interlocked his fingers, again supporting his chin on the balls of his thumbs. The pose seemed more practiced than spontaneous. "Don't you think I'm *aware* of that?" he repeated.

Tom shrugged. "If *that's* the case, you'll have to get *rid* of Colonial Concessions, won't you? And that goddamn Penal Health Services."

"Their contracts will soon be terminated. Can you say the same for yours? A pact with a killer is far more entangling."

"At least he can *offer* me a deal."

"You haven't heard ours yet."

"I'm not interested."

"Why not?"

"I owe Yoakum more than I owe you."

"*Do* you, Mr. Hemmings? And do you think Yoakum is a man without a price?"

"That doesn't concern me."

"Why not?"

"He may have saved my life," Tom snapped.

The Commissioner lowered his hands to the desk. His eyes, which were suddenly impenetrable, flashed as he spoke. "*Shouldn't* you be concerned, Mr. Hemmings. With your arrogance, at least? You *are* a bit of a snob, sir."

Tom felt his anger beginning to boil. "I *like* my arrogance," he muttered.

"I'm well aware of that, sir. But what would you have *without* it?"

Tom felt his chest tighten, his mouth become dry. *What would he have without his arrogance?* The question seemed to hover like a noose.

Tom spoke as though scalded. "Educate me," he muttered. "Give me a hint of what you want."

The Commissioner lowered his hands to the desk, a gesture so decisive that he appeared to be folding a poker hand. His eyes, now cool and distracted, roamed carefully over the aerial map at his fingers. He seemed to be absorbing strength from the miniature images of the buildings and streets.

"Are we returning to facts?" Tom asked dryly. He slowly leaned forward, inspecting the map between them.

The Commissioner nodded. "We are, Mr. Hemmings. What else can we do? I will give you only facts, sir, and no more of them than I think you can handle."

The Commissioner reached into his shirt pocket, removing a small pair of reading glasses. Putting on the spectacles, he squinted once more at the aerial map. The lenses, though paper thin, gave his face the authenticity of a scholar.

He spoke in a monotone. "We have *six* emergency squads on standby. Three more were bussed in last night from the state prison. This gives us an attack force of sixty men who for now will stay in the Administration Building."

"The palace guard," Tom said, sarcastically.

"Call them that if you want. But there is no point in revealing our strength in numbers. We have also bussed in a second team of sharpshooters. Most are positioned to shoot at the commissary. *And* we can rotate them hourly now. You have seen the armored personnel carrier?"

"Yes."

"That will also safeguard the attack."

"What about support services?"

"Done, Mr. Hemmings. We have notified the hospitals in Castleberg, Mooresville, and Farmington. All are on standby. Twenty ambulances are also on standby, units fully equipped with blood plasma, oxygen, and rubber shields for mouth-to-mouth resuscitation."

"And who will revive the noncombatants?"

"The Critical Incident Team for now. It has also been expanded. We now have three psychologists and twenty grief counselors. That should be enough to handle the phone calls from the families."

Tom pushed himself back from the table. "We seem to have all the components."

"All the components but one."

"What is that?"

"You already *know* what it is."

"A Judas?" Tom whispered.

"That's right. An inmate to help you create a diversion in the dormitory. Fewer will die if we take them by surprise."

"I don't think we'll *find* one. The inmates seem pretty tight."

"We *have* one already, Mr. Hemmings. And I think you probably know that."

"Who?"

"He calls himself the Deacon. And he says he'll talk only to you."

"At least he's discerning."

"Impatient would better describe him. I think you have had this date for a long time."

"When will I meet with him?"

"This afternoon in the gymnasium. You'll gain safe access through the Main Gate."

"And the Deacon?"

"He too will arrive there safely. Or perhaps he will send a messenger. But the snipers have been told to hold their fire."

"I'll try to remember that."

"Do, Mr. Hemmings. And do this as well. Create a diversion in the dormitory—I'm sure the Deacon will help you with that. Make sure the hostages are sequestered in your office. When the inmates are thoroughly diverted, *hide* in your office and give us a signal. At that moment, we will launch the attack."

The phone in the room had started ringing. The Commissioner answered it, and Tom could hear Hawkins' voice blaring through the receiver. The Commissioner nodded woodenly as though indulging an unwanted pollster at his doorstep. After a minute he grew impatient. "That we will *not* do, sir. We will *not* spank a baby with an ax." His ring finger gleamed, highlighting a tiny diamond as he placed the receiver on the desk. The gesture, an assurance that there would be no further interruptions, hinted at the gravity of what he was about to say.

"Were you discussing me?" Tom asked.

"No, Mr. Hemmings. Not *everything* is about you. I was referring to our campaign."

"And what if I refuse to take part in it?"

The Commissioner slammed the table with his hand. "You will be prosecuted as an accessory—an accessory to the murder of *four* inmates. You will stand trial alongside Yoakum. Is that what you wish, sir. To stand trial with Yoakum?"

"Fuck him."

"In that case, Mr. Hemmings, place me in your debt. At least I have offered you a better choice of devils."

"It seems that our devils pick us."

"And it's not always wise to resist them, my friend."

The Commissioner sighed and looked at the map. "Lets return to facts, Mr. Hemmings. We must take our facility back. That, sir, is a *fact*. The inmates have refused our terms. That too is a *fact*. That being said, we must execute our attack as cunningly as possible."

"By selling ourselves to the Devil, you mean?"

The Commissioner stretched then rose from the table. His motion was stiff, calculated, probably because the prolonged sitting had aggravated his back.

"Please keep your date in the gym, Mr. Hemmings. Let's plug up this dyke as efficiently as possible."

158

"Tame the tempest so to speak."

"Describe it that way if you wish."

"What if the tempest *needs* to blow?"

"You know *very well* what will happen, sir. I believe that is why you came to see me in the first place."

The Commissioner smiled as he finished speaking. He tilted his spectacles, rubbing the bridge of his nose with his thumb and forefinger. The glasses clung precariously to the tip of his nose.

The Commissioner drew a deep breath and smiled. "Do you think this is my first riot, Mr. Hemmings? Do you think I am threatening you without good reason? Do you think we cannot *control* an ill wind?"

Tom rolled his eyes. "And what will that bring us?"

"Better services, sir, once we get things under control. We will have *real* programs, *living* wages, *additional cells* for the zealots. That is the final fact, Mr. Hemmings, so you should be able to handle it. When the tempest is tamed, we will have a new inventory."

"I don't much like inventories."

"No, Mr. Hemmings. But it seems that you have taken one. Isn't that why you came to see me?"

"Like a prodigal son."

The Commissioner laughed. "Keep your date with the Deacon, Mr. Hemmings. He is your only friend."

III
TERMS

Who holds the Devil, let him hold him well.
He hardly will be caught a second time.
— Johann Wolfgang von Goethe

November 24, 2000
2:00 p.m.

The athletic office, a cramped cluttered chamber, seemed a messy location in which to await his confidant. But at least Tom felt safe in it—a feeling he had lacked when he had donned his Second Chance vest, dashed through the Main Gate, and crept into the gymnasium through the back entrance. The wattage from the desk lamp was softer than a candle, providing the room with a caressing glow—a glow that seemed to deify the football legends and basketball stars whose posters hung on the walls. The décor was so embracing that only the traces of blood on the floor reminded Tom of his mission.

The Commissioner had outlined the plan in great detail, but Tom still felt uneasy with it. It was perhaps the arrogance of the scheme—the assumption that its authors alone were adept at duplicity—that disturbed him the most. He was to reenter the dormitory under Chester's protection. At the urging of Chester, the hostages would be herded into his office where they were to be bound and blindfolded. The little man would then relay an offer to the inmates: amnesty if they surrendered within the hour. If the inmates did not choose to surrender, Chester would divert them with a speech. At that moment, Tom would lock himself in his office and phone the Control Unit. When the call was received, the dormitory would be plunged into utter darkness. The attack would then begin and Tom would free the hostages.

Remembering his contribution to the plan, Tom felt an unwarranted sense of triumph. It was *his* suggestion that the hostages be blindfolded. That way they would be clear-sighted the moment Tom removed their blindfolds and able to join to the attack. "Thank you, Yoakum," Tom muttered to himself. "Thank you for the idea."

So comforting was the room, so soft and caressing its glow, that Tom felt violated when the phone on the desk started to ring. He held the receiver to his ear, not bothering to speak until he heard a familiar voice at the other end of the line—a voice that barely competed with the background droning of a television. It was Chester, calling from Tom's office in the laundry dorm.

"Hawkins phoned me, sir. He asked me to call you up. It seems we have mischief to perform."

Tom sighed. "I had almost given up waiting for you."

"What do you want me for this time, sir?"

"You *know* what I want your for, Chester. To implement a plan that will salvage us both. We'll go over the details when we meet."

Tom heard a sharp intake of breath as he spoke, a suggestion that Chester may have changed his mind.

"Again you have overrated me, sir. I have told you before that your deliverance is beyond my power."

"I wouldn't call this mission a deliverance."

"Maybe not, Mr. Hemmings. But is it a demise? Our sins kill us only by degrees, sir."

Tom felt his pulse quicken. "I don't think I've *overestimated* you at all."

"How so?"

"Your powers are really quite remarkable. You could have used them to build yourself a fortune. You could have preached salvation from the highest of pulpits. You could have bilked thousands out of their savings and seduced their wives into the bargain. Why you have not done so is quite beyond me."

Again, Chester paused. The silence on the phone was suddenly profound, suggesting that Chester had just shut the door to the office. When Chester spoke again, his voice was louder.

"A deliverance, Mr. Hemmings, has spared me the worst of my demons."

"And yet you still speak for the inmates,"

"Better a spokesman than a Judas, sir. Being their spokesman is burden enough."

"The role of Judas suits you better."

Chester sighed. "There are limits to my chicanery, sir. Do not ask too much from a sick old man."

"How about a little honesty?"

"What can I tell you, sir? Were I speaking for most of us, I would say we are tired, scared, and sick of the entire business. I daresay we would have surrendered days ago were we not more frightened by the fanatics that command us than the horde beyond our gates."

Tom felt his face flush. "Look here, Chester. I can't hold the horde back for much longer."

"I am aware of that, Mr. Hemmings. One cannot expect temperance from Pharaoh's army."

"Then persuade the Muslims to execute terms."

"How do you propose that I do that, sir? If I tried they might execute *me*."

"Then let's get on with our goddamn plan. Time's running out and you're giving me the run-around. You said you were ready to barter."

Tom regretted his words as the phone went silent. When Chester spoke again, his voice was drier than powder.

"I'm sure that I did, Mr. Hemmings. But how can you tempt me without an offer? Your superiors refuse to *assign* me to the Farm Line, sir—they say I don't meet the criteria. They have offered me only some silly promise of amnesty."

Tom felt his stomach kick. *So Chester was bailing on him. So the facility would not give the Devil his due. So the comedy of errors was continuing. Once again, he had misplaced his trust.*

Tom stammered as he spoke. "Their stupidest decision of all."

"Perhaps it was their smartest. I am weary of even my treachery, sir. But another will help you, Mr. Hemmings—a man more patient than me. He knows the risks of betrayal and his terms are more meager than my own. I'm sure he will serve you better."

"Not where duplicity is concerned. You've pretty much set the standard there, Chester."

"For which they have paid me nothing."

"For which you wanted too much. What did you expect from Hittites?"

"The porch," Chester snapped. "It didn't seem like too much to ask for."

"Then I guess *you've* been screwed."

"Shall we call it an inception instead, Mr. Hemmings?"

"Of what?"

"Fortitude. The Hittites have impregnated me with a bit of spunk. From here-on-out, I shall prove a bulwark to temptation."

"A sensible choice," Tom sighed. "This facility is not worth your faith."

"Nor *yours*, Mr. Hemmings. So perhaps you shouldn't lecture me."

"I won't any more," Tom replied, a tactical duplicity of his own. Since Chester had become a haven to him—the only rascal he could bring himself to trust—he knew he would have to continue working with him even if it were at pauper's rates. And so he was disappointed by the acid in the little man's voice.

Tom held the phone tightly. "So where does that leave us, Chester?"

"With new beginnings, sir. I will become a respectable man and you will go on without me."

Tom hung up the phone, having no more to say, then instantly regretted this decision. He missed Chester's voice: not its piety—a pose that he hoped would prove false— but its sly and soothing tone. *How could he pull off the scheme without Chester? And who would his new Judas be?* The silence of the room, a profound yet sterile hush, had relinquished him completely to the hazards of second guessing.

His mission seemed so foolish to him now—so smug and lacking in anticipation—that he felt imperiled by the silhouette that fell suddenly across his desk. Tom looked towards the doorway and gasped. The man standing there seemed too thin to be substantial: a shadowy figure, practically consumed by the dimness of the room, he better resembled an angel than a cohort in mischief. It was several seconds before he recognized the intruder to be Hassan.

November 24, 2000
2:30 p.m.

T he thin man bowed, a trademark gesture that had become more disarming than courteous. It was no consolation that Tom—not Hassan—would have to initiate the discussion. Short Dog, the man's ever-present companion, was standing beside him, but even this muscular dwarf wore an attitude of supplication: a hangdog demeanor that implied not zealotry but the vulnerability of a frightened child. *They're lovers*, Tom realized—an observation that gave him no particular advantage. How could he expect to rely upon men whose most intimate loyalties lay elsewhere?

Tom nodded reluctantly, extending not an invitation to the men but an admission of mutual embarrassment. Silently, the pair glided into the room, their movements as graceful as those of geese descending. Even after they were seated, he continued to regard them as though they were other-worldly.

It was Hassan who spoke finally: a cordial but rather token effort to break the spell. His voice, soft and pliant, was like wind murmuring. "And how is Ms. Baumgardner?" he asked.

Tom shrugged. "You did her no favor by releasing her."

Hassan hesitated and then coughed. "Are you sure of that, Mr. Hemmings?"

"No. But why ask?"

"Isn't she a woman, after all? And do women *know* what is best for them?"

"Who am I to be sure about Sarah—or anything else for that matter?"

"If we failed her, I'm very sorry. She's a *cheap* woman, but Islam will forgive her. To an old sick Muslim she has been a treasure. And probably to you as well."

Tom smirked. "I agree with you there, but don't take it to heart. She told me I don't think properly."

Hassan smiled gently, rubbing his eyes as he did so. Once again he appeared reluctant to speak, a reticence that now seemed tactical. He was obviously there not to implement the plan, but to seek his comeuppance for the release of Sarah. Tom could only wonder how much more this favor would cost him.

Tom addressed the man sharply, hoping to break his parody of composure. "For someone not on our payroll, you seem rather smug."

Hassan laughed, a docile but sunless sound. "I hope that doesn't offend you, Mr. Hemmings. We are *enemies*, after all."

"No," Tom replied. "But you *did* offend Sarah. She thinks you're an even bigger pig than me."

Hassan lowered his eyes. "She's a woman, Mr. Hemmings. And women *do* take things to heart. That is why Islam must shepherd them."

Tom arched an eyebrow. "Don't shepherds devour their sheep?"

"They do, Mr. Hemmings—you know that already. And so *men* cannot be sheep."

"If we don't end this siege, Hassan, your Muslims will be *slaughtered* like sheep. Is that something you want?"

The thin man smiled. He stretched slowly, like a snake uncoiling. "Both men and sheep have that burden to bear. But their blood will not be on *my* hands."

Tom shook his head. "Just how pure is *your* blood?"

Hassan folded his hands. He bowed condescendingly before speaking. "I am HIV positive, Mr. Hemmings," he murmured. "*Must* you keep asking what you already know?"

"Yes. It explains your fool's passion for heroics."

"Passion no longer becomes me, Mr. Hemmings."

"Not even a lust for martyrdom?"

The thin man sighed. He drew a deep breath—an effort that seemed incompatible with his skeletal features. His sunken cheeks, the dark hollows of his eyes, seemed a barrier to sustenance of any kind. Hassan seemed to already be part of the afterworld: a state that afforded him not hope, not even contempt, but a seasoned amusement with all that he surveyed.

Several minutes passed—a pregnant interim during which neither of them spoke. Perhaps this was attributable to the charm of the man: a persuasive insularity that seemed to sanctify silence. It could not have been due to his conversion to Islam; spiritual rebirth was so common among the inmates that it could rarely be viewed as authentic. It would have in fact surprised Tom if Hassan—a third-time drug felon serving twenty years—had failed to embrace one of the jailhouse dogmas. Nonetheless, Tom felt naked before this lean man—a man who seemed determined to toy with him. As he looked into Hassan's eyes, his calm but impenetrable eyes, Tom knew he was staring into the heart of the void. And that the void had taken his measure.

Hassan coughed and sat forward in his chair. Against all expectations, he seemed ready to unmask or at least make the pretense of doing so.

"May I give you something, Mr. Hemmings?" Hassan reached into the pocket of his shirt and removed a piece of folded paper. His hand trembled as he dropped it on the desk, but his voice remained sarcastic.

"Don't read it now, Mr. Hemmings. You are already behind on your obligations. Save it until the attack is over."

Reluctantly, Tom picked up the paper. It was grimy, damp with perspiration, and he slipped it quickly into his hip pocket.

"The reflections of a lost king?" he asked, sarcastically.

"My swan song, Mr. Hemmings. Its value will grow once you've made me a martyr. Shall we call it the mother of poems?"

"The mother of all poems? I highly doubt that, Hassan."

"Read it anyway, Mr. Hemmings. If only to indulge a fool."

"Is this why you came here? To give me yet *another* lousy script? We have a job to do, Hassan. We need to sequester the hostages. We need to create a diversion. We need to *minimize* the casualties. Are you going to help me or not?"

"I will help up to a point, Mr. Hemmings. And I have one requirement."

"What is it?"

"I want you to also take the boy."

Tom looked warily at Short Dog. Although close to tears, the lad was still a true believer and therefore dangerous. He wondered momentarily if Hassan loved the boy—a thought he quickly dismissed as sentimental. "Take him *where*?"

"The Special Housing Unit."

"Why?"

"I no longer want him protecting me."

"Because he might succeed?"

Hassan laughed. "Not *everything* is about martyrdom, Mr. Hemmings. I simply want Short Dog to live."

Tom stared at the pair and he felt his anger growing. How could he be expected to bargain with a specter and a mute? "That's charitable of you," he said thinly.

Hassan lowered his eyes. "You *know* I am without charity, Mr. Hemmings. That isn't a privilege for mongrels and ghosts." The thin man yawned and shook his head. It was clear, from his attitude of superiority, that the void had endowed him with a cold but uncommon mind—a mind so penetrating that Tom could only bore him.

"Does that mean that you're just playing games?" Tom asked. Against his better judgment, he felt compelled to keep talking.

"It does," Hassan snapped. "Do you find that distasteful?"

"I don't much like games," Tom muttered. "And I don't much like ghosts."

"Then be wary of me, Mr. Hemmings. You can see I am little more than a shadow. My candle burned brighter when I was a pimp."

"What's that supposed to mean?"

Hassan smiled wearily and laughed. "Think about it, Mr. Hemmings. And then be glad for the darkness. It is charitable to us all."

"More so than the *Nation*."

Hassan nodded and coughed. "The guards *do* consider us a joke."

"That much I'll concede."

"Then also concede me the joke of my faith."

Tom looked at the man and felt suddenly repelled. He spoke angrily. "Why should *I* be generous to *you*?"

Hassan raised his head. "You would only be returning a courtesy. Aren't you also playing games, Mr. Hemmings? The plaque on your office door reads *Counselor*, doesn't it?" Hassan laughed grimly and folded his arms. "And yet, Mr. Hemmings, you can't even be honest with yourself."

As Tom's face reddened, Hassan dropped his eyes. "At least we have something in common, Mr. Hemmings. It seems you're no less of a shadow than me."

"I'm aware of the hoax."

"I doubt that, Mr. Hemmings. Not if you are clinging to it at all costs."

"This job," Tom spat, "is not worth clinging to at *any* cost."

Tom's anger, though confessional, remained focused on Hassan—a considerable feat since the man had evoked in him a grudging respect, a regard more spontaneous than anything he could muster for Hawkins or the Commissioner. He had not been prepared for the verdict of the void or the luster of an outlaw angel.

Hassan spoke impatiently. "*Will* you take the boy with you, Mr. Hemmings?"

Tom slowly nodded. He looked again at Short Dog. He wondered: *Was he truly witnessing an act of contrition?* The lad appeared frightened for good reason. Not only would he be a primary target for the E-Squads, but his pledge to a toxic priest had rendered him susceptible to a seed even deadlier than dogma. In all probability, the boy had already become a host to the AIDS virus.

"Why do you bother with the Nation of Islam?" Tom asked. "We studied that bullshit at the academy. It's nothing but comic book crap."

Hassan shook his head. "And what does that matter?"

"It insults us both."

Hassan shook his head. "Yet our *personal* dole will be grand, Mr. Hemmings. Fools will proclaim us heroes. But only because there are *worse* things."

"Like what?"

"Like those who believe in nothing."

"That's a hell of a statement, coming from a drug addict."

"No longer, Mr. Hemmings," Hassan murmured. "Once I smelled like a corpse from all the meth I injected. Eventually, when even my veins had collapsed, I injected the poison through my tongue. I would say that forgives me a mongrel's reprieve."

"Your faith is a fraud."

"I know it is, sir. But doesn't that make it a gentler bile?"

"Not to me!" Tom snapped. The man's confession, which might have once been sincere, struck him as shopworn— like the intimacy of a jaded lover. Hassan rubbed his eyes as though ridding them of sleep.

"Why *not*, Mr. Hemmings? Is there more to be said for Colonial Concessions. Or the flunkies who sent you to con us. Don't you feel bribed, Mr. Hemmings?"

Tom shrugged. "*You* bribed me with a woman, didn't you?"

"That I *will* not apologize for. Not if it helps save the boy."

"I told you I'd take the boy. Did you want a receipt?"

"No, Mr. Hemmings. That would leave too much evidence of my pact with you."

Hassan was now looking directly into Tom's eyes. He was clearly unimpressed by the worth of Tom's soul—a commodity for which Tom still hoped the Devil would pay any price.

"I will sequester the hostages for you, Mr. Hemmings. And I will say nothing about your silly plan. *These things* I will do and nothing more."

"You're supposed to be a Judas," Tom snapped.

"And *you* a negotiator in good faith. But since that is not the case, I don't care to be your Judas. You deserve no more than I'm offering, Mr. Hemmings. I am overpaying you as it is."

Again the man bowed, closing his eyes as he did so. He appeared to be summoning a higher power—a gesture so incongruous that to watch it was almost amusing. But Tom still felt trumped by the thin man's charade: his sordid pact with the Commissioner could not challenge even this pantomime of prayer.

Tom shook his head sadly and looked at his watch. "If you won't help me, who will, Hassan?"

The second shift whistle, a faint but sudden blast, caused Tom to flinch. Under the circumstances, the ritual of another shift change seemed irrelevant. But it was a starker ritual that came suddenly to his mind: an execution he had attended at the state prison several years ago when he had been a member of the Critical Incident Team. His job had been to debrief the executioners—the tense correctional officers within the glassed-in chamber—but his sympathies had extended more intuitively to the condemned man: a youthful African American who had been convicted of committing a gang-directed murder. The boy had declined to wear a sack on his head, preferring to make eye contact with some Muslim ministers in the gallery, and had sat obediently in the chair—eager to please this small audience as the leather throngs were tightened around his ankles and wrists. The electrodes, when applied to the boy's polished temples, seemed almost ornamental, so it had come as no surprise that he remained alive even after the secondary jolt of electricity had been administered. It had taken four jolts to finish him off: an effort so desperate that it had seemed almost conciliatory when the spasms finally began and the body slumped forward in the chair. It was not until guards carted out the corpse, frozen in instant rigor mortis, that Tom had started to feel overmatched—not by the odor of dung and scorched flesh so much as the Draconian weight of duty. He had left the room quickly and gone to the visitor's bathroom where he had thrown up.

The whistle blew again. He looked at Hassan. The thin man smiled agreeably as though he were indifferent to premonitions. It was his impartiality that made him seem comely, as though he were not an adversary but a sympathetic friend. Such was the trickery of the abyss.

Tom spoke apologetically. "A false alarm."

The thin man chuckled. "Don't you *want* the guard to change, Mr. Hemmings?"

The remark, although vague, was not devoid of irony. Tom felt his jaw tighten. "No," he replied. "Not if you're talking about inmates running the asylum. That wouldn't be too sane."

"No, Mr. Hemmings. It *would* be too sane. But *Islam* suffers *fools* as well as women."

"I don't want your sufferance. I want your support."

"I'll pray for you then."

Tom shook his head sadly. "Your prayers would only diminish me more."

Hassan laughed politely, an empty concession. His expression was too studied to convey spontaneity or even mirth. "The Deacon will come back to you," he murmured. "He will come to you tomorrow in the chapel. Once the second shift whistle has blown."

"The Deacon? I thought he washed his hands of me."

Hassan laughed. "Did you think you would be rid of him so easily, Mr. Hemmings? He is not a charlatan but the king of charlatans. Even you are not unworthy of the Deacon."

"I'd rather work with you."

Hassan shook his head. "A shadow cannot help you, Mr. Hemmings. You want somebody more substantial."

"And that would be the Deacon?"

"It would. He's a stouter man than me. And in ways far wiser."

"Oh great, a wiseguy."

Hassan laughed again. "He is no less than what you deserve, Mr. Hemmings. Thankfully, he is also no *more*. So be grateful for men like the Deacon."

The man rose slowly from the table, an indication that their conversation was over. The whistle, as though trumpeting his departure, blew sharply once again. "Shall

174

we play out our script, Mr. Hemmings?" he asked. "We *do* have a battle to get on with."

"You mean a rebellion to squash."

Hassan smiled wryly. "A rebellion in which *you* are the despot, sir. No wonder you don't wish to fight it."

"I'd just as soon not. But what else can be done?"

"Nothing that would exceed the script. So play your part well, sir. Islam demands commitment even from its enemies."

"The script is still a lie. And a *trite* one at that."

"That is all the more reason to play your part well. Remember that it has been performed before—countless times. And by far better actors than we."

The man's wry expression reminded Tom that he was still being mocked. "I'll honor my role," Tom said flatly.

"Do that, Mr. Hemmings."

Hassan remained standing as the telephone began to ring. Lifting the receiver, Tom heard Hawkins' excited voice. The message from the captain—that they would soon be rotating the snipers—suggested it was time to end his collaboration. In the event of a miscommunication, Hassan could end up getting shot on his way back to the dormitory.

"He's leaving," Tom said. He replaced the receiver.

Hassan, intuitive to the content of the message, smiled thinly. "Haven't you betrayed me yet, Mr. Hemmings?"

"No." Tom shrugged. "But there's always tomorrow."

"I was rather hoping to end things today."

"Then *you* need a competent Judas as well."

"I do. But I won't fault you should you rise to the occasion."

"That *is* generous of you."

"No, it's not, Mr. Hemmings. I'm really rather desperate. Were despots to falter then martyrs would also fail."

The man folded his arms and looked past the desk. His expression, now cool and trancelike, suggested that he was already focused upon the fray to come: a battle not of glory but betrayal. At that moment, Tom felt as though the man were his brother. The terms, after all, were the same for them both.

Hassan cleared his throat finally and said, "Take the boy."

November 24, 2000
6:00 p.m.

It was late when Tom left the Administration Building. His debriefing, a tactical conversation with Hawkins, had so exhausted him that he regretted that he had not waited for the captain to leave the facility before slipping out of the gymnasium. He had been impressed only by the ultimatum Hawkins had given him: an angry assurance that the attack would be launched the following evening whether Tom created a diversion or not. When told that Chester had bailed, Hawkins had rolled his eyes. "Okay, Hemmings, we'll *put* that fucker on the Farm Line. That is if he does the job *right*. But he'll go to the *hole* if he don't. And he'll stay there till he rots."

The thought that the battle might take place without him was only briefly liberating: casualties, after all, would be unacceptably high and the Prison Review Board, in an inevitable search for slackers, would certainly treat him severely if he failed to con the inmates. It was therefore the memory of Short Dog—the expression on the boy's face when he had turned him over to the Special Housing Unit— that gave Tom his only true feeling of reprieve. The boy had looked at him with such gratitude, such obvious relief, that Tom felt as though he had somehow rescued him from a dungeon. That he had in fact delivered him to one in no way diminished his sense of accomplishment, and he had watched with exaggerated pride as the range door hummed shut, sealing the boy indefinitely within the heavily secured building. Not even Brewer, after patting the boy down, succeeded in dampening Tom's sense of triumph. "Don't expect no cigar, Hemmings," the big man had grumbled. "This kid used to have himself a set of *balls*. Now he's just a punk like you." Tom's response, that he was only trying to minimize casualties, earned him yet another sneer from

176

Brewer. "I don't *give* a shit, Hemmings. How's that going to help the union."

The imminence of the attack was driven home to him as he walked towards his car. Several National Guardsmen, pimply adolescents wearing starched khaki uniforms, were cleaning M-16s beneath the guard tower. The sight seemed ludicrous since they would probably be on standby until the lockdown phase of the operation. But it was clear that the pieces were now all in place—that there would be no further postponements. The attack would be launched the following day whether Tom was part of it or not.

He drove slowly back to Castleberg, taking the service route once again. The countryside seemed anemic to him now—a drab precursor to winter—but the leafless trees were sufficient, at least, to give him a sense of homecoming. Although he had traveled the route only yesterday, he felt as though he had been gone for a long time.

It took him ten minutes to arrive in Castleberg—a redundant destination since the streets seemed no less depleted to him than the countryside. This may have been due to the sluttish demeanor of the taverns or an excess of barren storefronts, but a more likely explanation was that the town seemed to exist as a relic. Lethargic in its stillness, impenetrable in its silence, it offered no echo to the predatory growling of the Wal-Mart trucks along Highway 17. He turned on the car radio, a quick defensive gesture, but was not entertained by even a bluegrass favorite. The song was "Rank Strangers," a Stanley Brothers epic, but the tune only haunted him as he navigated the quiet streets. He drove reflexively, his attention on the music, and the car, perhaps on its own accord, delivered him to Sarah's house.

Her car was not there, but he knocked on the door anyway. Hearing no response, he pressed the handle, discovered the door to be unlocked, and went inside. Despite the intimacies he had shared with Sarah, he felt like a burglar and so it relieved him when he confirmed that she was not at home. Not only would this spare him from his obsessive

177

embarrassment, but he would have an opportunity to go for another jog. Retrieving his sports bag from the car, he changed rapidly, almost fearful that she would come home and catch him in the act. After hanging his clothing in the hallway closet, he slipped out of the house, stretched quickly, then began running along the shoulder of the road.

He jogged eastward along Highway 17, intent on avoiding the college campus which he now associated with Lieutenant Perkins. He did not doubt that the lieutenant, staid and rule-bound while living, would also prove territorial in death, and so he felt a growing sense of relief as he distanced himself from the town. Soon even the Safeway and the car dealerships were behind him, and he felt the embrace of true solitude—a sensation that only increased when he veered onto a dirt road, a forested three-mile trek that would eventually hook to the west and return him to the town.

Entombed by the sycamores and cottonwoods, he slackened his stride: a tactic he hoped might retain him forever in the twilight of Indian summer. After awhile he started to breathe raggedly, overmatched by a steep rise that meandered endlessly among the trees, but he was disconcerted only when he finally cleared the ridge and spotted the twinkle of distant streetlights. He descended the hill slowly, ploddingly, his stride so deliberate that he was mystified by an explosion of movement in front of him. It was only the hindquarters of the animals—a cluster of bounding white lumps—that convinced him that he had merely scattered a herd of deer. The racket died quickly, insulated by the trees, and was soon replaced by the rhythmic beating of his stride.

He sat down when he reached the bottom of the hill, stretching lazily until the vigilant croon of a hoot owl convinced him that he was shirking. He paused long enough to recover his breath, then he rose to his feet, shook loose a cramp in his leg, and trotted slowly in the direction of the town.

He approached Sarah's house from the edge of the woods, jumping over a dry creek bed and some abandoned railroad trestles before spotting the house once again. Given the length of his run, the sense of arrival it had provided him, it disappointed him to discover that Sarah was still not home—that the cottage was not even illuminated by a porch bulb. He saw only the pickup truck near her driveway—a dented unkempt vehicle sitting in the pallid wash of a streetlight. A tiny red glow—the eye of a cigarette—was floating within the cab, a suggestion that a reception was awaiting him after all. Inebriated by his run—perhaps to the point of recklessness—he walked boldly towards the truck. This time he was ready for Yoakum.

November 24, 2000
7:00 p.m.

The red glow leaped from the truck and then burst into pieces upon the sidewalk. The sparks were so distracting that Tom did not notice Yoakum until after a door to the truck slammed shut. He had forgotten that they had business to discuss, and so it annoyed him that Yoakum was grinning impishly as he walked towards him.

"You've outrun the rabbits, Mr. Hemmings. An' *that* you can take to the bank."

"I would," Tom replied, "if I had an account."

Yoakum grinned broadly and pumped Tom's hand. "You got yerself a *purse* anyhow. An' a good woman's purse is *better* 'an gold."

Tom groaned. "She doesn't consider me an investment."

"That makes it all the sweeter, sir. You're collectin' the cream without buyin' yerself the cow."

Tom crossed his arms across his chest. "She wouldn't appreciate you calling her a cow."

Yoakum wagged his head. "She don't appreciate me anyhow, Mr. Hemmings. A woman like that is *particula*r, sir. But she knows a *real* gennelman when she sees one."

Tom shrugged sheepishly. "I don't think being a gentleman is helping me."

"Then best you *stop* thinkin'. There ain't no *percentage* in thinkin' too much. Things come down to the same in the end, don't they, sir?"

"And what end is that?"

"Simple, Mr. Hemmings. Ladies you court, scum you get rid of, fools you outwit, and friends you look after. Especially if they're as good a friend as you." The man struck a match; the flame struggled feebly between his palms. When he had lit another cigarette, he tucked the spent match into the band of his field cap.

"When's the missus comin' home?" Yoakum asked.

"What makes that *your* business?"

"The rabbits, Mr. Hemmings. I need some time to talk to ya. Did Hawkins and them ask you about the manhunt too?"

"No," Tom replied. He lowered his eyes. "But I think they suspect that the shoot wasn't righteous."

Yoakum smoked slowly. He watched the smoke curl. "They *always* suspectin', Mr. Hemmings. But suspectin' won't get 'em too far. As long as you didn't tell 'em nothin' we'll be fine."

"I'm not really sure *what* to tell them. You shotgunned Hopper's lover and that's all I know about it."

Yoakum chuckled. "That's 'cause I thought he had a *rod* on him."

"But didn't you fire the pistol as well?"

"I might have at that, sir. I'd have been a fool *not* to. When you're pickin' off scum buckets you gotta be *resourceful*."

Yoakum winked and continued to smoke. The circuitry of his comments—his chronic refusal to divulge too much information—seemed considerate rather than evasive, a kindness to a cohort who was already out of his depth. Tom could only marvel at this curious man, a Machiavellian monster to perhaps everyone but himself. He therefore spoke impetuously.

"Was killing those Disciples a personal vendetta? Or were you acting in the line of duty?"

Yoakum grinned broadly, exposing his tobacco stained teeth. "What difference does it make, sir? A man's duty is to himself, ain't it now? An' to them he holds dear to his heart."

"Convince the Commissioner—not me," Tom snapped. "Maybe it will stop him from burying you."

Yoakum laughed. "You think he's capable of it, Mr. Hemmings? He was only a teacher a few years back. That was in Joliet before he became a commish." He spat contemptuously then shook his head. "Preachers and teachers. They don't make good supervisors, do they, sir?"

"So maybe he's done with me," Tom replied wistfully. "Maybe he'll order me *not* to go back into that dormitory. Not until we've taken back the facility anyway." Tom looked into the darkness as though an angel might appear.

"Now don't you take *that* to the bank, sir. If they ain't done with me then they ain't done with you."

"What would you suggest?"

"Be ready for 'em when they lean on you, sir. Now if they say they got a witness, don't worry. That just means they're gettin' desperate. If they say they've traced the guns just laugh. Both of them Glocks have been filed to the quick. There ain't no serial numbers on 'em. An' they can't use what you tell 'em in confidence against you. Not unless they read you your rights first."

"It might be *less* trouble to tell them the truth—or some version of it anyhow. It *might* even be expedient."

Yoakum groaned and shook his head. "Sir, the smart thing for them ain't the smart thing for you. 'Cause none of 'em hold ya dear to their heart."

Tom shook his head, unable to disguise his sarcasm. "I would rather you loved me less."

Yoakum grinned. He pinched out the cigarette, sucking his fingers as he did so, then slipped the butt into the pocket of his jacket.

"Ya saved my neck, sir. An' that's a plain fact. So whatever happens there's one thing you can count on. Ol' Henry Yoakum will be coverin' your back."

"The same way you covered Sarah's?"

Yoakum shrugged, diverting his gaze to the street. "I don't know what she told ya, sir. But it's gotta be Gospel comin' from a woman like that."

"She said you once dropped a dime on her."

"That I did, sir. I played the brass against her. But a kitchen dorm is *dangerous*, Mr. Hemmings. It ain't no place for a lady like Sarah."

"That's not quite how she tells it."

"I'm sure it's not. But it's the same kinda favor *you* done her, ain't it, sir?"

Tom looked into the distance. "I suppose that's true," he mumbled.

"Ain't no *need* for supposin'. Look out for your friends, sir, and let it go at that. 'Cause it's them who love you who'll be takin' care of you in the end."

The pock-faced man smirked, then clapped him smartly on the shoulder. The gesture left Tom cold, perhaps because of the crisp evening air and the clinging dampness beneath his sweat suit. He was shivering when the porch bulb went on, bathing the driveway in a sharp yellow light.

Tom shook his head sadly. "That bulb's on a timer."

Yoakum chuckled. "Hang in there, Mr. Hemmings. Your evening's just begun."

November 24, 2000
8:00 p.m.

Tom showered quickly, put on a clean sweat suit, and then went to the living room to watch the evening news while he waited for Sarah to return. Her television, a Zenith portable, was parked on a bookcase behind a stack of Harlequin romance novels, a location so incidental that it took him several minutes to locate it. Turning on the set, he found the reception unrewarding: ghosted and lacking flesh tones, the images failed to solidify even after he had adjusted the rabbit ears. The news was dully familiar, a mention of the presidential election, which was still stalemated by the Florida vote count, and an update of the continuing standoff at the penal facility. Since a clear picture did not seem necessary, he sat down on the couch, put up his feet, and waited. His impatience to see Sarah now bordered on panic: he remembered that her children were with relatives in Rockville and that she had made no promise to be home that evening. His discomfort increased when the news hour ended, but the program that followed, a *Full House* rerun, was so numbing to him that he failed to react even after he heard the slamming of a car door in the driveway. It was not until the front door opened that he rose hastily from the couch and turned off the television. He felt as though he were concealing evidence.

She was carrying a bulging grocery sack, a burden that obstructed her view, reassuring him that she hadn't witnessed his choice of television programs. Setting the bag upon the couch, she smiled and crossed the room. Her kiss was quick though yielding and he could feel the heat of her exertion through her thin summer frock.

"There's two more bags in the car."

"Shall I fetch them?" he asked.

"You *could* do that," she laughed. "It ain't that big a job. Nothing like taking inventory, anyhow."

She was talking on a cell phone when he returned from the car with the rest of the groceries. Her voice was soft but impatient enough to assure him that the conversation would soon be over. "Just leave 'em with Harry," she said finally. "It's not like he doesn't *deserve* to be bugged. I'll come get 'em in the morning." She shut off the phone and dropped it on the couch.

"Kids," she said wearily.

"You saw them today?"

She nodded. "And one of 'em has the chicken pox. Can you believe *that?*" Her tone of voice was reproachful, as though he were somehow to blame for the matter.

"I've *had* the pox," he said lamely. "You could have brought them home with you."

"Why?" she snapped. "You wanna adopt them? Anyhow, I had a job interview this afternoon. Couldn't have 'em taggin' along, could I?"

"Is Wal-Mart that strict?"

She nodded then sighed, apparently irritated by the question. "But they *still* want to make me an assistant manager. Now ain't *that* a hoot?"

"What did you tell them?"

"I told 'em I wouldn't be *nobody's* snitch. I told 'em to just put me behind a register like they did last time. They said they would think it over and probably call me on Monday."

He sat on the couch while she went into the kitchen and put away the groceries. When she returned to the living room, she stretched contentedly, slipped off her sandals, then snuggled beside him on the couch. Her kiss was soft but obligatory, and she pushed him away when he started to undo her dress.

"*Behave* yourself, skipper. And maybe I'll fix you some dinner."

"I'm taking inventory," he replied. "You *said* you had no other use for me."

She chuckled then poked his ribs. "What I *said* is it ain't happenin' twice. And I *meant* what I said." She adjusted the strap to her dress. "You're *still* thinkin' with the wrong head, skipper."

"Why is it the wrong head *tonight*?"

"I can't really say for sure. Maybe it's got something to do with that Hassan fella."

"Would it surprise you to know that I talked to him today? We negotiated in the gym."

"Why would *that* surprise me? And what did he tell you this time?"

"He also assured me that he was nobody's snitch."

She snorted. "But fawnin' and lyin' don't bother him none. It didn't even bother him to turn me over to you like a two-bit whore. An' just so he could get himself a favor."

"I don't think of it that way."

"*That* don't surprise me either. Not with the head *you're* thinkin' with." She sat up stiffly, tucking her legs beneath her buttocks. "You *did* him that favor, didn't you?"

"It wasn't that much of a favor," he said, guiltily. "I just took the kid off his hands."

"The runt, you mean." She shook her head. "*That* wasn't a favor, skipper. At least not to the officers who gotta work in there. When he reaches his full growth he'll end up killin' one of 'em."

"Not if they keep him in the hole. I turned him over to Brewer."

"I'll *bet* you did. And what *else* did you turn over to Brewer?"

"I didn't turn over our secret."

"You didn't *have* to. If Hawkins knows you been shackin' up here, the whole damn place knows."

"Why does that matter?" he blurted. "You told me you were easy."

"It's not bein' *easy* that I mind, skipper. Since that's all men are good for, I may as *well* be easy. But bein' easy don't make me no whore." She folded her arms as though guarding her breasts, but the posture made her seem statuesque rather than foreboding. He desired her all the more.

"To me you're a Godsend," he whispered, hoping he didn't sound desperate.

"Now that's a *fine* way to put it. Didn't God send *Jesus* a whore too?"

"I'm still going to think of it as something special."

"And it'll *stay* special," she snapped. "Just as long as it don't happen twice."

She rose from the couch and went into the kitchen. After a while the aroma of chili, a spicy yet common meal, reminded him of the banality of his imagination. It was therefore dejection, the folly of having idolized his lust, that convinced him to turn on the television once again. *The West Wing* was airing, his favorite program—perhaps because it *also* ennobled the pedestrian.

"Leave it on if you like," she called from the kitchen. "But dinner's ready."

They ate silently at the kitchen table, the sound of the television the only accompaniment to the tinkle of cutlery. The meal, though slightly scorched, was a comfort to him: if not a prelude to passion, it at least offered him the consolation of domesticity. He was therefore unaffected by their lack of conversation and ate slowly, hoping that by doing so he could prolong the moment. But Sarah had eaten just half of her food when she pushed her bowl aside.

"So when are you going back into that dorm?"

"I don't know that I am," he lied. "There's nothing more to negotiate for. The inmates are standing firm."

"Now who told you that? A couple of bojacks?"

"Yes."

"They're conning you, skipper. Even Yoakum will tell you that."

Tom made a face. "Well, they've fooled *me* anyhow."

"I doubt that anything fools you, skipper—not unless you want it to. You're going back in there, aren't you?"

He sighed. "If the Commissioner says to, what else can I do?"

"You don't *need* to do anything. I've told you that once already. None of this is *your* concern. Tell them no. *N. O.*"

"It *might* save a few lives if I do go back in there."

"Don't bother, skipper. You'll probably end up savin' the *wrong* lives."

"Maybe I'll work some at Wal-Mart," he joked. "That could make you my boss. I'd *have* to listen to you then."

She laughed. "You wouldn't last long at Wal-Mart, skipper. 'Cept maybe in Sportin' Goods."

She rocked back on the kitchen chair, putting her hands behind her neck, and he felt her bare feet in his lap. Reflexively, hoping to convince her of his subordination, he began to massage her insoles. She chuckled, amused by the transparency of the gesture, and watched him as he worked. After a while she spoke softly.

"Keep your head on straight, skipper. You *don't* know what to expect in that dorm. There ain't no honor among bojacks."

Later, reclining together on the couch, they watched the remainder of *The West Wing*. The Rob Lowe character, a self-righteous staff assistant, afforded him a fleeting glimmer of trust: a hope that illusions were something he might count on, after all. It was Sarah who helped him recover his perspective.

"Lowe *ain't* no hero," she said. "Sleepin' with two girls at *once* is what he did in *real* life. That's his personal business, I suppose, but why did he have to *film* it?"

The irritation in her voice, probably a reference to her own loss of privacy, made him feel suddenly contemptible. Still, she barely resisted when he put his arm around her and stroked her breast through the loose fabric of her dress. Her lips parted slowly, indulging his kiss, and her palm, as though dramatizing the capture of her breast, pressed upon the back of his hand.

"Don't do it, skipper," she murmured softly. "You wanna be *stuck* with me?"

The gravity of her request, its appeal to good sense, only intensified his desire. Releasing her breast, he stroked her thigh slowly, massaging it randomly until his fingers, as though by accident, slipped beneath the elastic of her panties. She was wetter than he had anticipated, but her fluid seemed too resilient, a slipperiness intended to quickly expel his finger. He sat back obediently when her hand pushed gently against his chest.

"I give *up*," she said. "But it's gonna be on *your* head, skipper."

She slipped off the couch, taking his hand as she did so, and he followed her into her bedroom. A bulb woke dimly as she stooped beside a night table, bathing the room in a glow that was too revealing—not because of the garishness of the floral wallpaper but because of the large collection of stuffed bears perched upon the dresser and bed, a sight so startling to him that he felt as though he were about to desecrate a nursery. He therefore took comfort in the businesslike manner with which she undid the straps to her dress, allowing the garment to puddle at her feet. Her breasts, small and depleted, provided him with an additional sense of empowerment, and he slipped quickly out of his sweat suit when she pulled back the bedcover.

"The sheets need launderin'," she murmured.

She eased quickly beneath the covers, jostling a glass on the night table and causing it to topple to the floor. The clatter was so loud that it seemed to be terminal—an admonition that would surely restore her better judgment.

"*Now* look what you made me go and do."

He picked up the glass, placing it back on the night table before joining her beneath the covers. When he reached for her, he was relieved to discover that she had already removed her panties. Her mound, soft and soapy, enveloped his fingers while her mouth, perhaps determined to have the last word, crushed possessively onto his own. Her shudder again seemed an act of revulsion, a spasm so quick, so spontaneously triggered, that it made him feel expendable.

Gently, he stroked her thigh, hoping to renew her interest, but it was she who took the initiative, removing his briefs with a hasty tug and then mounting him objectively. Her core was so warm, so unbearably slick, that he regretted that she hadn't fitted him with a condom: the dull barrier might have given him an opportunity to impress her with his skill. Instead he felt vulnerable, overmatched, and he attempted to distance himself mentally as her hips jerked furiously into his own. She moaned and then stiffened, perhaps chastising her body for abandoning her—an emotion he shared when his own climax mingled sharply with hers. Thankfully, she hovered above him, keeping him inside her while her tongue, darting in and out of his mouth, preserved the momentum of their coupling.

When he had slipped out of her, she rose from the bed and left the room, returning after a minute with a large terry towel that she placed between his legs. The gesture, a belated act of intimacy, was reassuring to him, but he was hoping for a compliment instead. He tickled her playfully as she snuggled beside him once again.

"That *had* to be special," he murmured.

She laughed and then poked him. "It *better* be special, skipper. It's all we got in common."

November 24, 2000
11:00 p.m.

Anightmare awoke him, a cold invasive sensation. He was drowning in pitch black water, water surrounded by darkening cliffs. But he was familiar with the nightmare, and he felt only tedium when the walls of the stone quarry were replaced by the dim company of the stuffed bears. It was not even midnight according to the digital alarm clock, but he knew he would not fall asleep again soon. The room was too stuffy, the sheets too abrasive, and he could hear the perpetual growling of the trucks along Highway 17. He slipped from the bed, slowly so as not to awaken Sarah, and made his way to the living room.

The light in the kitchen was still burning, illuminating the crowded bookcase that supported the television set. He stooped, searching compulsively for something to read, but was uninspired by the contents of the shelves: detective digests, more Harlequin romances, and two narrow hardbacks whose titles—*The Land Fish* and *Father Flanagan, Friend to Youth*—convinced him to leave them unopened. It was therefore inertia that drove him to the hallway closet where he fumbled about in his sports bag, retrieving finally the small square of paper from the liner, the paper Hassan had given him. He carried it cautiously to the kitchen, resisting the urge to wash his hands, and unfolded it at the kitchen table.

The poem, a composition entitled "Pale Men," was barely legible and so he studied it carefully, examining the idiosyncrasies of the letters as though attempting to break a code. When he had mastered its first line—*Arise pale men ...* —he sighed at its sentimentality, the necessity of ideologues to cast avarice as destiny. Since such sentiments had founded and preserved nations, he could scarcely begrudge them to a jailhouse convert, but he studied the poem with a profound reluctance, grateful that its brevity—five short verses—would sufficiently honor his promise to Hassan. When he had deciphered the first two lines he paused,

189

knowing that he was again delving too far into the void. The poem was truly a swan song, a dark infectious anthem, and he could picture Hassan, his face grim with passion, revising it for the hundredth time in a corner of the dormitory.

Arise pale men and wrest yourselves a stake
Where coin as dark is lent to lesser rakes

He pushed aside the paper, feeling the sudden implosion of a migraine, an obstruction to his vision that he attributed to providence rather than fatigue. Returning to the living room, he turned on the television set. The eleven o'clock news was presenting a breakthrough to the Florida stalemate, a vote from the canvassing board in Miami-Dade County to cancel the recounting of the votes. Clearly the decision was coerced—a response to Republican strongmen who had stormed the election center—and it made him feel incensed. His sense of mission could hardly survive if overlords showed their true colors. The artlessness of the Florida rout, its feudal assumption that a few votes could cancel out thousands, would give too much voice to his detractors, their caustic insistence that he was championing a foreign cause. Disgusted, he turned off the television and returned to the kitchen table.

The page was less watery now, and so he retrieved a pencil and notepad from the kitchen counter. Seated at the table, his eyes back in focus, he began copying out the verses. He worked slowly, as though defusing a bomb, and was grateful when the pencil, perhaps guided by an intuitive spirit, started moving on its own accord. When he was finished, he sighed. The poem, though a gem, served only to depress him further, not by its timbre—the infectious cry of the disinherited—but its ultimate naïveté: the trite and exorbitant failure it prescribed.

He read.

Arise pale men and wrest yourselves a stake
Where coin as dark is lent to lesser rakes
Where consecrated yokes in silence borne

190

Belie the silence of a quieter morn.

Arise pale men. Adulterate the shame
That lamer men are born to entertain
That fawners have assuaged with loyalty
And paler men its enemies must be.

Awake pale men and lend your vacant stare
Where sight is bartered for a cheaper ware
Where heists are purged that desecrate the strong
And stronger heists are urged to carry on.

Arise pale men. Offend no property
Derived of temperance, born of sanctity
That leaves your penance to its rightful court
And proffers no vile ransom to support.

May usury give way to prouder lies
May anarchy assume a clearer guise
May smoke and cinder consecrate the skies
That lame may limp and pale men may arise.

November 25, 2000
Noon

Tom slept through the morning—a shallow yet dreamless sleep—and would probably have slept longer had Sarah not awakened him. The sight of her was disarming: her hair, bound tightly with curlers, accentuated the leanness of her face, but the severity of her expression was tempered by her hand upon his shoulder. It was clear from her touch, the lightness of her fingers, that she had woken him reluctantly. He rose slowly from the bed, surprised that he hadn't heard the ringing of the telephone himself.

"It's *rude* of him to be late," he murmured.

She looked at him quizzically.

"The tramp," he joked.

191

"It's Etta," she snapped. "But she's *all* the tramp that *you* need, Skipper."

He dressed slowly, taking the time to button his shirt before padding into the kitchen. His procrastination was self-indulgent, but he still felt wickedly empowered when he saw the receiver dangling feebly from the wall. Feeling reckless, he lifted it to his ear.

"It's the smithy," he said.

"Mr. Hemmings ...?" Etta Johnson's voice was warm and melodious, awakening yet again his fantasy of palm trees and pounding drums. He looked about for Sarah, his face growing warmer, and was thankful to see that she had left the kitchen.

He spoke softly into the receiver. "You have me."

"The fact is we *don't* have you, sir. You're five hours late and you haven't called in. We *were* growing rather concerned about you."

"Thank you," he said. "I'd forgotten the time."

"*Did* you, Mr. Hemmings? Then why do you seem to be gloating?"

"I've been thinking with the wrong head," he confessed. "But that's all the more reason for your concern."

"Well, you *are* in our prayers, sir. But we're still expecting you."

"And the real serpent? Is he expecting me too?"

He heard a pause, an indication that Etta, on some vestal level, was sharing in the joke.

"Are you talking about that strange little man? Yes, Mr. Hemmings, he's expecting you this evening in the chapel."

Tom's heart sank. So Chester would assist him with a diversion, after all. "The chapel," he murmured. "That's a hell of a place to marry the Devil."

"The Devil, Mr. Hemmings. My, but that does sound ambitious. Isn't it enough that you're taking advantage of that poor woman?"

"I am," he said. "But it isn't enough."

"Then consider a *woman's* advice, sir. Leave Mrs. Baumgardner alone. She's somebody who needs *help*."

"Would an enabler do just as well? I'm *that* much at least."

"Don't be smart with me, sir. You must *surely* be aware that sex is an opiate to Mrs. Baumgardner. You may as well be giving crack to a prostitute."

"I'm partial to crack," Tom replied. He reached for the percolator and poured himself a cup of coffee. It was several long seconds before Etta responded.

"Does *rudeness* console you also?" she muttered.

"Not entirely," he confessed. "Perhaps I *do* need your advice."

"You need *instructions* even more, Mr. Hemmings. And your orders do *not* involve Sarah. We are giving you *only* what you can handle."

He paused, consoled by the snub that Etta must have received from the Commissioner. Since the plan to take back the dormitory—*the full extent of the plan*—could not possibly have been revealed to so opinionated a woman, he felt somewhat inoculated to her censure of him. What more could he wish for, when Judgment Day came, than a jurist who had not been fully appraised of his sins? He decided to test her.

"Heroics I can handle."

"Spoken like a typical man. But are you good for anything *besides* heroics? You're *job* is to be a messenger."

"And not a bedfellow to a charlatan?"

"That's right," she snapped. "Under *no* circumstances are you to re-enter that dormitory."

"Why not?"

"Because policies *should* be remembered from time-to-time. We don't *need* another hostage in there."

"I feel like a hostage already."

"Don't exaggerate, Mr. Hemmings. That woman is too overwrought to have turned you into a hostage."

"She has captured me nonetheless. You might say I've been booked."

"You already *have* a booking."

"But not an engagement."

"As I said, sir, we are keeping you within your limits. I should think you would be grateful for that."

"And what message am I to deliver?"

"Amnesty, sir. Amnesty and a steak. For those inmates who are willing to go immediately into deadlock."

Tom snorted. "*Some* surrenders are *too* cheaply bought."

"Do you really *believe* that? I don't think you do. Most of those men are hypocritical, sir. Many have told me privately that they actually *welcome* the controlled movements. Phrase the offer properly and the majority of them will go *gladly* into deadlock."

Tom clenched the receiver. "Even when the amnesty isn't real?"

"Yes."

"That would make *me* a hypocrite."

"*Would* it, Mr. Hemmings? Why? You're an intelligent man who chooses to reside in a trailer. You are a prodigy who squanders his time on jogging and one-night stands. You would only be hypocritical if you offered them anything *but* deadlock."

Her cold observation served only to irritate him, not because of its accuracy but because it invaded his sense of pride. It was his intelligence, after all, that should have delivered him from the travesty of duty.

"Thank you for setting me straight," he remarked.

"I *forbid* you to be coy with me, Mr. Hemmings."

"Coyness is all I have to offer."

"Then save it for your conquests."

"And not my conqueror?"

Again he heard silence, a pause so prolonged that he found himself missing the cold authority of her voice. He suddenly regretted having relegated her to the role of a dominatrix.

"Mr. Hemmings?" she said finally.

"Yes?"

"Don't you think I'm *capable* enough to be a super-intendent?"

"I do. But I also think of it as a demotion."

"And why is that?"

194

"I would rather see you as an earth mother."

He heard a faint splutter, a noise that sounded almost like a chuckle. Since he was accustomed to thinking of her as a diva, her concession to his wit served only to disappoint him. When she spoke again, her voice was reassuringly cold.

"Did I hear you right, Mr. Hemmings? An *earth mother*?"

"You heard right."

"Then clearly it's time that you *came* down to earth? You have real business to attend to, Mr. Hemmings—not schoolboy daydreams."

It was the mettle in her voice, not her reference to duty, that weakened the last of his will. Her sense of mission, though lacking in creativity, was clearly less sullied than his own.

"When do you want me?"

"At six p.m. sharp."

"Six it will be," he said, wearily.

"Well and good, Mr. Hemmings. And *please* be on time."

November 25, 2000
12:30 p.m.

He slipped the receiver into the cradle, slowly so as to cushion the sound, and went into the living room to rejoin Sarah. Perched upon the couch, her hair still in curlers, she was squinting over the page he had copied out the previous evening. Her expression was critical rather than inquisitive, as though she were examining a piece of contraband, but he was glad to see her focused on something other than his conversation with Etta.

"Hassan give you this?" she asked finally. "I seen him doin' some scribblin' back in the dorm."

He nodded. "It's his swan song. He calls it 'Pale Men.'"

"Just 'cause he's dying don't make him no swan, skipper."

"Well, he *is* a strange bird."

Sarah giggled. "And doesn't that *tell* you something?"

"It does," he replied. "It tells me to honor fallen angels. It tells me dark beauty can bind."

She shrugged, ignoring his attempt to compliment her. Tossing the page aside, she picked up a small basket that lay beside her on the couch. "Better get rid of it," she muttered. "Before it gets *you* in a bind. So what were you talkin' about so long with Etta?"

"Bedfellows," he confessed. "She says I can't have any."

Sarah groaned. "I'll *bet* she did. What she *probably* told you was to keep out of *my* bed."

"She did say you were vulnerable."

"Well maybe I *need* to be now and again. Or maybe she's just hard up. My virtue's a strange thing for *Etta* to be protectin'."

"That is kind of funny."

"No, it's not, skipper. What's funny is how you were talkin' to her. Like maybe you seen her picture in *Hustler* or somethin'."

Tom felt his cheeks burning. "I meant nothing by it."

"I don't guess you did. But *that* only makes it worse."

Slowly, as though handling eggs, Sarah began removing the curlers from her hair, placing them one by one into the basket. Her breasts, which were braless beneath her sweat shirt, jiggled as she worked, a sight so arousing to him that she may as well have been undressing. He suddenly felt like a peeper.

"Your virtue is safe with me," he said, lamely.

"What's *that* supposed to mean?"

"That we're wild yet innocent—much like the lilies of the field."

She laughed, shaking her head. The basket was full and she set it beside her on the couch. "That's just the problem if you ask *me*. You're a little too *used* to the field."

"Then take me in," he blurted. "Make me an honest man."

"Now don't get heavy on me, skipper. Do yourself a favor and keep on behavin' like a pig."

"Deny me that option and claim your revenge." He held out his hands to her. "Surely, I'm still worthy of punishment."

"Don't tempt me none," she griped. She closed the basket, rose from the couch, and kissed him softly on the chin. "Anyhow, I kinda *prefer* you as a pig."

Later, as she lay alongside him in bed, he looked at her naked reflection in the dresser mirror. The sharpness of her hips, the empty sag of her breasts, gave her body a shopworn quality that somehow belittled his passion for her. That his feelings were still genuine—that his string of one-nighters seemed frivolous now—struck him not as a revelation but a forewarning that he was dangerously out of his depth. His recent confession to Etta—"I've been thinking with the wrong head"—was suddenly an even greater embarrassment to him.

Sarah was nibbling his neck now, a gesture so intimate that his trepidations were instantly dashed. "You still thinkin' about Etta?" she asked.

"I'm not," he replied.

She laughed. "You're not much of a liar, skipper. I can't say it matters though."

"Why say that?"

"Because she's not going to be *around* much longer. Not if Brewer an' them have their way. Hawkins don't care for her either—the pig."

"That doesn't make sense. I thought you didn't like her."

"I *don't*. But that don't make *Hawkins* no saint."

She snuggled beside him, encircling his waist with her leg. His seed, leaking warmly from her crotch, felt uncomfortably sticky upon his hip. "I don't *need* to make sense to you, skipper—not if you're going back into that dorm. It don't look like sense will impress you none."

"I've got no choice," he replied.

"Why? 'Cause you're tight with Etta?"

"That isn't it."

"Is it because the Commissioner's blackmailin' you?"

His voice was barely audible. "Yes."

"You're lyin' to me again, skipper. He don't have a case and you know it."

"I'm inclined to believe that he does."

Sarah snorted. "That's 'cause you want to be a hotshot hero. But *you* ain't to blame for what *Yoakum* gone and done."

He shook his head. "You don't know the whole story."

"I don't need to," she said, pushing away from him. "'Cause he tried the same crap out on me. It was after he shot that joker in the kitchen dorm."

"What did he tell you?" Tom raised his head so he could look down at her.

"Can't you *guess*?"

"That the two of you had to keep tight?"

"That's right, skipper. He even suggested we sleep together. 'To help us stand firm against the brass' is how he put it."

Tom's head sunk back down to the pillow. He tried to speak sharply, but knew that he sounded hollow. "I'm *glad* you refused him."

Her voice grew sarcastic. "I'll *bet* you are—since you're so noble and all."

The springs grumbled as she sat up in bed. Retrieving her sweatshirt from the floor, she pulled it over her breasts. "*Now* will you quit perving on me? I'm no longer a buxom woman, you know."

He rolled toward her, one hand behind his head. "I don't care."

"Well *I* do. It's like you're lookin' for a reason to run on back to Etta."

"*Duty* is my mistress—not Etta."

"You're *still* bullshittin', skipper. You *oughta* let 'em put you out to pasture. I *told* you that once already."

"It's too quiet in a pasture."

She tugged at the sweatshirt, releasing her hair from the collar as she did so. When she spoke to him again it seemed like an afterthought. "What does *that* mean?"

He shrugged. "Call it fate or the tide of events. Call it the claim of an unholy wind. All I know is that the travesty of action is preferable to the silence of the void."

She chuckled. "Well ain't you *somethin'*, talking all flowery like Chester. All *I* know is my kids need fetchin'."

It was later, when they were sitting together at the kitchen table, that Tom realized the full dimensions of the void—an abyss that included not music or odes but the drawl of a siren over whom he could exercise not the slightest pretense. It was only her charity—her willingness to accept him as the rube he most certainly was—that gave him some semblance of definition, a compass too meager to equip him adequately for the no-man's-land he had entered. But his lifestyle had nonetheless come to an end—not in a flight of glory or the hail of bullets to come, but in this small incidental kitchen with a woman too worldly for him to impress. Sadly, he remembered the words of Hassan, the man's bleak but empathic admission that his candle had burned brighter when he had been a pimp.

Tom ate slowly, deliberately, as though the warmed over chili was a matter requiring careful concentration. This was not to avoid conversation with Sarah, but because the meal, in too many ways, had acquired for him the solemnity of the Last Supper. Sarah, sensing his preoccupation, sat quietly as he ate, ignoring her bowl as though engaging in a hunger strike. It was not until the meal was over and she had scraped and rinsed the bowls that she spoke to him again.

"It ends tonight, doesn't it?"

He nodded. "It's time."

"Time for *what*?"

"For the Hittites to storm the fortress." Tom gazed out the kitchen window. "I guess it should have happened before now."

She put down the dishtowel and folded her arms. "That's Chester talkin'—not *you*, skipper. What do they *need you* for?"

"To arrange a diversion in the dorm. Diversions are the one thing I'm good at."

"Accordin' to who? Etta?"

"She doesn't even know that I'm going back in there." He focused his gaze on Sarah's lean face. "Anyhow, you told me to keep away from her."

She shrugged and shook her head. "Too bad you never *worked* a dorm, skipper—like me and Yoakum done."

"I *have* worked a dorm," Tom snapped.

"For a couple of weeks maybe. An' probably not at night."

"It was the *second* shift."

"Then you *should* know what you're gettin' yourself into. It shouldn't take *Etta* to knock some sense into you." Sarah sat down again at the kitchen table. Her eyes, bright and disdainful, locked boldly onto his own. "Have you really forgotten what it's like?"

Tom rolled his eyes. "Remind me. Maybe I'll remember."

"It's the *bojacks* who do the divertin'. And it happens when they think someone's tryin' to sell 'em out. Seen 'em do it more than once. They'll raise a ruckus in the shower or someplace then wait for the dorm officers to go break it up. An' while that's happenin' they do in the snitch. Usually they cut his throat like a chicken."

"Yoakum told me as much."

"Course he did, skipper. That's how he *controls* his snitches. He tells 'em he'll expose 'em to the whole dorm if they don't tow the line for him."

"Are you telling me Etta is right?"

"I'm not givin' her that much credit. But you're chancin' it if you think you can hustle a laundry dorm. An' if you're workin' with a snitch you *both* deserve killing." Disdainfully, Sarah rose from the table and disappeared from the room. A half hour later she returned, wearing jeans and a light windbreaker. A purse, tucked beneath her elbow, suggested that their conversation was over.

"Go if you're goin'," she snapped. "At least you'll be puttin' one over on Etta."

Tom looked up from the kitchen table. "Is that a good thing?"

"Probably not. But if it keeps that bitch in her place it's good enough for me."

"That sounds rather petty."

"What do you mean by that?"

"At least I'm nobler than you."

She shrugged. "I'd rather be petty—if that's what you want to call it. The whole problem here, in case you haven't noticed, is that everyone has a damn good reason for what he's doin'. An' that even goes for the bojacks."

Her remark, its inverted but irresistible logic, gave him a moment of hope. "And what do you hold sacred?" he asked.

She shook her head sadly and looked at the floor. "Now what do you want me to tell you? You want me to tell you it's *you*?"

"Yes."

"Don't worry," she said. "I ain't holdin' you sacred, skipper. You wouldn't want the responsibility. But go con those bojacks and some asshole will."

"Why am I here if I'm such a lost cause?"

"You ain't a lost cause, skipper. You're a *pig*. And a pig is something I can handle." Sarah came over, squeezed his hand, then kissed him lightly on the neck. "It's time for you to go," she said. "Time you became hotshot hero. You're too damn lazy for anything else."

He wanted to hug her desperately, but his better instincts prevailed. After all, who was he to pledge himself to so sharp and spirited a woman? He had come too far already and the hammering of his heart had surely resulted from great and exhaustive flight. He swallowed past the lump in his throat. "Will you welcome me back when it's over?" he asked.

She shook her head. "Quit askin' those questions, skipper. There ain't no point to 'em. Anyhow, I'm gonna be in Rockville."

November 25, 2000
6:00 p.m.

His return to the prison gave Tom a fleeting sense of liberation: a sensation inconsistent to the advanced state of the siege, its aura of dark and malignant finality. The snipers on the roof, whose numbers had almost doubled, impressed him more than ever as a flock of carrion birds while the attack force, now swollen to over fifty men, struck him as an army of seasoned mercenaries. Lounging like hirelings in front of the Administration Building, their shotguns seemed too dusty, their blue uniforms too rumpled, their waists too fattened with tear gas canisters and cartridge belts. Surely, they had families to worry about. Surely, they wanted to go home alive. But their faces, as they watched him stroll by, were tense and noncommittal. He felt like a dead man walking.

The chapel, when he approached it through the east gate, also seemed foreboding to him: thick and heavily columned, its stained glass windows protected by bars, it better resembled a bastion than a refuge. Only a flirtatious comment from Etta—the one person who *had* spoken to him—provided him with a moment of levity. She had squeezed his elbow after briefing him in her office and had smiled indulgently. "You *are* a piece of work, Mr. Hemmings. *Earth mother* indeed."

He ducked into the chapel through the back door. Passing through a narrow foyer, he could hear music: a stern measured cadence that lacked the buoyancy of his cherished bluegrass. The hymn grew louder as he entered the assembly hall, so dominating the acoustical chamber that he did not at once notice its source: a cassette player parked on the foremost pew where his informant sat awaiting him. Were it not for the scent of tobacco, a rich rather chocolaty aroma, the hall would have struck him as utterly inhospitable. It therefore seemed an act of charity when Chester, noticing him at last, shut off the cassette player. It was time for the two of them to discuss their strategy. It was time to create the diversion.

Tom strode slowly towards the pews, more disturbed by the silence than the music, and seated himself on the pew beside Chester. Reluctant to speak, he studied the man, wondering obsessively how he had managed to acquire a smoking pipe.

"Still clouding the void?" Tom said, after a moment.

Chester nodded. "That I am, Mr. Hemmings. But not from conviction, sir. I am simply a vain and talkative man."

"But not without gifts, I see."

Chester sat solemnly, clutching the pipe in both of his hands. His fingers were shaking, his hair was unkempt, and his face looked as pale as his starched kitchen whites. He sucked the stem slowly and the smoke continued to bellow. "Gifts I have not earned," he said finally. "Think of it, sir. I'm an old rascal, an unrepentant sinner, a man who has abandoned his followers."

"And yet you sit listening to Bach."

Chester took another puff from his pipe. "The rarest of gifts, sir, and a fine example of God's mercy. Who am I to deserve Bach?"

The question, a reminder of his own rakish bounty, caught Tom unprepared. He slouched back in the pew, grateful for the gray indifference of the church. "For a man without grace, I've been lucky myself."

Chester frowned. "Does that mean you're sleeping with Mrs. Baumgardner, sir?"

"I am." Tom chuckled to himself. "She's all the windfall I can afford."

Chester shook his head. "Gifts should not carry a *price*, Mr. Hemmings. Remember the words of Jeremiah. 'Lift up your *eyes*. Like an Arab in the wilderness you have polluted yourself with harlotry. Therefore the spring rains will not come.'" Chester took another puff. "I speak from experience, sir."

"There are worse things than droughts."

"There are, Mr. Hemmings. And perhaps that is why I have been given this reprieve. Even in my hour of desolation, the Lord has comforted me."

"With Bach?"

"No, Mr. Hemmings. With a few good words from the Book of Sirath. 'What is too sublime for you seek not. What is beyond your strength search not.'"

"Isn't that a Catholic text?"

Chester's face colored. "And what of it, sir? Am I not a turncoat?" Again he sucked the pipe stem, a few prolonged puffs that seemed to ease the trembling in his hands. His eyes began to narrow, perhaps in deference to the haze.

Tom shook his head. "We *will* be saving lives."

"For what purpose, sir? God has decreed their harvest."

"And why is that? To punish the nonbelievers among them?"

"No, Mr. Hemmings. God's love is indiscriminate. I am surely proof of that."

Tom gazed at the stained glass windows surrounding them. He shook his head. "I, for one, can't figure out why."

Chester shrugged. "Who am *I* to say. I know only that his Kingdom is forever merciful. The Lord will exact just a fraction of his due while the misers—those who fix their scales for cheating—will demand to be paid in full."

Tom slumped in the pew. "Are we back to the Hittites?"

"We are, Mr. Hemmings. And woe unto them. The Lord has sworn by the pride of Jacob that *never* will he forget a *thing* they have done. The Book of Amos, sir."

Tom squirmed impatiently. "Aren't you a little heavy with the scripture today?"

Chester sighed. "I wish that were true, Mr. Hemmings. But scripture is not heavy to a charlatan."

"Yet you garnish every word of it, don't you, Chester?"

"Sadly I do, sir. But you already know that I'm a voyeur as well."

"Well, at least you can see the big picture. At least you're helping us take back the dorm. You're doing the right thing, Chester."

"But for the *wrong* reasons. I would rather be zealous than wise, sir. My path would be narrow, my suffering swift, and the Kingdom of Heaven thereafter my own. Such are the rewards of blindness." Chester tapped his pipe on the edge of the pew, knocking the ash to the floor.

"The *farm* will be your reward," Tom snapped. "Why not let it be enough?"

"It will have to be, won't it, sir? A farm where no farming is done—where the soil lies untilled and will not yield its strength. A most fitting prize for an impotent man."

"Submission brings safer rewards," Tom confessed.

"Alas, we reap what we sow, Mr. Hemmings? Shall we call it the Land of Nod?" Chester dipped into the pocket of his shirt, removing a pouch of Red Man tobacco. Fitting the pipe between his teeth, he filled up the bowl then quickly struck a match. The flame bobbed feebly before vanishing into another cloud of smoke.

"How are things in the dorm?" Tom asked.

"Bad, Mr. Hemmings. How else *could* they be? The Aryan Brotherhood and the Disciples quarrel constantly among each other. The Muslims—they just ponder and pray. But everyone still wants amnesty for the death of Lieutenant Perkins and everyone still wants reliable commissary—if only to pay their debts on time. A strange matter, isn't it, sir? Were it not for the generosity of Captain Hawkins we would all be famished right now."

"The generosity of *Hawkins*?"

"We traded two sick hostages for a load of supplies— soup and Spam mostly and a few boxes of cigarettes. The cigarettes alone were a bargain. They cost fifty dollars a pack on the black market now."

"How about a steak as well? Will any of them surrender for a steak?"

"At the expense of his life? I doubt that, Mr. Hemmings. Under the circumstances, Spam will do."

"How are the remaining hostages?"

"Better than might be expected. For the most part, they sit around playing cards and drinking tea. And they wager with the Aryan Brotherhood on the football games. They're in your office right now, sir, tied up and blindfolded. Hassan gave that order an hour ago. I guess Hawkins must have phoned him."

"What about weapons?"

"I don't think there are any more—not in the dormitory, anyway. But then again, I do not seek to know too much."

"And Hopper?"

"A frightening young man. We still have him tied to his bed. *Him* you can take off our hands any time." Chester swore softly then struck another match. The pipe, which had gone out, was now more of an irritation to him than a solace. He lowered his head, guiding the flame carefully while the stem remained rigid between his teeth.

"Can't you just toss him out?"

"We cannot, Mr. Hemmings. Not without forfeiting God's mercy. The boy is a mongrel who wants to die."

"You threw out some Disciples, didn't you? Before all this shit hit the fan?"

Chester lowered the pipe. "God will forgive us for *that*, Mr. Hemmings. Sir, they wouldn't stop talking about going back to Africa. We had simply had enough of them."

"I hear some of them snuck into the commissary. And that one of them took a shot at us."

"If you say so, Mr. Hemmings. Again, I do not seek to know too much."

Chester rose from the pew and then walked over to a small desk parked beside the altar. Slowly, methodically, he emptied his pockets, placing several letters and some photos into one of the drawers. He relinquished the items slowly, ritualistically, like a man making a deposit at a bank.

"Mementos of your wife?"

Chester nodded. "We must all hold something sacred, sir—if only for the sake of duty. We were wed for forty years."

"You were lucky."

"I know that, Mr. Hemmings. Yet my memory of her is empty. She's a mirage to me now and perhaps she always was."

"Sounds like *forsaken* duty."

"I suppose it was, Mr. Hemmings. But there is much to be said for a wasteland, sir. For forty years it protected me from loathsome mischief. Is it any wonder that Moses remained so long in the desert?" Chester closed the drawer slowly, cautiously, an act not of reverence but forfeiture. But his face was relaxed when he returned to the pew.

"You *do* remember the plan?" Tom asked. "I'm sure Hawkins discussed it with you."

"He did. I'm to ask the inmates to surrender peacefully for a steak. Perhaps a sermon will convince them to do that, sir."

"And if they surrender?"

"*You* will instruct them to march out the front door. Hands upon their heads."

"And if they don't?"

"I'll encourage them to debate the matter. While they're quarreling among one another the dorm lights will go out and Pharaoh's troops will strike."

"Until then the hostages stay in my office. Tied up and blindfolded."

Chester nodded and remained standing. "And so we are not without grace, Mr. Hemmings. Since sight is a liability, we can do them no greater favor."

Tom again squirmed in the pew; it was becoming uncomfortable to him. "You're speaking facetiously."

"No, Mr. Hemmings. For *once* I am sincere. I long for the cover of darkness myself."

"Spoken like a true thief."

"A thief, Mr. Hemmings, but not without temperance. After all, I have stolen only a fraction of what I could have."

Tom shook his head. "No more bullshit, Chester. If the lights go out, make a run for my office. I'll be waiting for you there. Knock three times and I'll let you in. And I'll tie you up once I've untied the guards. Nobody will know you're a turncoat."

Chester folded his arms. His gaze was now distracted, condescending, as though he had deigned to take comfort in the stained glass window that glittered anemically at the back of the church. He tapped his foot impatiently. "Shall we get on with it, sir?"

Tom rose from the pew, not bothering to answer, and followed the little man from the assembly hall back into the dingy foyer. They departed the chapel through the back door, then crept through the alleyway between the dormitories and the perimeter fence. The buildings, though old and crumbly, were sufficient to shield them from the sharpshooters.

IV

SMOKE

The light was departing.
The brown air drew down ...
—Dante Alighieri

November 25, 2000
7:00 p.m

Tom clutched Chester's arm at the entrance to the dormitory. "You *do* remember the plan," he repeated. "Ask them to surrender. Divert them if they don't. That's when the lights will go out."

Chester sighed stoically then patted Tom on the shoulder. "Yes, Mr. Hemmings. I *remember* the plan. It is hardly so intricate that an old man would forget it."

"Well, make sure you follow it," Tom muttered nervously.

Cautiously, Tom followed Chester into the dormitory. The huge but familiar room was suddenly intimidating to him, perhaps because the remaining hostages—all nine of them—were now sitting in his office tied to chairs. Showcased behind the Plexiglas window, they looked like stuffed monkeys on display. The men looked so helpless, so utterly degraded, that their blindfolds seemed to be a gift. That the dorm was otherwise disorganized, a neighborhood of noisy inmate cliques, did little to alleviate Tom's sudden rush of fear: the suspicion that neither he nor Chester had the ability to create a successful diversion. He hoped the sequestration of the hostages was a signal from Hassan, a sign that the thin man would help them round up the inmates, but Hassan, praying alone at one of the game tables, only nodded when Tom locked eyes with him: a look that conveyed neither solace nor familiarity—only an empty acknowledgement that Tom had come back to the dormitory. Were it not for Gabriel Grant, who was also sitting alone at a game table, Tom would have believed himself to be a phantom; it in fact seemed an act of clairvoyance when Gabriel, noticing him finally, rose from the table and bolted towards him.

"His *feet* smell, Jackson!"

211

"Whose?"

"That Hopper dude. His *feet* smell. Make him wash his *feet*, Jackson!"

It took Tom a moment to notice Hopper. The boy, who still looked like a leper, had been bound to a chair in the television area—probably so the Muslims could keep a better watch over him. The boy looked both feral and dispirited, his features so shrunken, his eyes so hollow, that he seemed unaware of even the televised football game, a rowdy contest between the Patriots and Raiders. Remembering his link to Hopper, the role he had played in killing the boy's lover, Tom could only appreciate the vigilance of the Muslims: these taciturn men, in all probability, were preventing him from getting hurt.

Tom looked at Gabriel, shaking his head. "Forget about Hopper. He's not your concern."

"But his feet *smell*, Jackson."

"I don't know what else to tell you, Gabriel."

A suggestion more practical than his own floated from the crowd in front of the television. "*I* do! *Kill* the little motherfucker! Let him rot and stink some more!"

Tom felt Chester's hand upon his elbow. "End this discussion, sir. End it *now*." The little man was guiding him in the direction of Hassan. As they approached the game tables, Chester's voice grew calmer. "Don't *stray* from our plan, I beg you, sir. It is hardly *our* privilege to wash the feet of beggars."

Hassan, rising slowly from the table, bowed his head. His face remained cold and inscrutable as Tom nodded back.

"Thank you," Tom muttered.

"For what, Mr. Hemmings?" The man's voice was without inflection.

"For securing the hostages."

"We have bound them with mere strips of sheet," Hassan murmured. "Every half hour we loosen the knots. That *isn't* the fortune of sheep, is it now?"

"Your martyrdom is assured."

Hassan shook his head. His expression had become bitter. "Only *saints* may be martyred, Mr. Hemmings. Pimps are simply exterminated. And we both know that I have *never* been more than a pimp."

"Today you did better."

"Did I, Mr. Hemmings? Then today you must strike me down."

"You *do* know the plan," Tom murmured.

"I do."

"Then you know that you don't have long to wait."

Hassan smiled thinly. His face seemed haunted as he gazed towards the bed pods. A small group of Muslims, having finished their evening prayer, were drifting towards the game tables. Hassan shook his head and sighed. "We *all* know we will soon be attacked, Mr. Hemmings."

Tom lowered his voice. "You said you'd be silent about that."

"And did you think my silence would make a difference?"

Chester, shuffling impatiently, pulled once again at Tom's elbow. His expression was stern as he interrupted the conversation. "Silence is far too resonant, sir. And for that very reason, Mr. Hassan is permitting me to speak. Perhaps my words, vain though they may be, will tame the hush."

Tom's heart was now pounding. "I only hope that you're inspired," he murmured.

Chester nodded grimly. "Angels will loosen my tongue, Mr. Hemmings, as they have always done. Consider it yet *another* undeserved gift." The man seemed profoundly sad, as though he were submitting not to inspiration but to the dictates of an iron destiny. Chester's voice began to quiver. "Will you help me up onto a table, sir?"

Tom nodded, accepting Chester's hand, and was surprised by the heaviness of his little body. The man's joints crackled like a rifle salute as he scrambled to a standing position on top of a game table, but the sound was not a commanding one. The crowd that now surrounded them seemed too diverse to control, the blood-red headbands of the Disciples too stark a contrast to the discreet beanies of the Muslims and the polished skulls of the Aryan Brotherhood. Not even the crowd noise from the television, a cheer for a winning field goal, seemed to diminish the tribalism of the inmates. Only Hopper, who was now looking desperately about, appeared to have his own identity: a useless gift since his stare was like that of a trapped animal. Tom shuddered and looked away, but not before noticing that the television area was empty—that the roar from the football game had been replaced by the virile theme song from *Cops*.

Hassan chuckled softly and patted Tom's back. "The game was close, Mr. Hemmings."

November 25, 2000
7:30 p.m.

The dorm was now silent, the clamor of the television having given way to the potent hush of the crowd, a silence too dark and brooding to seem accessible to the platitudes of an aging homilist. Chester, perhaps sensing the power of the void, began to tremble as he looked among the vacant faces. His skin was now clammy, his brow damp, and he clutched a small Bible in his hand as though it were an amulet. Even when he spoke, his words seemed irrelevant, a pitch meant only for backwoods meeting tents and the crisp applause of the converted.

"Gentlemen," he began. "We have proven ourselves to be charitable hosts. But *dare we now host* the prophet Isaiah?" He opened the Bible and started to read, but his voice, which seemed suddenly too large for him, only accentuated his fragile appearance. His reversion to his persona therefore seemed desperate, not calculated, as though he were drowning without a life vest. But it was still a heroic moment, an assertion so rash, so utterly careless, that it could only have been born of a profound self-weariness.

Chester lowered the Bible. Looking complacently at the crowd, he appeared to have been drugged by the sing-song cadence of the verses—so much so that not even the wooden stares of the Muslims seemed to affect him. His voice

214

swelled as he continued speaking, his delivery so patented, so rhythmic, that he no longer looked at the scripture.

"Gentlemen," he snapped. "Prophecy is cruel. And therefore true justice belongs to the Lord. Better we should *weep* for those who decree inequity, for those who sanctify plagues, for those who lay waste to the wretched. How will they hide when the locust return to roost? Where will they stash their crippling wealth? Truly, *nothing* will remain for them but to crouch among the prisoners and fall among the stricken for God's anger will not be dissuaded."

What the fuck was this? Tom wondered. The little man was straying from the script. Instead of placating the inmates, calming them with the word of God, he was using the Bible like a sword. Had he forgotten the purpose of his mission or was he simply trying to rivet the attention of the inmates?

Tom felt betrayed as Chester closed the Bible. The little man's eyes were now filled with humility and sadness, yet he also seemed invigorated by the mention of epic sin. His voice remained strong as he continued speaking. "Because they neglect our sick, because they steal our pittance, because they punish our sins sevenfold, let them *hear* the word of Jehovah. There is ever a time when weighted scales and swindled grain will cease to acquit the reaper's scathe, when the rain will lay rust to his stolen blade, and when the very earth will disparage his seed and spit forth a harvest of rage."

The words, though well rehearsed, seemed like hailstones striking a window pain, a knocking too lyrical and repetitious to merit the responses that rose randomly from the crowd. "Let *go* my people!" a deep voice thundered, generating several bursts of sarcastic laughter. "The bitches took my *shorts*!" a second voice cried. "Like it *isssss*!" a third party hollered, probably one of the Disciples. "Say it like it *isssss*, Deacon!"

Chester, still buoyed by the scripture, slowly raised his hand, a gesture that was somehow sufficient to restore the room to silence. The aplomb with which he stood upon the table, the confidence with which he now faced the rabble, had given him a dignity that overrode even his broken promise to the facility—his pledge to con and not rally the inmates. *At least he betrayed us with a kiss,* Tom thought bitterly. He wanted to tap Chester's knee, implore him to tone things down, but his hands were shaking with fear.

Chester reopened the Bible and read. His voice was soft and melodious now, and he dispensed each word as though it were a jewel. "Gentlemen, the Book of Revelations," he said. "Behold a pale horse, the bearer of Death, and Hades and tribulations follow him. But know that the Devil throws some into prison *only* that they may be tested. Be faithful unto death and you will reap the crown of life everlasting."

"Like it *isssss,* Deacon!" the same voice shouted. An enforced silence had otherwise settled upon the crowd, an acquiescence that seemed attributable less to the power of Chester's speech than the watchfulness of the Muslims who had now formed a circle around him. Hassan, still standing among them, looked particularly formidable, his eyes so calm, his face so ashen, that he could well have been one of the seraphim conscripted to set loose the plagues.

Chester, his voice now hoarse, began to cough. One of the Muslims placed a plastic water bottle in his hand and he drank from it deeply as though attempting to douse a flame. The liquid finally lubricated his throat and his words rang clearly as he continued speaking. "I say to you now, don't *heed* the Great Harlot—she who would strip you of even your shorts. Her nails have grown brittle, her breasts limp and foul, and her favors bring only disease. Neither should you fear the storm, for it is God's own storm and will topple the lofty more swiftly than the low. And when the winds are spent and the torrents swept away, another storm will follow and another and another until the idols have been crushed, the lenders scattered, and Babylon has been rendered unto dust. And on that day, the sun will split the clouds and startle the land with a strange and ghostly light."

"*Leeead* me to the harlot!" a loud voice exclaimed. "Split *her* instead!" another voice called. More laughter rippled throughout the crowd, but the levity seemed forced, anemic, like the prepackaged chuckles of a television sitcom. The

216

moment belonged to Chester—no one else—not because of
destiny, not even because of hysteria, but because he alone
had been foolish enough to seize the tiller of nationhood.
Having gained the underrated element of surprise, he was
simply without a serious competitor, an advantage for
which he appeared to be grateful. His gaze held steady as
he looked upon the crowd and his voice became suddenly
tender.

"Some of you are not willing to make a stand," Chester
continued. "If that is the case, depart—I beg you. Mr.
Hemmings will escort you safely to a holding range where
you will be given a warm cell, a blanket, and a steak, though
perhaps not a stake in heaven. Heaven, after all, is for men
of faith and courage. But depart, I beg you, you who are
afraid. We do not wish to see you harmed."

Chester waited and watched. Not a man stirred, a
response he must surely have anticipated. After a minute,
he shook his head sadly and tucked the Bible into his hip
pocket. He continued to speak.

"Those of you who stay," he said. "I will address you
hereafter as brothers. For there is not *one* among you so
wretched, so vile, so tainted and forlorn that this day will
not mitigate your sins and make you a brother to us all. And
whatever taxes you on this day will only make you dearer
and you will not fall, but an angel will catch you, restore
you with the blood of the lamb, and deliver you, a newborn
child, to the fraternity of heaven."

"Like it *isssss*!" the same voice shouted, a commendation
that somehow seemed unworthy of the speech. Even the
smattering of applause, the slow clapping of a dozen pairs
of hands, seemed a meager response to such blundering
courage, the compulsion of a single man to cast himself,
however clumsily, as Bethlehem's provident beast. It was
therefore the very absence of noise that gave the little
man his validation: the cessation of derision, however
enforced, seemed a comedy less than a sublime suspension
of selfishness. Chester, aware of his triumph, perhaps even
sensing the transience of the moment, leaned forward to
conclude his speech.

"Gentlemen," he said. "I am surely the poorest of speakers. I have stumbled on my words, shaken like a child, and stolen the language of wiser men. It must truly be a bondsman's blessing that a tongue so pathetic as my own might raise you to the glory of the angels. Though mortal servility might have proved wiser, our sovereign is so blind, his ransom so vile, that he has stolen from us even the tolerance of saints. And so let fire be our faith and fortune our master and let angels make dear our depleted accounts. Let us drink this cup joyously, my brothers, and pledge to it our hearts, our courage, and our renewed honor."

The little man tottered as he finished speaking, clearly exhausted, and his hand trembled as he drank again from the water bottle. His speech, though a masterstroke, had cost him too much; he looked visibly shaken now and his perch above the throng made it seem as if he were standing in the shadow of a noose. But the spell of his sermon continued to linger, resonating in the reticence of the crowd, the renewed clapping of several pairs of hands, and the towering presence of Hassan whose expression, grim and determined, seemed to be one of prayer. *Let it begin*, was the message in his face. *And let it be now—when souls are buoyant and ready for flight.* The homage of the crowd, a formidable illusion, persisted even when Gabriel Grant, doubtlessly a vestige of Babylon, spoke suddenly from the edge of the room. His comment, vulgar and mercifully brief, was like the frantic honking of a goose.

"You stole my soup, Jackson!"

November 25, 2000
Game Time

Tom ducked into his office and slipped the radio from his belt. It would be foolhardy to remain any longer among the inmates, to offer them the false promises of immunity, or to gamble on the judgment of the sharpshooters should he dash out of the dorm. Things were

218

getting out of control and he had to stay safe. But at least the inmates were diverted in the game area.

Depressing the squelch button, he gave the signal. "It's game time," he murmured. His voice was so low that he doubted that it had carried above the hand clapping in the dormitory. Hearing no response from the Control Unit, he felt a shiver of panic. Had he forgotten to energize the charger? He plunged the radio back into its sheath and quickly locked his office door.

The lights in the building suddenly went out. The phone on his desk began to ring, a petty scolding that only irritated him as he pocketed his keys. The telephone could not compete with the racket in the dormitory: cries, curses, Plexiglas shattering. The attack was underway.

He groped blindly for the phone, guided by the ringing. When he found the receiver, he pressed it against his ear. "What?!!"

"Hemmings?" It was Hawkins.

"Here I am!" he replied.

"Yer office secure? You out of the loop?" The captain sounded frantic enough to be bullied.

"A cuckold is *always* out of the loop."

"Now this ain't the *time* to be ribbin' me, Hemmings."

"Why not?"

"*We're* the ones packin' hard-ons tonight."

Tom patted the keys in his pocket and sighed. "What good does that do someone out of the loop?"

He knew he was speaking hopefully. The dormitory was so dark he could see only semblances, outlines too shadowy to be captured by the searchlight combing the barred windowpanes. Another crash, followed by more glass tinkling, gave him a moment of hope: the glare from the searchlight was now more intense—evidence that the main window to the dormitory had been shattered. He could now hear the noise from the compound outside: hasty commands, the growl of the personnel carrier, and the *pop pop popping* of the first tear gas canisters.

He returned the receiver to his ear. "How long till the inmates are fucked?"

"A few minutes more oughta do it," Hawkins said. "We've taken 'em by surprise—thanks to you and that Chester fella. But a couple of them bojacks need packin' in before we take back the dorm."

As Hawkins spoke, Tom could hear the cover fire of the shotguns: a booming so rhythmic—so measured—that it suggested target practice rather than battle.

"The ones in the commissary?"

"Not *them*, Hemmings. They ain't even shootin' back at us."

"Then who?"

"Some fuckers from yer dorm. We seen 'em herdin' hostages outside. Must've been the tear gas that drove 'em out. That and the smoke from the mattresses they're burnin'."

"The hostages are in my office."

He could hear Hawkins grunt, a virile sound that bordered on a chuckle. "The ones they haven't knifed, maybe. One of 'em just *castrated* a hostage, Hemmings. Cut off his balls an' ate 'em Mau Mau style."

Tom gripped the receiver tightly. "*No one's* had his nuts severed, Hawkins. The hostages are in my office—*all tied up.*"

"If they're tied up, Hemmings, they *oughta* be severed. It's time you cut 'em loose, dontcha think?"

It was the excitement in Hawkins' voice, its utter lack of constraint, that convinced Tom to attend to the hostages. Dropping the receiver, he ambled across the room, his hands out in front of him to absorb a fall. He was startled when his hands touched flesh: a discovery that brought him neither pride nor relief, only an embarrassing reminder that he had not finished his job. He removed the man's blindfold then the gag. The wrist bindings were more of a challenge: the cloth had been soaked in water and the knots were harder than stone. His fingers ached as he attacked the knots and he heard a snapping in one of his knuckles. His hand went entirely numb.

"Rajah ..." It was a feeble sound, an old man's voice—sullen but ineffectual, moody yet acquiescent. The man had mistaken him for Hassan.

"I'm here to release you!" he snapped.

"I know that, Rajah. But tea and a biscuit is what I'm wantin'. It ain't too much to be askin' for, is it?"

Tom tugged at the bindings, working them loose, but the man did not rise from the chair. One of his hands had sprung free of the knots and was gripping Tom's wrist like a vise. Tom helped the old man to his feet. "Untie the others," he whispered—a command he could only hope would be obeyed. He returned to his desk and started groping about, but the phone was now buried in darkness. His fingers had thawed when he finally found the receiver; the knuckle howled as he spoke.

"They'll be packing in a minute or two." He was speaking facetiously but Hawkins seemed immune to ridicule.

"A minute is all we need, Hemmings."

"What's happening now?"

"We've already captured the commissary. The bojacks were passed out in there—drunk on *pineapple jack*. Soon we'll be takin' the *dorm* back too."

"Did you get their rifle?"

"It ain't in there, Hemmings. Some fucker must have run off with it."

A boom, another crash, and the clamor of barking dogs suggested that Hawkins had miscalculated yet again. Already, there were officers in the dormitory, their arrival announced by drifting flashlights, heavy footfalls, and the dull thudding of batons. A blaze of light hit him, blinding him momentarily before continuing its trajectory, an orbit accompanied by a ringing shout: "*On yer bunks.*" The afterglow blanketed his eyes.

Tom spoke into the receiver. "It's over."

"What makes you *say* that?" Hawkins yelled.

"The dorm's lost its heart. They're clubbing these bojacks like seals."

"If they're still clubbin' 'em, Hemmings, how can it be *over*?"

"Well maybe it *ought* to be."

"Don't lecture me *now*, Hemmings. Coddlin' won't help 'em none. If they get jacked up, we'll have to smoke five times as many."

"Why don't you get them some *pineapple* jack?"

Hawkins groaned. "Hemmings, you ain't there to *baby sit* the bojacks. You're there to *free hostages*. How're they doin' anyhow?"

Tom lowered the phone and looked towards the hostages. His eyes, again accustomed to the gloaming, could see several forms shuffling around the office—men moving so stiffly that he felt he was witnessing the resurrection of the dead. The hostages seemed deaf to the renewed clamor in the dormitory: screams, thuds, the booming of shotguns—all signs that the struggle was accelerating. He had anticipated the counterattack—he had even been prepared to take pleasure in it—but the chill of intuition now paralyzed him.

Tom lifted the receiver. "The hostages are loose."

Hawkins grunted. "And payback's gonna be a bitch. Now wait for my signal then open the door for 'em. It's *time* them old fellas kicked ass."

"But they're *older* than time."

"Maybe so, Hemmings. But they're still good men. Most of 'em are Korean War vets and vets ain't squeamish about a fight."

The door to his office was thudding like a war-drum. Tom squinted, attempting to identify the hammering, and realized it was coming from outside the office. He did not know if it was a guard or an inmate, but he felt no compulsion to let the person in. He instead felt a surge of rebellion, anger so familiar to him that it almost amounted to nostalgia. Tom called softly to the hostages as though he were soliciting ghosts.

"We taking the dorm back, fellas?"

"Fuck 'em up!" one of them shouted, perhaps the heartiest of the Korean vets.

"Who's poundin the door?!!" another demanded. "If it's *Perkins* kick his butt."

And if it's Chester, fuck him, Tom thought.

Tom mumbled sarcastically into the receiver—"Whenever you say, Hawkins." An explosion of glass quickly killed his derision: a direct hit upon his office window, it obliterated all thoughts of contempt. He had not heard the shotgun, the most likely cause of the impact, but the din of battle was deafening now and tear gas was scalding his eyes.

A passing glare stunned him, the narrow eye of a flashlight, and Tom dropped the receiver as though it might incriminate him. His keys were irrelevant now, but he clutched them tightly and leaped towards the door. The pounding had stopped but he felt no reaction—he could only grope blindly for the lock.

He inserted a key, twisted the handle, and stumbled out into the dormitory.

November 25, 2000
Game Time

Tom felt as though he had stumbled into the first circle of hell: a smoky under-region that was only vaguely horrific since it offered some hope of deliverance. This was perhaps due to the probe of the searchlight; the theatrical glare streaming through a dormitory window lent a symbiotic quality to continuing pockets of battle, as though the combatants were engaging in acrobatic displays. His vision was further softened by the prick of the tear gas in his eyes, a benevolent ache that moderated the shadows and gave the dormitory an airy glitter. He was therefore unimpressed when he tripped over something soft but rigid; the obstacle, a fleshy inmate in kitchen whites, only added to the harmony of the room. The man's hands stretched towards him as though trying to calm him, a timely gesture since the face was as sculptured as a statue's and bore an expression of utter peace. The man's wound, a tiny dot upon his shirt, seemed no more than a food stain, a blot too incidental to merit either empathy or alarm. Tom stepped over the corpse and began to move cautiously towards the back of the dormitory.

"*Cole slaw.*" The cry, though senseless, was loud enough to startle him. He looked back at the dead man, half-expecting him to rise, but the demand had come from an inmate with a more stunning wound. The man's jaw, dislocated and dangling, gave him the toothy gape of a crocodile, a queer parody since the injury had not compromised his ability to speak. "*Cole slaw,*" he repeated shrilly. "*Cole slaw.*" The man lunged as he spoke, seizing Tom's forearm with such authority that Tom felt like a felon when he resisted. He pulled back desperately, freeing his arm, and the man, off balance, staggered past him and vanished into the haze.

Frantic to forget the incident, Tom looked around the dormitory. A plan had now formed in the back of his mind. If he could unlock the staff entrance, which lay beyond the last of the bed pods, he could make his escape through the alley behind the building. He did not think of this as abandoning the field of battle but as a sane response to friendly fire; there was no indication that the attack was succeeding or that his rescuers were capable of striking with precision. He could see only shadows, hear only curses, see only patches of lingering smoke. Something buzzed past his ear—more glass exploded. A split second later he heard the distant report of a rifle. An onslaught of lava invaded his bowels and he fought back the urge to shit as he ducked into the inmate bathroom.

"Drop that cigar!" The cry floated aimlessly throughout the dorm—a cry Tom could not comprehend. But he froze, as though chastised for his cowardice, and was grateful when a sight in the bathroom distracted him. An obese inmate was kneeling on the bathroom floor, tugging at the pants of a slender officer who had been knocked unconscious. The inmate was watching Tom like an owl and his eyes were watery with fear. The man bowed his head and started to weep. "Drive me to *Jesus*, sir."

Tom could make out the baton lying beside the officer and, knowing instantly that the inmate wanted to be

224

stopped, picked it up and struck him on the shoulder. The blow was harder than he had intended—he could hear the collar bone snap—but the man only shuddered with gratitude. "Thank you, sir. Thank you." Tom hit him a second time, grazing his skull before striking his neck, and then forced himself to drop the baton. The inmate, oblivious to the blood ribboning his forehead, continued to grovel. "Thank you, sir. Thank you." He was masturbating furiously as he wept.

Another shotgun blast, followed by the renewed barking of dogs, drowned out the whimpering of the inmate. It was the sound of reinforcements: an unwelcome surge since Tom did not wish to be rescued with shitty pants. Reluctantly, as though betraying a friend, he abandoned the weeping inmate and ducked into one of the toilet stalls. His bowels erupted the moment he sat on the stool and he finished his crap in seconds. He then tightened his belt, flushed the toilet, and stumbled from the stall.

A gang of Disciples, involved in an act of retribution, blocked his exit from the bathroom. Two lanky boys were holding down a stout boy, a Disciple whose red handkerchief had slipped down over his eyes. A fourth boy, a head taller than the rest, was methodically striking the stout one, delivering the blows with impatient commands. "Keep your head up, Jerome! Take your whuppin' like a *man!*" The stout boy raised his head and the tall boy cracked his knuckles upon his skull. Clutching his hand, the tall boy howled with pain. "*Motherfucker,*" he screamed. He kicked savagely at the stout boy, disloging him from the grip of the other two Disciples. Quick as a hare, the stout boy bolted from the bathroom and melted into the dormitory.

The tall boy, noticing that Tom was watching him, displayed his sore hand. "It *hurts*, Mr. Hemmings," he griped. He wiggled the fingers then spoke as though embarrassed. "He stole my *tobacco*, sir. Didn't want to *pay* me for it."

Tom replied, "Follow me." His order seemed cocky under the circumstances, but the tall boy, blinded by his pain, trailed him obediently from the bathroom. It was not until they were half way across the dormitory that a beef-faced officer sang out to them.

"Lets *see* them hands!" The officer looked sympathetic in the half-light and the tall boy, relieved, pointed his hand towards him. When the shotgun bellowed the boy grabbed his stomach. He staggered drunkenly, as though imitating a man with a bellyache. "Oh my!" he laughed. He was clutching his gut like a halfback on the dodge, but a football-shaped bundle spilled through his hands. The boy wrinkled his nose, repulsed by the stench of undigested Spam. He sat down slowly upon the floor. "Jerome broke my knuckles, sir!" He slipped the injured hand into his pants, removing a knife that was too slick for him to hang onto. The weapon dangled from his fingers then clattered harmlessly to the floor.

"*Mr. Hemmings*?" The officer's voice was panicky now. Tom nodded, holding his hands high as he backed away from the injured boy. The officer, assured that Tom wasn't an inmate, waived him aside. "Ya seen nothing, sir," the man muttered; he cracked the shotgun, ejecting a trapped shell, then he fired another blast at the boy. "Jerome!" the boy shouted. "You *fucker*, Jerome!" He curled into a ball as he began to die.

The officer cracked the shotgun once again. "Ya seen nothing, sir," he rasped. "I'm a UAW man—just like yerself, Mr. Hemmings. Now you best get outta here, sir." The man clapped him on the shoulder, yodeled with excitement, and dashed towards the far end of the dormitory.

The dogs were now louder, an insatiable barking that suggested the E-squads were taking control of the dorm. But the din of battle still persisted: the thuds and cries had in fact intensified, rendering comical the hysterical protests of a cornered inmate. "Don't let him chew *me*, officer!" the voice cried. "It was Short Dog what hit you with that soup can."

"Stop lyin' to me, Rashad! I seen ya stab my buddy!"

"Take care of yer *buddy*!" a louder voice hollered. The order was followed by another shotgun blast.

"Get outta here, Hemmings! We told you that once already!" The command was superfluous: caught now in a surge of bodies, a wave of retreating inmates, Tom was being buffeted steadily towards the back of the dormitory. He stumbled and was about to fall when someone grabbed him from behind with a bear hug, walloping the air from his lungs. Tom responded quickly, instinctually, driving his fist into the man's testicles then spinning towards him when his grip relaxed. He struck the man's nose with the heal of his hand and was astonished when the bone broke. The sound was like a walnut cracking.

The inmate, a burley Muslim, looked at him reproachfully. "I just wanted some Winstons!" he groused; the man sank to his knees and stared frantically at the floor. "Whew," he said then rolled onto his back.

Tom knelt, preparing to help the fallen inmate, but was knocked flying by a blow from a baton. The dorm spun like a carrousel, hot lights exploding as though celebrating the recapture of the dormitory. Tom extended his palms to block the next blow, but felt only the wetness on the floor, an oily pool that was soaking his knees. The body beside him was waxy, serene, and he looked at it with bewilderment. It was the body of an officer—not the inmate he had struck. The man's head was pulpy but his eyes were remote—unaffected by even the porridge of brain matter leaking from his nose. He seemed to be superior to the battle. Tom lifted his hands, sniffing compulsively at the sticky liquid that covered them. It was chicken soup.

"Thompson?" The voice belonged to an elderly officer who had lingered behind the attack force. The man was sitting on a bunk, looking tenderly in Tom's direction. Probably, he was one of the hostages.

"I'm Hemmings," Tom snapped.

"Pardon me, sir. But I thought you was Thompson." The man was holding a saucer in his hands as though he were awaiting a cup of tea. "You *know* he went fishin' without his hat. Wanted to catch himself some largemouths."

Tom shook his head. "I'll send him back to *fetch* it."

"*Would* you, sir?" The officer looked relieved. "A man oughtn't go fishin' without his hat, you know." He dropped the saucer, a piece of skull, and rose slowly from the bunk. "Dern you, Claude Adkins," he muttered angrily. "There was worms for the diggin' too."

Repulsed, Tom looked away from the officer. The staff entrance, although probably blocked by the retreating inmates, remained a fixation to him: an outlet more logical than the front door where he was sure to be targeted by a sharpshooter. Slowly, heroically, he rose to his feet, but was lost in a sudden implosion of lights. The lights became subtle as he stumbled through the dormitory, the brightness replaced by sinewy haze and the macabre vestiges of battle. Bodies, visible now in the half-glow, lay all around him, their features so bent, so comically twisted, that they looked like broken dolls. But there were sights more startling than the bodies: an effeminate boy was braiding the hair of a corpse, a sallow-faced man was painting himself with shit, a jowly inmate, his bowels heaped tidily upon his lap, was dabbing his face with shaving lotion. The man called to Tom as he passed. "Jonah!" he cried. "Keep the cow in the *barn*, Jonah!" He looked like a butcher displaying tripe.

The smoke thickened as Tom approached the staff entrance, and he could now smell lighter fluid. He could also smell meat, slightly scorched meat, a gentle reminder of his meals with Sarah. Quickly, Tom fumbled his keys from his pocket, panicking when he was unable to feel them. But the keys were in his hand, mocking the cottony sensation in his fingers. He picked out the key to the staff entrance and clutched it tightly.

A cheesy smell buried the smoky aroma, alerting him to the presence of a huge inmate: a paunchy perspiring man completely naked except for a chef's hat on his hand. The man was hopping from foot-to-foot, watching him with vacant eyes. He rubbed his genitals and spoke. "Dish it up, pardner!" he snarled.

Tom froze. "*Back off, asshole,*" he warned.

The man cackled. "Open the *door* is all I meant. We only cook squealers in here."

Tom's stomach bucked as though kicked by a mule. "What the fuck are you cooking?" he gasped.

The man smiled sheepishly. "Trixie," he said. "But she shouldn't be *givin'* blow jobs. She's lousy with AIDS and the biggest snitch in the dorm. Hassan said leave her be, but we hadda torch her for *everyone's* sake. She smells like *bacon*, don't she, sir?"

The playfulness of the man, his ghoulish sense of humor, filled Tom with horror. Frantic, he stabbed the key into the lock, but pain crippled his hand when he tried to turn it. The smoke was so thick now, his panic so blind, that he felt as though he had been tied to a stake. But his grip did not weaken. The bolt started creaking. Slowly, the door rolled open.

November 25, 2000
8:30 p.m.

Tom stepped out into the alley, closing the door behind him then locking it with a final twist of the key. The act suddenly seemed foolish: the alley was filled with effigies, not allies, phantoms so ominously cloaked by the haze that he suspected he had cut off an avenue of retreat. His apprehension only grew as he plunged into the smog and staggered in the direction of the sally port. He had stumbled no more than a half dozen paces when one of the forms, perhaps sensing his vulnerability, drifted towards him.

A harvest moon made the form look angelic: the features, small and child-like, were slow to develop, while the haziness gave it an almost celestial quality. Tom's attitude therefore remained one of hope, even when he recognized the hollow eyes, the sunken cheeks, the weak receding chin. That Hopper was limping emboldened Tom further; his own injury, a tight lump at the base of his skull, had provided him with the bond of empathy, an advantage he had surely been lacking during the manhunt.

Hopper halted, grimacing as he did so. His voice was soft and nasally, and he was favoring his right leg.

"Say, mister!"

"I hear you."

"It may as well be now, mister."

"Not here," Tom replied. "We can get out through the sally port."

Hopper nodded sullenly. Their brief exchange appeared to have unnerved him. "I guess it don't matter much where," he muttered. Hopper reached into his pocket, removing a large red rag with which he wiped the soot from his face. The handkerchief, which he had probably borrowed from a Disciple, made the swastika on his boney wrist look comical. "I wish you'd go on ahead of me, mister. I don't wanna look at your face."

"Be careful what you wish for."

The boy spat. "Fuck being careful. Being careful got me *hurt*."

"Don't hold yourself at fault."

"It *weren't* my fault," Hopper whined. "One of them marksman did it. Shot me down like I was a colored man. And all I was doin' was runnin' from the dorm."

"You don't have much further to run."

"I *can't* run, mister. You go on ahead. I'll try to catch up to you."

Tom turned away from Hopper, not wanting to talk to him any more, and stumbled in the direction of the sally port. Behind him, he could hear the hobbled pace of his pursuer, but the sound was soon drowned out by heavier footsteps. A cloud of inmates passed him, men running so swiftly that Tom could only believe himself to be of superior courage. He was therefore insulted by the collision: the impact, a stinging blow to his shoulder, caused him to stagger and almost fall. "What asshole bumped me?" he demanded, his question unanswered as the inmates, indistinguishable from one another, disappeared into the night. When he clutched his shoulder, Tom realized he was bleeding. The seepage was warm, generous, and soothed the aching in his fingers. He could not feel his other hand at all.

"Sarah," he said, perhaps too reflexively. The mention of her name embarrassed him and so he was comforted when his surroundings began to recede from his senses. Soon only the pressure upon his back, the hard wet surface of the ground, reminded him of his predicament. He moaned, not recognizing the voice as his own, and tightened his grip on his shoulder. In the serenity of the moment, he was incurious as to who had shot him.

A smokey presence was approaching him now. Thankfully, it was not Sarah. He would need a tamer emissary to guide him to the afterworld: a place where his life, his heroic but regrettable life, ran the risk of too jaundiced an inventory. It therefore did not interest him that the presence was a kindly one; he could sense its fastidiousness as well: a self-righteousness that could only fare him poorly in the world to come. The intruder was Perkins—unmistakably Perkins—and he had always despised the man.

Perkins' presence was soon overpowering, but Tom was not impressed by its manifestation. He could see only the boots intermingling with smoke, boots moving so slowly, so cautiously, that he began to doubt that he was the object of their approach. He was far more aware of a hovering ray of light: a stabbing beam that made his eyes water and alienated him even further from his chaperon. As the beam became harsher he closed his eyes prayerfully, not opening them until he felt the solicitous tug of fingertips upon his wrist, the prepossessing hand upon his forehead, but even when he opened them a vestige of light still remained, a sharp but inauthentic glare too imprinted upon his retinas to fade. Even so he could finally distinguish his rescuer: the melted brow, the heavily pocked cheeks, the ferreting eyes that were somehow more tender than pious. "Mr. Hemmings ..."

He clung to his wound and groaned with relief. It was Yoakum who had come to fetch him.

November 25, 2000
9:00 p.m.

"Sit up tall, Mr. Hemmings. Won't do ya no good to keep lying down, sir." Yoakum eased Tom to a sitting position and mopped his forehead with a dry towel. "At least it was a *clean* shot, sir. Went right through the both of ya."

Tom shook his head, pleasantly confused until Yoakum motioned with the flashlight. Pausing twice, the patch of light illuminated first a Glock, which appeared to have been discarded, and then Hopper's prone body. A dark puddle, broader than a table top, encircled the boy, but he was distinguishable only by the swastika on his wrist; his head, pulpy on the right side, suggested that a shot to the left temple had instantly paralyzed his shooting hand. Tom shook his head then looked away. Only the predictability of the sight, its numbing familiarity, prevented him from gagging.

Tom's throat was parched and he spoke with difficulty. "You might have missed *me*."

Yoakum smiled feebly. "I apologize for that, sir. But the boy needed dustin' and quick. I *shoulda* smoked him before I left the dormitory day-before-last. But that goddamn Hassan wouldn't let me."

Tom nodded as Yoakum spoke, understanding only dimly what the man was saying. "Was he trying to shoot me for real?" he asked finally.

Yoakum lifted his pant leg. His throw-down, another Glock, was still strapped to his shin. "What do *you* think, sir. The little fucker musta hidden that pistol—maybe in one of the air vents—*before* Hassan even tied him up."

Tom shrugged. "You told me I think too *much*. You told me to stay dumb."

"Well *too* much thinkin' will *make* a man dumb. The point is he can't hurt us now, sir."

Tom heard the towel rip—a sound so sharp that it made him flinch. It was several seconds before he realized that Yoakum had wrapped his wound and was fitting him with a sling. "I'll miss him ..." Tom muttered for some obscure reason; the wound was beginning to throb, its pain as unforgiving as a toothache. "But I'll leave his soul to Perkins."

Yoakum tugged at the sling, elevating Tom's hand. The pain began to ease. "Now *that's* the way to look at it, sir. But that little scum bucket ain't *worth* missing."

Tom felt the need to joke. "What didn't you miss him with?"

"A Mini-14, Mr. Hemmings. I won't use no blunderbuss when it comes to protectin' my road dog. But let's keep that between you and me."

"Did you get it from the commissary?"

Yoakum chuckled and shook his head. "Be friendly to me, *please*, Mr. Hemmings. You're startin' to sound like *Perkins*, sir." He pulled the sling tighter then strapped Tom's arm to his body with another strip of towel. "You *sure* that Perkins is dead and buried?"

The alley grew darker as Yoakum helped him to his feet. The man's voice was now distant to him and he listened without reaction. He felt as though he were stranded in thickening fog. "It's over now, Mr. Hemmings ... We're roundin' up the last of 'em. But I still need to get you out of here, sir ..."

Tom stood for a moment, allowing the fog to ease. "What about *friendly* fire?"

Yoakum patted him reassuringly on the back. "Don't worry about *that*, sir. They're expectin' you home for dinner. I told Etta I'd be fetchin' you from the dorm."

November 25, 2000
9:15 p.m.

The pain in Tom's shoulder had become unbearable, but it was the German Shepherds that commanded his attention as Yoakum guided him through the compound. Their rabid barking assaulted him like hammer blows, depriving him of the benevolence of shock and distracting him from the warm glow now emanating from the streetlights. Although the dogs had been arranged in a perimeter circle, they seemed oblivious to the protocols of surrender; instead, they were straining at their leashes, ignoring the shouts of their handlers as they lunged at the naked inmates stumbling single file from the laundry dorm. Only the blare of a bullhorn—stern robotic commands—competed with the clamor of the dogs and gave the battle a semblance of finality.

"KEEP YOUR HANDS ABOVE YOUR HEADS," the metallic voice repeated. *"HANDS UP WHERE WE CAN SEE THEM. NOW KNEEL DOWN IN A STRAIGHT ROW."*

A group of officers, some swinging clubs, were shackling the inmates who had already fallen to their knees. The beatings seemed excessive, but Tom shuddered luxuriously when he heard a baton crack bone.

"Ya all right there, Mr. Hemmings?" Yoakum said.

He nodded, allowing Yoakum to support him as he walked. "Nothing a hospital dinner won't fix."

"Well, a *banquet* is what you deserve, Mr. Hemmings—helpin' us round up the bojacks like you done. Hawkins himself said as much."

"And what are the bojacks' deserts?"

Yoakum laughed. "Boloney sandwiches—that's what *they'll* be gettin'. And they coulda had a steak."

A shotgun boomed, toppling a skinny inmate as he attempted to scramble from the circle. The man, only slightly wounded, clutched his genitals intuitively and began flailing about with his legs. "Don't aim no lower, guv'nor!" he shouted, a cry that produced bellows of laughter from the guards. It looked as though the man were performing a skit.

Yoakum shook his head. "Trigger-happy fools," he muttered. "Not *all* them bojacks *need* dustin', Mr. Hemmings."

"How would *you* know?"

Yoakum laughed. "This much I *do* know, sir. That fucker still has *balls*."

A troop of paramedics, granite-faced men pushing gurneys, was now overtaking them. Men lay on the stretchers like bundled beef, bloodied beyond recognition as they glided in the direction of Control Unit where the ambulances awaited. The movement of the gurneys was eerily silent, and Tom felt relieved when one of the injured, possibly a mental patient, began tugging at his bandages. "*Apollo*." the man shouted. "I demand to speak to *Apollo*."

"Did you brief the Commissioner?" Tom asked.

"I did," Yoakum said. "And you know what he said? He said ya plugged up the *dyke—you* and that Chester dude. But don't let him make you no deputy Commissioner."

"I would *prefer* not to be rewarded."

"Well you did piss off Her Highness, Mrs. Johnson. But that's because she's got the hots for ya. She told me to get you out of that dorm and *quick*."

"Etta's hots won't set well with Sarah."

"I expect not, sir, Sarah bein' a lady and all. But don't be humorin' Etta instead. Keep your mouth shut and *none* of us will feel the heat."

"I wouldn't mind heat if it's coming from Etta."

Yoakum laughed loudly. "Listen to yer road doggie, sir. Right now ya couldn't *handle* that much pussy."

"My thanks for plugging the *dyke*," Tom snapped. The Main Gate was open now and the sight of the parking lot startled him. But the illusion of rescue was still precious— far more embracing than the rites of duty. He did not need Etta's blessing; he did not need Perkins' approval. Such godly sanctions were moot to a man with his stiffs safely buried and the unflinching support of his road dog.

Tom paused momentarily, tightened his sling, then accompanied Yoakum through the gate.

December 1, 2000
3:00 p.m.

Tom recuperated in the Indianapolis General Hospital, a beehive of a facility where he was granted a private room, perhaps in concession to his notoriety as a dyke plugger. The room seemed unmerited, but he still welcomed the privacy; unplugging the phone beside his bed, he asked the nurses to leave his door closed whenever possible. He even avoided the news on television, preferring to receive his information from Yoakum who visited him daily. It was through Yoakum that he learned that the Commissioner had ordered a three-month lockdown of the facility, that Hassan and the surviving Muslims had been trucked to the Maximum Control Complex in the town of Carlisle, and that the contract with Colonial Concessions was under serious review. He learned also that Sarah was probably still in Rockville, a conclusion Yoakum had come to after visiting her house on three consecutive evenings and finding the porch light off each time. Since Tom had not tried to contact her himself, he took Yoakum at his word. And he believed she had discarded him wisely.

"She'll come when she's ready, Mr. Hemmings," Yoakum said. "But not a day sooner, I'll bet. All this dirty business is a bit much for a lady like Sarah."

"I doubt that," Tom answered. "She prefers *pigs*."

"Well, Etta ain't as particular, sir—I'm tellin' you that right now. She's coming in to see you herself since you ain't answerin' yer phone."

This news was more than Tom wanted to process. He rolled his eyes. "My trough is running over," he snapped.

Yoakum smirked. "That's all well and good, Mr. Hemmings. But don't be spillin' the beans."

Tom sighed, exasperated, and attempted to readjust his sling. The numbness had not left his fingers, leading him to believe that he had suffered nerve damage in his shoulder. "What good is Etta to me? I can't even jack."

Yoakum scratched his chin thoughtfully. "I apologize again, Mr. Hemmings. But it could have been much worse, sir."

Tom tried to flex his fingers. "That *isn't* much consolation."

"Maybe not, sir. But don't go mountin' Etta just 'cause ya can't jack off. I'm tellin' you that 'cause your hand will be fine. I told the doctors I wouldn't settle for nothing less."

"And what's *your* prognosis according to Etta?"

Yoakum chuckled dryly. "Hell's bells, Mr. Hemmings, they're investigatin' *everyone* right now. Even the bojacks and they ain't *worth* investigatin'. So they ain't gonna rule out me and you."

"I have an engagement right here," Tom said. "I need to recover the use of my hand."

Yoakum squeezed Tom's wrist tenderly. "I know that, Mr. Hemmings. But ya got another engagement with Etta. So don't be goin' soft on me."

"How can I? I can't even jack."

"Then you got no business with Etta."

"What makes you so damn sure of that?"

"I'm yer road dog, sir, and I'm tellin' you straight. You don't need to be in bed with no ball buster."

Tom shook his head, annoyed once again, not by the artlessness of Yoakum's remark so much as its contentiousness—the man's rigid assumption that he was undeserving of a heartful fantasy.

"Maybe not," Tom said finally. "But earth mothers are another matter."

Yoakum lowered his eyes. He seemed deeply amused. "Mum's the word then, ain't it, Mr. Hemmings?"

December 2, 2000
10:00 a.m.

Tom was sleeping soundly the following morning when Etta came to visit him. He awoke quickly to her cough, but it took him a full minute to shake off the sluggishness caused by the morphine. In the hazy interim, he was slow to notice the sag of flesh beneath her jaw, the dishevelment of her blouse, or the dark circles beneath her armpits. And he was barely assaulted by the gaminess of her perfume—at least not until after she had tucked her skirt behind her legs and seated herself on the chair beside his bed. She seemed buoyant—ephemeral—and when she spoke her voice was like a rich melody.

"So, Mr. Hemmings. How are you today?"

"How well could I be? An angel has come to fetch me."

She smiled and rubbed her eyes. "Mr. Hemmings," she said. "Try to remember that I'm a mother of four. I have stretch marks and cellulite thighs. I have had two face-

237

lifts and a tummy tuck. So isn't it time you punctured your schoolboy fantasy?"

"My canon's not up to it," he punned.

She laughed, perhaps too politely, and patted his forehead. Moving methodically, as though catering to an infant, she fluffed the pillow behind his head. "Your bed needs raising, Mr. Hemmings," she said. "But not your canons."

"What will I have without them?"

"A bit of perspective, sir. Something you have shown very little of so far."

"A *bit* of perspective would suit me just fine. I want just enough to remain on your leash."

"I know that, Mr. Hemmings. But your doggishness does *not* flatter me. I rank very low on your totem pole, don't I?"

"Ah, but Etta, you *have* my libido."

"But not your affection. That seems to belong to a broken woman and a goatish little man who calls himself a pastor. And what do you know about Yoakum, sir?"

"He's my road hound."

"Does that mean you trust him?"

"As far as dogs go."

"Mrs. Baumgardner claims he's a *pig*, sir. But more importantly he's a blackmailer, a drug trafficker, and a murderer."

Tom winked slyly. "All I know is he saved my bacon."

Etta shook her head. "The man *did* shoot you, Mr. Hemmings. Does that make him deserving of your loyalty?"

"That was an accident."

"Possibly, Mr. Hemmings. Or maybe he was giving you a warning. Hasn't that even occurred to you, sir?" A cell phone was chirping as she spoke, a trill that belied the severity of her tone. She frowned and dipped into a pocket of her purse. After hitting the silencer, she looked at him sternly, as though holding him responsible for the interruption.

He seized the advantage. "Is warning me *your* prerogative only?"

"Mr. Hemmings," she snapped. "What I am giving you is an opportunity—not a warning."

Tom blinked several times. "To abandon my road dog?"

"For starters, yes. He *will* be going to prison."

"And where will that leave me?"

She pocketed the cell phone, smiling tightly. "That's rather up to you, isn't it, sir? But I *am* offering to keep you on my leash."

"That won't shrink my canon."

"Perhaps not, Mr. Hemmings. But I'm going downtown to help with the investigation. I'm being reappointed as ombudsman and I need a fact finder. Someone to ask questions and write notes."

"Sarah *said* they'd be getting rid of you."

"Never mind Sarah," she snapped. "Unlike Sarah, I can *handle* adolescent men. You could do her no greater favor than to accept my offer."

"I may just as well. She has cut me loose."

"You're accepting the job?"

He shrugged, attempting once more to flex his fingers. "I'll take my stand with you," he said.

"Please do *not* take a stand, Mr. Hemmings. You have taken too many of them as it is. And they're all one-nighters from what I have heard."

Tom shrugged and grinned guiltily. "There's a lot to be said for one-nighters," he muttered.

Etta sighed. Her palm, moist and maternal, was resting once again upon his forehead. "I believe you know better than that. Just *look* at your consorts. A popinjay pretending to be a priest, a blackmailer pretending to be a stalwart, and a slut pretending to be your wife. These are mercenaries, Mr. Hemmings—not companions. And I think it's their very depravity that attracts you."

Tom sighed heavily. "I do have history with them."

She arched her eyebrows. "*History* you call it? I don't think so, sir."

"What else would it be?"

"Not history. Remember that I have *lived* a bit of history."

239

"Are you still trying to puncture my fantasy?"

"Not with history, sir. It has too fine an arc."

"... Which inclines towards justice. I know. I have read Luther King."

"Then don't profane him, Mr. Hemmings. Call your exploits whatever else you wish, but do not call them *history*."

"The Commissioner told me I did rather well, creating that diversion and all."

Etta rolled her eyes. "The *Commissioner*? He's the biggest *popinjay* of them all. And a *very* unprincipled man. I have seen his kind come and go far too many times."

"At least he gave me a plan."

"A plan? Was allowing you to marry the Devil a plan? Because that's what you did when you broke my instructions." Etta flung her purse upon the floor. "You should *never* have entered that dormitory."

Tom tried not to laugh. "So I married the Devil? Oh well. It beats a one night stand."

"Not in your case, Mr. Hemmings. Not when marriage suits you even less."

"And I was hoping for some permanency."

"No, Mr. Hemmings. You were hoping to become a hero. And unfortunately you have succeeded."

"A joyless ambition, I realize now. That comes from being unmarried, I guess."

Etta sighed sensuously, folding her hands—a gesture that drew his attention to a wedding ring on her finger. "Where else *could* it come from?" she said finally. "Had you ever been married you would know that inmates are like *children*. They are woolgatherers, like you, and prefer to be kept within the limits of their daydreams. Offer them an ultimatum and a forbidden treat and they will grovel at your feet like puppies."

"Forbidden rewards," Tom sighed. He could feel his erection beneath the sheets. "They are not inconsiderable, are they?"

"Not to an adolescent. But grownups can resist them, Mr. Hemmings."

Her scent ripened as she rose suddenly from the chair—"You're flushed, Mr. Hemmings"—and adjusted the thermostat on the wall. Returning to his bed, she pulled his blanket down to his waist and then tucked it carefully into both sides of the mattress.

"Exposed would better describe me," he said.

She laughed throatily and readjusted his pillow. "Mr. Hemmings," she said. "You are far too transparent to merit exposure."

"Then why do you want me for your snitch?"

"What makes you think I *want* you?"

"You offered me the job."

"Isn't that something that *you* want? A cheap atonement and a marriage of submission? Or would you prefer that I let you rot in here?"

"I'll rot either way."

She shook her head, pressing her palm upon his forehead once again. "I have spoken to your doctors, Mr. Hemmings," she said. "They told me your hand is going to heal. And you'll have your discharge in a few days."

"That's imminent *if* my hand heals."

She smiled gently then kissed him upon the forehead. "Not if you find better use for it, sir."

"And what should I do in the meantime?"

She laughed. "In the meantime, I suggest you sleep."

She was gone when he awoke, an empty consolation since her perfume still lingered like a presence. Her bouquet, its overpowering staleness, belittled him even in her absence, even as he lay in the semidarkness of the room and surrendered himself to the drip-drip-dripping of the morphine. It was only his infantile need for a tit that allowed him to hope for a loftier shame, an abasement he could at least call on his own.

He had to admit it. He ached for Sarah.

December 5, 2000
10:00 a.m.

She arrived on the morning he was scheduled for discharge—an untimely visit since he had already dressed himself and packed his bag. The effort, though exhausting, had rejuvenated his instinct for flight, an impulse that overruled the stiffness in his hand and the stagnant aroma developing within his sling. At that moment, he was almost grateful for the sling: it allowed him to hug her with only one arm, an embrace that reciprocated the coolness of her kiss. Her faded jeans and red hunting jacket reminded him that winter had come.

"It's hard to squeeze you, skipper," she said. "But that don't surprise me none."

He spoke hopefully. "I had almost given up waiting for you."

"Is *that* why you let her in?"

"Etta?"

"I can *smell* her, skipper, so don't try and wiggle out of it." Her chin seemed sharper, her anger rehearsed, and she had lost weight. Gingerly, as though doing the bed a favor, she sat upon the rumpled sheets. "We need to talk."

"That's not what I was hoping to hear."

"Course not, skipper—that's why you're a *pig*. I told that to Etta, you know, so she wouldn't come around pestering you. A fat lot of good *that* did."

As he sat down beside her, she clutched his good hand, interlacing her slim fingers with his.

Tom chuckled and rolled his eyes. "Does that mean you're no longer beholden to Etta? You said she once did you a favor."

She squeezed his fingers, causing him to wince. "You'll be holding *yourself* if you say that again. At least that'll be the case if *I* have anything to say about it." She dropped his hand and rested her palm on the inside of his knee. Having demonstrated her advantage, she smiled tightly.

"Are they putting you in a watchtower?" he asked

242

Her eyes narrowed. "Joking won't save you, skipper. No more than lying will."

"But you *are* going back to the Farm."

"Yes."

"Then I'm not really lying, am I?"

She glared and removed her hand from his leg. "Well, that's not saying a whole lot, is it? I already told Wal-Mart they could kiss my ass."

"So when do you start tower duty?"

"In about a week. I passed my debriefing, you know? Now that was a *real* joke. Those Muslims treated me like a queen while I was in there—a whole lot better than Etta and them *ever* did."

"I fared somewhat better with Etta."

She groaned. "You need to cut her apron strings, skipper. 'Cause you can't blow dust in Etta's eyes—not like you did with the bojacks. You and that Chester creep."

"I guess we deserve your contempt."

"You *deserve* worse than that. *Chester* they oughta hang."

"We've dusted enough of them already," he said.

Sarah shrugged. "Well, they should've shot Chester while they had the chance. He created a *ton* of paperwork—stirrin' up the bojacks the way he did. It'd serve you right if they made *you* do it."

"Well, I *did* get shot. Doesn't that salvage me?"

"Not unless you're a ghost, it don't." She sighed impatiently and then opened her purse. "Anyhow, I brought you something. I got it from Wal-Mart." She dropped a large envelope onto the bed.

"I need nurturing—not cards."

She shook her head. "I ain't your wet nurse, skipper. I already *got* two kids to look after. That's why we gotta talk."

"About what?"

"Cutting strings."

"Oh," Tom said, dropping his eyes. His heart was sinking like a stone. "And who's my successor?"

"Harry, if you need to know. He ain't much to brag on, but he's *still* their father. I'm lettin' him move back into the house."

He reached for her hand, grateful when she didn't resist, but his voice was now angry. "The *boozer* is coming back into your house?"

"Well, he won't do it sober, that's for sure. But he *will* keep my brats in line while I'm working third shift. And he *will* pay my car off."

"That's generous of him."

She chuckled tonelessly. "It's 'cause he feels guilty, skipper, so I wouldn't call it generous. But it's a whole lot more than I can trust *you* to do."

"I'll miss you," he murmured.

She snatched her hand away and glared. "Why? Are you in that big a hurry to get rid of me?"

"*Yes*, if you're taking back the boozer."

"He's moving back in—that's *all* I said. I didn't *say* I was going back to him."

Tom's heart skipped a beat. "Why not?"

She wrinkled her nose as though noticing something stale. He pulled the sling defensively against his body.

Sarah sighed. "If you really *must* know he wets the bed. And I won't sleep with *no one* who wets the bed. I told him that too."

"And he's *good* with that?"

"Of *course* he's not good with it. He just doesn't have a *choice*."

Feeling vindicated, he stroked the back of her neck. He then picked up the envelope from the bed. "A marriage of submission," he said. "There's a lot to be said for them."

"A lot that's *petty*," she snapped. "But he's gettin' no more than what he deserves. And I'm happy to dish it out to him."

"And what about me?"

Sarah winked and laughed. "Don't worry, skipper, you'll get your punishment too. I can't exactly hang you, but I *can* keep you hanging around."

Tom let the envelope fall from his fingers. "Like the specter at the feast."

Her voice grew bitter. "That about describes it, skipper. It'll probably suit you just fine though—that's the only problem."

"I thought you stopped believing in ghosts."

She shrugged and shook her head. "There wouldn't be much *point* to that, would it? Not when ghosts are all I can handle."

She kissed him tenderly, causing him to shudder, not from desire so much as the longevity her kiss implied: the intimation that their affair, however stolen, would last for a long time. After a moment she pushed him away. Slowly, as though handling a contact lens, she picked up the envelope he had dropped.

"Here," she said. "I'll help you open it."

February 21, 2001
8:00 a.m.

It was snowing on the morning he drove back to the Hill, the flakes, hard and gray, leaving a patchy blanket upon the rutted farmland and the freshly-tarred service road. Tom's hand, strengthened by ten weeks of therapy, gripped the steering wheel comfortably, but the harsh winter sun irritated his eyes and he squinted as he drove. His wound had healed and his instincts were sharper, enabling him to turn down Etta's offer and instead take a job as institutional investigator, a position that would let him spend most of his time secluded in the Administration Building. It was Hawkins, in his new capacity as provisional superintendent, who had offered him the job, deeming it his reward for instigating the successful capture of the dormitory.

"So she booted you out of her house?" the captain had said while visiting him in his trailer the previous day. Not waiting for an answer, Hawkins had continued speaking. "It's just as well, son. It's just as well. You got something comin' for risking your neck and *Sarah* ain't the one to provide it."

Aroused by the hope that he could still be near her, Tom accepted the job on the spot, a decision that caused Brewer to phone him within the hour. *"Turn in your union jacket,"* the big man thundered.

"Fuck you," Tom replied. "It was *Yoakum* who had my back, not you."

"Then go join the Teamsters, Hemmings. You don't need to be comin' to *our* meetings no more."

The sight of the Hill eased his irritation: the narrow arch checkpoint, the empty vocational shops, the scarred rooftop of the Administration Building were mitigated by the snow, a thickening descent that gave these drab structures the serenity of relics. The electric gate opened wide to admit him, a motion so sudden that it startled him. He drove slowly past the gate, reluctant to scar the snow, and parked in front of the Administrative Building.

Tom's new office was a cozy room on the upper story of the Administrative Building, and he was especially grateful for the herringbone carpet that Hawkins had had installed for him. He ignored the backlog of paperwork—death reports that needed finalizing—and spent the morning decorating the room with pictures and props that he'd loaded into his car. The pictures, Gauguin prints from an art dealer in Indianapolis, were clearly ostentatious, the Tahitian nymphs a poor complement to a pair of mounted bass he had caught in the quarry, but he still hung the pictures alongside the largemouths. So engrossing was the task, so satisfying his sense of rebellion, that it was not until noon that he slipped from the office, entered the prison compound, and walked towards the Special Housing Unit.

Tom awaited his cohort in the carpeted chamber at the hub of the Special Housing Unit. The walls of the room were packed tightly with law books, a musty decor that seemed fittingly pretentious: the books were too outdated, after all, to interfere with the conduct adjustment hearings that were held there twice a week. He sat patiently at the conference table, enjoying the prolonged silence of the room. Although the cell ranges were practically empty, it was an hour before a range officer brought Chester in to see him.

The little man was wearing shackles, restraints that seemed totally bogus: the waist chain, the handcuffs, even the dragging leg irons in no way contributed to an aura of defeat. The man's face was fleshier, his color was restored, and his belly bulged tightly within his red jump suit. He did not resemble an agitator so much as a country squire familiar with good living.

Chester stood quietly in front of the table, standing stock still until the officer had removed the shackles and left the room. He then nodded meekly and straightened his sweatshirt, tugging at the cloth as though willing it to stretch. When he spoke, his tone was humble.

"Dare I speak for the dead, Mr. Hemmings? Or shall I simply hang my head?"

"Why be silent *today*?"

"*Today*, Mr. Hemmings, *you* are the host. And I am still grateful for undeserved gifts."

"Sarah says they should hang you."

Chester shook his head and frowned. "They can do it only once, sir. *One* hanging for a dozen mortal sins. That too would be an undeserved gift." Releasing the hem of his sweatshirt, he sat beside Tom at the conference table. "How often do you see her, sir?"

"Frequently. She comes by each night before starting the graveyard shift."

"Then she's flattering us both, Mr. Hemmings. But it's better I remain forsaken than be carried to a better life. A prophet's demise would enshrine me beyond my worth."

"Would it? You were as *articulate* as a prophet."

"And what of it, sir?" The man's voice was shaky. "Were I mute, I might have ascended to the salute of cannons. But because I'm articulate, I am lost. That which I would champion today, I would too easily talk myself out of tomorrow."

"Either way you'll be compensated."

Chester's face flushed. "Then let my reward be a meager one, sir. Assign me to the greenhouse where I might sit alone and feed the pigeons. For once, Mr. Hemmings, I am grateful for the paltry wages of sin."

"You were prudent yourself to survive the attack."

"It was none of my doing."

"Whose was it—the Lord's?"

"No, Mr. Hemmings. I've fallen too far from His grace. And so I remain in the belly of the whale."

"While pigeons partake of a feast."

Chester shrugged. "Strange, is it not, that my words have flown others to His harvest. I am jealous of even the pigeons, sir."

"Your suffering is well-deserved."

"It is, sir. But as I have said, His greatest works are performed through sinners."

"How did you survive?"

"I fainted, Mr. Hemmings. I was exhausted, having delivered my epiphany to nobler men. The guards captured me before I heard a shot."

"You were fortunate."

"I would rather be grateful than fortunate, sir."

"Be grateful you didn't have to witness the attack. The battle was like thunder in a morgue. You're a fool if you think there was anything *sacred* about it."

"Without faith, Mr. Hemmings, morgues would be unbearable. And so I prefer to be duped."

"Faith would have *made* it intolerable," Tom snapped. "My only salvation was that I had no faith to lose."

Chester lowered his head. He seemed relieved. "It is not your *only* salvation, Mr. Hemmings. Be consoled that you are not alone in your grief. My unworthiness has sequestered me also."

"That and the lie you told. You were supposed to calm the inmates—not rile them up."

"That, Mr. Hemmings, was the spirit of Jeremiah. But perhaps I've recited him too many times." Chester lifted his sweatshirt, removing a Bible from the waistband of his pants. The book, broken at the seam, fell open when he laid it upon the table. He read wearily and without inflection. "'You have duped me, O Lord, and I let myself be duped. Violence is my message—derision my cup. I say to myself I will speak your name no more. But it becomes like a fire burning in my heart. I cannot hold it in.'"

"After all that's happened, you *still* believe that?"

"Unfortunately, I do. But the message is mightier than the vessel." Chester rose from the chair, his joints cracking sharply. Rubbing his wrists, he walked over to the law books. Chester glanced at the titles, skipping from volume to volume as though searching for a misplaced reference. "I *have* heard the thunder, Mr. Hemmings," he said finally. "It filled up the ranges these last three months. Midnight screams, men beating bars, cells slamming shut at all hours of the night. And they took my statement a half dozen times."

"The donation of an empty vessel?"

"A murmur in the void, sir. A void that speaks louder than even the thunder and grows more expansive with each passing day. Do you know I'm the only one left, Mr. Hemmings? They moved the other inmates to securer prisons."

"You'll fare better without them. And they without you."

"Probably, sir. But only because the inmates have coronated me. They *still* consider me a true prophet. An heir to a new nation."

Tom chuckled. "You'll just have to live with their reverence, Chester."

"Reverence, yes, but spare me the crown. It may as well have thorns."

"More men would have died had you not distracted them. That much I'm still sure of."

"And that only adds to my burden, sir. I have cheated even the Lord—deprived him of his full and rightful harvest. I should have warned the inmates that Pharaoh's troops were approaching." Chester fingered the books as though tuning a piano.

"Perhaps you'll find peace on the Farm Line," Tom muttered.

Chester again shook his head. Abandoning the law books, he returned to the table where he stood stiffly at attention. He appeared to be awaiting an invitation to sit. "I *will* accept my reward, Mr. Hemmings. *That much* I can lay claim to."

"Consider it a true profit."

"Not a *true* profit, sir, but an ample one. The wages of mischief are thankfully very small." His hand trembled as he reached again into the waistband of his pants. The envelope he removed was thin and unaddressed.

"*Another* message?"

"Hassan," Chester replied. "He was among the first to leave. He said to give you this."

"Condolences, I suppose." Tom pocketed the envelope.

"I haven't read it. There are *limits* to my indiscretions."

"But not to your rhetoric."

"Fortunately, sir, I have not done it justice."

Tom smiled grimly. "That's why you'll be going to the Farm Line."

"Thank you so much, Mr. Hemmings. The Lord has also been gracious to me. It's a blessing that I sowed so little fruit—that my seed was cast upon nettles and rock."

"You're *thankful* to be a charlatan?"

"No, Mr. Hemmings. I'm thankful my cup is empty. I'm an old man, sir, and cannot carry a cross."

Tom smirked. "I could give you a hand."

Chester sighed. "Do not bother, Mr. Hemmings. I will meet my maker soon enough. And until that time I will tend to smaller gardens."

The man remained standing, his eyes upon the floor. His resignation to his reward seemed almost a courtesy; clearly their rapport, a bond now strengthened by fire and ash, did not require the validation of a favor. That Chester was still a confidant to him also seemed irrelevant, a confirmation not of friendship but the abject poverty of Tom's soul.

Tom nodded politely and rose from the table. "The pigeons will be grateful," he said.

February 21, 2001
4:00 p.m.

Tom went ice fishing later that day, returning to his trailer with a stringer of bluegills he had caught at the water reservoirs. The outing had failed to invigorate him: the ice, thickened by an early winter chill, had supported his weight with the apathy of stone, and the bluegills had solidified the instant he unhooked them, not struggling until later when he thawed them with tap water from his kitchen sink. He cleaned the fish quickly, salting the fillets before dropping them into a pot upon the stove. As the fish began to steam he watched the news on television, a habit he had resumed since the Penal Farm had fallen from the attention of the networks.

Later, when he had eaten the fish, he slipped a cassette into a VCR player he had bought at Wal-Mart the previous day. The tape, a *Kung Fu* rerun, riveted his attention, perhaps because its protagonist, a fistic mystic in the Land of Nod, unflinchingly championed the polemics of action—an option he yet found preferable to the silence of the void. He watched the tape in its entirety: the plot, though utterly predictable, remained a sanctification of faith—an assurance that even the stalest of scripts were to be taken seriously. It was ten p.m. when Tom turned off the television, but he finally felt ready to retrieve the letter Hassan had written him.

He opened it and read.

Mr. Hemmings.

I have better served you as a pimp than an adversary and so I hope that this message finds you well. I do not mean this in the spirit of Islam (though Islam would surely demand it) but because I still have a grain of pity for you. And therein lies the shock of my martyrdom: It has not been a blaze of glory but a pyre that burns feebly and without illumination. I have

251

*glimpsed the world to come, after all, and
have found it to be as tedious as this one.*

*Thank you for saving the boy. You did
not really save him and both of us know it,
but he is still the fondest of my distractions.
In a world filled with shadow and fluttering
graves, it is larvae that best entertain us.*

*Take care, Mr. Hemmings, and embrace
the flicker. I hope to precede you in passage
at least. Perhaps we can share a chuckle in
the netherworld.*

Hassan

When Tom had re-read the letter, he took it outside to
destroy. He was anxious to burn it quickly, and so he was
grateful that he had been given permission to do so. It was
snowing once again, a thick stinging shroud that made him
want to hurry. He worked expeditiously, folding the page into
a tight steeple before clearing a space for it on the ground.
He struck a match and shielded the flare between his palms:
flame licked hungrily at the paper. The fire warmed his
hands, as through reciprocating the care he had given it, and
the letter withered rapidly.

He shivered when the snowfall did not dim—when the
gloaming persisted, defying the dead ashes and tinting the
flakes with a phosphoric glow. He wiped his hands quickly
then rose from the ground. Convinced he was now worthy
of foxfire, he did not flinch when he noticed the twin orbs in
the distance or heard the muffled explosion of the tires upon
gravel. The graveyard shift was an hour away and Sarah was
coming to meet him.

Although the letter had been destroyed and his secrets
seemed secure, he preferred the memory of conflict to the
tedium of closure. This was not due to a restored sense of
ethics or even the need for penance; it was only because the
events that followed the riot were utterly confining in their
predictability. But he was learning to discredit his instincts,

having exposed them as initiatives for which he had little real talent, and so it was his nostalgia for battle that allowed him to yield gratefully to the mundane.

As the Commissioner had promised, the contracts with the privateers were terminated, a decision that seemed hopeful since their services would be returned to the Department of Corrections. The lockdown, however, remained in effect, another wise decision as it would probably be months before the hospital and commissary would operate at their traditional levels of dependability. But Tom's date with the Devil had still captured the day: the appropriations budget, which had been fattened by an emergency session of the state legislature, was so generous that he was forced to congratulate the Commissioner on his foresight.

Another predictable event was the lionizing of Lieutenant Perkins. The governor, who was unfamiliar with either the man or his spirit, had awarded him a posthumous medal of valor, proclaiming him to be the real hero of the siege. Fortunately, the award ceremony did not broadcast the ambiguity surrounding Perkins' death: further investigation in fact seemed pointless since Yoakum, when he had stormed the gymnasium, had most likely done away with Perkins' killer. Tom was therefore relieved when Yoakum was awarded a medal as well and he rather welcomed the rumor that the pock-faced man would soon be promoted to the rank of lieutenant. It especially consoled him when Brewer took the gossip seriously.

"*Promote* that son-of-a-bitch," Brewer sneered, "and they can lock us *all* up for insubordination!" That Brewer had already been insubordinate—he had convinced three members of his squad to disobey the attack order—seemed irrelevant to the big man, perhaps because the matter had only cost him a week's suspension from work.

The death toll from the insurrection was also foreseeable—not the numbers, which were substantial, but the ratio of inmates to officers killed. A total of twenty-three inmates had lost their lives while only two officers besides Perkins had died. One of them was a squad sergeant who had suffered a head wound during the capture of the dormitory: a needless death since the man had been targeted by a rooftop sniper after inexplicably removing his helmet.

The second fatality, a female officer assigned to the Northeast Watchtower, was not even a direct statistic of battle: she had accidentally shot herself in the liver while loading her Mini-14. The inmates, to the contrary, had all been deliberately targeted. The majority of them had fallen defending the dormitory, but Tom no longer regretted the fact that he had been unable to save them. The men were rebels, after all—disaffected souls—and would probably have gone on to do desperate things had they managed to live. Even Gabriel Grant, killed by a shotgun blast during the first minute of the attack, did not move Tom to compassion; he instead felt consoled that the shoot had been righteous, that Gabriel had brought it on himself by dashing towards the point squad while waiving a spray can of Lysol. Since no family member claimed Gabriel's body, Tom authorized it to be buried on Boot Hill, an inmate cemetery located near the water treatment plant.

Etta Johnson, not to his surprise, did not stay long in her position as ombudsman; she had held the job for less than a month when she was given the superintendent's position at the Campus, a picturesque women's prison located near the town of Rockville. She did write him regularly, flirtatious letters that smelled of her perfume, and so she remained prominent in his fantasies at least. In her absence, Harold Hawkins continued on as provisional superintendent of the Farm. The Hawkins months, as Tom later described them, impressed him as basically equitable since the captain leaned equally on both the unions and the inmates.

"You gotta hammer 'em *all*, Hemmings," the captain instructed him. "Being an investigator ain't for the *pussy-whipped*."

"Like you hammered Yoakum?" Tom had replied, laughing when Hawkins flushed.

"His day's comin', Hemmings, his day's gonna come. I ain't done with the cocksucker yet."

Despite Hawkins' warning, Tom did not take the investigator's job very seriously: a symptom, perhaps, of his growing preference for limbo over action. He began taking more days off, filling them with lengthy jogs, rabbit hunting, and fishing trips to the quarry. He started to play better tennis, his game unaffected by the lingering slackness in his hand (the looser grip in fact improved his serve). He started renting movies: James Bond classics, martial art melodramas, and generous doses of pornography. And he continued to sleep with Sarah, content to stay pussy-whipped despite the threat to his career. She came to see him almost nightly, curling up with him for a few short hours before heading off to work the graveyard shift, and so he grew less intimidated by the permanence of their relationship. Her moody concessions and wounded kisses were in fact a validation of his insubstantiality.

Tom's pedigree, if he were to claim one, could only be found in Chester: a legacy less than the final measurement of his indigence. Still, he took the credit when the little man was transferred to the farm crew, an announcement made by the Classification Committee the same afternoon Tom had visited him in the hole. He suspected his satisfaction was undeserved: that Chester, ever meticulous in his manipulations, had enlisted him as only a minor player in his scheme to again till the soil. In spite of this, Chester honored him the next day when he drove past the farm crew on his way to work. Watching Tom pass, the little man stopped the tractor he was driving, stood up in his seat, and saluted him fiercely. Chester soon became a fixture on the farm crew, his tact and courtesy a buffer to his reputation as a renegade priest. By spring, he was moved to the top of his pay scale.

Glossary Of Organizations, Technical Terms, And Slang

AFSMCE: American Federation of State, Municipal, and County Employees. Members wear green cardigans and are regarded as suck-ups by the Teamsters and the UAW.

American Gospel Party: Pseudo religious organization that advocates racial separation and a profound distrust of government.

Aryan Brotherhood: Prison gang identified with white supremacy. Members have shaven skulls and Swastika tattoos.

Bojack: Slang for inmate or lout.

Brass: The prison command structure. Captains, lieutenants, and sergeants are considered to be "the brass."

Buy the farm: To die, usually in a violent manner.

Central Office: The planning and policy branch of the Indiana Department of Corrections. It is located in downtown Indianapolis.

Christian Coalition: A faith-based organization founded by Pat Robertson in 1989. The Christian Coalition is dedicated to preserving family values and American sovereignty.

Classification Board: A three-member panel responsible for assigning and reassigning inmates within the facility. The guidelines for inmate assignments are strict. Inmates convicted of sex crimes and forcible felonies are rarely allowed to leave the Hill.

Colonial Concession Company: A multistate corporation that sells commissary items to inmates. The items are substandard and sold at inflated prices.

Conduct Adjustment Board: A three-member tribunal that administers sanctions to inmates charged with rule violations. Sanctions may include taking away an inmate's good time and/or segregating him in the Special Housing Unit. Inmates charged with rule violations are entitled to representation by inmate advocates and due process protocols.

Control Unit: A module responsible for telephone and radio communications throughout the prison. It is situated so that officers assigned there can see most of the comings and goings on the Hill.

Correctional Academy: Training academy located in Westville, Indiana. The Correctional Academy provides training in self-defense, assault tactics, and hostage negotiation.

Devils Disciples: An inmate gang identified with drug dealing and violence. Members are recognizable by the red handkerchiefs they tie around their foreheads.

Dropping a dime: Informing.

Emergency Squad (or E-Squad): A tactical unit responsible for breaking up inmate fights and responding to other emergencies. Members are equipped with shields, spit shields, Second Chance Vests, and batons. During riots, they also carry shotguns.

Farm Line: A group of inmates who are permitted to work on the prison farm and dairy. Since they are allowed to leave the Hill, this is a highly-coveted assignment.

Fish Line: Newly-arrived inmates who are yet to be assigned within the facility. Fish Line inmates are placed in the Segregation Unit behind the Control Unit while awaiting assignment.

Foxfire: A bioluminescence created by fungi in decaying wood. Sometimes, it is extremely bright.

The Great Harlot: A creature in the Book of Revelation symbolic of the Roman Empire.

The Hill: The tightly-fenced inner compound of the prison. Only inmates eligible for honor assignments, such as the Farm Line, are permitted to leave the Hill.

Hittites: An ancient race who built empires in Asia Minor and Syria. In the eyes of the American Gospel Party, Hittites is a fitting term for a conspiring elite who are stealing America from its rightful heirs.

The Hole: Slang for Special Housing Unit.

Investigation Office: An institutional office responsible for investigating staff and inmate misconduct.

K-9 Unit: A unit consisting of German Shepherds and their handlers. The K-9 Unit is used to sniff out drugs planted within the prison. Since many inmates fear the dogs, it is also used to restore and maintain order.

Key Room: A room in the Administration Building where keys, firearms, and batons are stored.

Mini-14: A high velocity semiautomatic rifle generally assigned to officers manning the watchtowers.

Muslims: An inmate organization committed to prayer and self-betterment. Members may be orthodox Muslims or followers of the more radical Nation of Islam. They wear white beanies.

Nation of Islam: A separatist organization founded in Detroit, Michigan in 1930, and widely promoted by Elijah Muhammad. Elijah's early teachings included the belief that the African American was the true inheritor of the earth, while the white man was the devil and the product of a failed experiment. Elijah's sexual misadventures eventually contributed to a rift within the Nation.

Penal Health Services: A nationwide corporation that provides privatized health care to prisons. It has come under media attack due to services considered to be substandard and in violation of the Eighth Amendment's cruel and unusual punishment provision.

The Peter Principle: A twofold principle formulated by Dr. Lawrence J. Peter in 1969. It states that members of any hierarchy rise no higher than their level of incompetence. It also states that organizations tend to eliminate both the incompetent and the super competent.

Philistine: Inhabitant of ancient Philistia. The American Gospel Party uses this term to define a conspiring elite—a privileged cast that is godless, exploitive, and averse to the American spirit of fair play.

Porter Line: A group of inmates assigned to the Porters' Room located behind the Administration Building. Porter Line inmates deliver messages and escort other inmates around the facility. The Porter Line is considered an honor assignment.

Prison Review Board: A watchdog organization at the Central Office level. The Prison Review Board assures that Indiana's prison practices comply with the law.

Rabbit: Slang for escapee.

Redcoats: A derogatory term for prison staff with membership in the United Auto Workers.

Remington 870: Tactical shotgun commonly used in police work and to quell prison riots.

Reserve E-Squad: An emergency squad in the early stages of training.

Road Dog: Slang for partner.

Sally Port: Double-gated entranceway to a prison compound.

Sandman: Term for obliviousness.

Screening Office: An institutional office that is responsible for evaluating disciplinary reports on inmates. When a report is deemed credible, the Screening Office forwards it to the Conduct Adjustment Board for disposition.

Second Chance Vest: Bulletproof vest.

Skinheads: Inmates recognizable by their shaved heads and white supremacist philosophy. Skinheads are usually members of the Aryan Brotherhood.

Special Housing Unit: A heavily-fortified building where inmates with serious disciplinary problems are housed.

Teamsters: International Brotherhood of Teamsters. Although a truckers union, the Teamsters have also been active in recruiting prison staff. Teamster members wear black jackets.

Trafficking: The illegal sale of contraband, usually alcohol and drugs, to inmates by staff members.

Trustees: Inmates entrusted to perform janitorial duties in the Administration Building and the Special Housing Unit.

United Auto Workers: The International Union of Automobile, Aerospace, and Agricultural Implement Workers. Since many auto plants have relocated to third world countries, the UAW has focused upon recruiting prison staff. Members wear bright red parkas.

Work Release: An honor assignment. Inmates selected for work release are placed in halfway houses under the supervision of the Department of Corrections. They reside in the houses at night and work jobs in the community during the day.

Acknowledgements

First, I would like to thank my wife, Mary Hanna, my mother, Catherine Barker Hanna, and my mother-in law, Mickey McClure, for supporting me in my ambition to become a published writer. To them, I have dedicated this novel. I am also grateful to Clyde James Hanna, my late father, who instilled in me a love of books. "Learn to read," he advised me, "and you will never be lonely."

I would like to express my appreciation to Lisa Meltzer Penn and Audrey Kalman for their sharp edits on the manhunt chapter. Their observations have enabled me to look at the entire book with a more critical eye. I am grateful to the following members of my critique group: Ann Foster, Chris Wachlin, and Bardi Rosman Koodrin, for their comments on my short stories. I am a better writer because of them. And I am particularly grateful for Elise Francis Miller for her thorough proofreading of the entire book.

I would like to thank George Jansen, the first to read my book. His observations were vital in helping me establish my story line and ground my characters. I am obligated to Marty Sorensen for appointing me fiction editor of The Sand Hill Review. My literary eye is clearer because of Marty. And a big thanks to Elliott Mao for her tireless work in designing the maps of the prison.

I would like to give special thanks Tory Hartmann, my publisher, friend, and chief editor. I am deeply indebted to her for her editorial vision and her business savvy in getting the book into the hands of readers. She has had the impact of an angel.

Made in the USA
San Bernardino, CA
19 February 2014